I0771379
Svalla
Coast
Iridian
Coast
Mosshollow
Ferra
Mountains
Copperholm
Frostfern
Valley
The
Greywood
Pinehaven
Derca
Frostmere River
Wayford
Ironspine
Ridge
Azure
Islands
Brightwater River
Millvale
Willowbrook
Thornwick
Cedarholt
Mistmere
Goldbrook
Bramblewood
Copperdale
Aldermere
Willowmere
Southmarch
Neosilica
Rosen
Bay
VALDAES
0   50   100   150 miles

Mosswood Apothecary - Spotify Playlist

PLAYLIST

Riptide – Vance Joy
Bloom - Bonus Track – The Paper Kites
Spiller - Instrumental Version – Cécile Corbel
Motion Sickness – Phoebe Bridgers
Like Real People Do – Hozier
Merry-Go-Round of Life – Joe Hisaishi
Celeste – Ezra Vine
Grow as We Go – Ben Platt
(You) On My Arm – Leith Ross
Ho Hey – The Lumineers
SFU – Cayley Spivey
Home – Edward Sharpe & The Magnetic Zeros
Escape Artist – Zoë Keating
First Day of My Life – Bright Eyes
Mystery of Love - Demo – Sufjan Stevens
Northern Attitude – Noah Kahan

The Curse – Agnes Obel

Flickers – Son Lux

Daydream – Youth Lagoon

The Moss – Cosmo Sheldrake

Warm – SG Lewis

Erase Me – Quinn Christopherson

breathe again – Joy Oladokun

Giver Taker – Anjimile

My Body Is a Cage – Arcade Fire

yeti – Paris Paloma, Old Sea Brigade

Devil's Spoke – Laura Marling

Cherry Wine - Live – Hozier

The Funeral – Band of Horses

Cosmic Love – Florence + The Machine

Run Boy Run – Woodkid

Liability – Lorde

Hide and Seek – Imogen Heap

The Garden – Mirah

Gloria – The Lumineers

Gale Song – The Lumineers

Sæglópur – Sigur Rós

I Will Follow You into the Dark – Death Cab for Cutie

King – Florence + The Machine

Shake It Out – Florence + The Machine

In the Woods Somewhere – Hozier

Mystery of Love – From Call Me By Your Name – Sufjan Stevens

Contents

For the queer people who wished they could see themselves in tales of magic and adventure—may you find your spark, your enchanted forest, and your chosen family home.

Introduction

JOIN MY NEWSLETTER

to always know new releases and updates!

(all the cool magical people are doing it)

The Principles of Alchemy

Graduation day at Flamel University should have been filled with joy. Instead, dread and tears clung in the air as potential graduates failed their finals in front of the public. Rowan Mosswood watched in horror as automatons carried the third student off the stage in Cobalt Square and tossed them into the back of an ambulance. This time, an ambitious student attempted to translocate a pound of gold but miscalculated the destination point. Needless to say, the gold didn't go where it should have. It ended up fused inside their arm.

Cobalt Square was packed, crammed with students, the public, and a slew of news and business automatons recording the events. This was a highlight in the bustling city of Neosilica, the day Flamel released only a handful of students. Scouts throughout the city would descend on graduates the moment they stepped off the stage, eager to scoop them up before their competitors. However, many others in the crowd were more interested in watching for explosions and injuries that might force the dean to end the day early.

Rowan adjusted his baggy sage-green button-up shirt, the same color as his eyes, and rubbed his tanned hands together. He wasn't ready for this. Not by a long shot. The memories of his last attempt still haunted him. He hadn't been ready for this two years ago when he last attempted to graduate. Granted, botanical alchemy had fewer risks than other disciplines, but last time he embarrassed himself when he accidentally created a rapidly growing invasive type of sentient fungus. The crowd had to flee when it overtook a news automaton and started beating a portly businessman over the head. Of course, the dean had to step in. He dismantled nearly a decade of mechanical alchemy, leaving behind only a heap of fungus-infested metal. Rowan spent nearly a year tracking down and crawling into rather unseemly places to find and eradicate the remaining mycelium.

He tapped his foot, looking back at the line of

students. Hundreds, all waiting for their turn to get on stage. Some camped out the day before to ensure the dean would see them. Rowan wasn't as desperate, but he had arrived before sunrise when the city was oddly quiet save for the whirring of maintenance automatons making their rounds through the cobblestone streets. He'd spent his morning watching the sun crawl past the towers of metal and glass that stretched high into the sky, their modern facades meshing with the old stone buildings and carefully preserved parks below only a few blocks away. Here in the industrial heart of Neosilica, anything green was kept at bay—confined to the gardens of Flamel University or the manicured grounds of Rosen Park, where wealthy citizens could escape the relentless horizon of metal.

Four people were ahead of him now, and he'd have nothing to show if she didn't hurry up. He pulled at his collar, sweat beading on his brow. He was going to fail again.

Shouts came, just in earshot. "Ugh, gross! What is that? Stop pushing!"

Rowan stood on his tiptoes and spotted the sea of students parting, plugging their noses as purple hair bobbed between them.

Marley, a short Black woman with a silver nose ring and a thick pair of overalls on, appeared in front of him, plugging her own nose as she held up a burlap sack. "You're lucky we're friends."

Rowan couldn't agree more. After nearly two years at Flamel with no friends, he'd found Marley, and she'd made his next four years worth it. He swiped the burlap sack from her and stuck his hand inside, fishing around until his fingers wrapped around a glass jar.

He shut his eyes and begged the universe, "Please, please, please have worked." When he pulled it out, the jar was nearly empty, with only a small blue seed at the bottom. "Yes!"

"You gonna tell me why you have a bag of manure in your bedroom?" she asked.

Rowan tucked the small jar in his pocket. "The jar had to sit somewhere dark and quiet. Not all disciplines are refined metal and containers of oil, you know." He winced, thinking about the state Marley must have found his room in—piles of texts stacked like towers across his floor, dried herbs hanging everywhere, and, of course, the bag of manure.

"I nearly died!" Marley shouted at him, arms flailing. "How can someone have that many books just thrown on the floor? Why haven't you packed?"

Rowan shook his head. "After last time, I'm not hoping for much. Just that the dean might pity me and keep me for another two years."

Marley grunted, pulling out a bottle of liquid silver from her pocket, and turned it over. "I mean, would it hurt you to switch disciplines? Nano and quantum are out of the question, but metallurgic alchemy is still in high demand. I heard the dean has a quota to pass each year or his donors will stop funding."

"Would if I could," Rowan said. "But my mom wanted me to do this. I owe it to her. 'The world will always need botanical alchemy, even if they don't know it.' She taught me everything she knew about healing salves and teas, but she still dreamed of the day I'd learn the 'real magic nature has.' Too bad now all I want in life is to have my own shop somewhere making the same things we used to make back home."

"But Neosilica doesn't need that, not now that we have nano and quantum. Did she even see an automaton before she passed?" Marley asked.

Rowan dropped his head, remembering his life in a small house just outside Neosilica, in what the older folks still called the Rosen District. "No, she didn't."

Marley lightly punched his shoulder. "Ignore what I said. You're right. And you've got the talent. No matter what the dean or that piece of garbage ex-boyfriend thinks."

Rowan's cheeks flushed as that pretentious, know-it-all Calder Steelwright with his big, dumb, perfect jawline and platinum hair surfaced in his mind. He looked down at the ground and said, "Thanks."

Marley punched his shoulder. "Hey! None of that self-wallowing. You've got a diploma waiting for you, and you're gonna kill it. So just get—"

"Next, we have Marley Argentum," a booming male voice, Dean Vayu, called from up on the stage.

Marley turned and glared at Rowan. "You signed me in before you?"

"Seemed like the right thing to do at the time," Rowan said.

Marley rolled her eyes and hopped up on the stairs. "We're both graduating this year and finding us some sugar daddies to fund our research. You hear me?"

"Yeah, yeah. Good luck!" Rowan shouted.

Rowan watched as she jumped up on stage. She nodded to Dean Vayu, a tall Black man in purple robes, before pulling chalk out from behind her ear and deftly drawing a sigil on the stone slab in the center of the stage. The dean stood behind her, scribbling notes on a clipboard as she worked.

Before Rowan knew it, Marley uncorked and poured out the contents of her bottled silver on the slab and placed her hands on the sigil.

Blue light glowed from the slab, and Rowan shielded his eyes. Moments later, the crowd let out a cheer. Rowan peeked behind his fingers, spotting a small silver ferret hopping up into Marley's hands.

She held it up for the dean and said, "This is still a prototype, but this sigil and silver combination allows for automatons without seams. I think with a few more resources and years, I could work something larger."

Dean Vayu held out a hand, running a finger along the ferret, then nodded. He traced a sigil in the air with his finger, purple light trailing behind, while his other hand pulled a blank piece of paper from his robes. When he was done, the light descended onto a sheet of paper.

"Marley Selene Argentum," Dean Vayu shouted out to the crowd. "By demonstrating your mastery in your selected discipline, I am proud to grant you this seal of approval, denoting you as an Alchemist of the Metallurgical Arts of Flamel University. As you step into the world beyond these halls, may your accomplishments reflect the excellence of our beloved university."

Dean Vayu handed over the certificate to Marley. Marley grinned from ear to ear, looking back at Rowan and waving it in the air before walking off the other side. Two men and a woman, all dressed in suits, flocked to Marley the moment she stepped off stage. Behind them were a group of recruiters in military dress, their uniforms adorned with the azure and silver insignias of the Island Coalition. They'd been approaching every metallurgical graduate, desperate for alchemists who could help harvest the rich veins of reactive metals that had sparked the ongoing conflict. He hoped whatever they offered Marley wouldn't be worth it.

A crew of rusted automatons raced to the stone slab, pouring water over the top and scrubbing it clean of any residual markings. As they did that, Dean Vayu flipped through his clipboard, sighed, cleared his throat, and said,

"Next, for his second attempt, we have Rowan Mosswood."

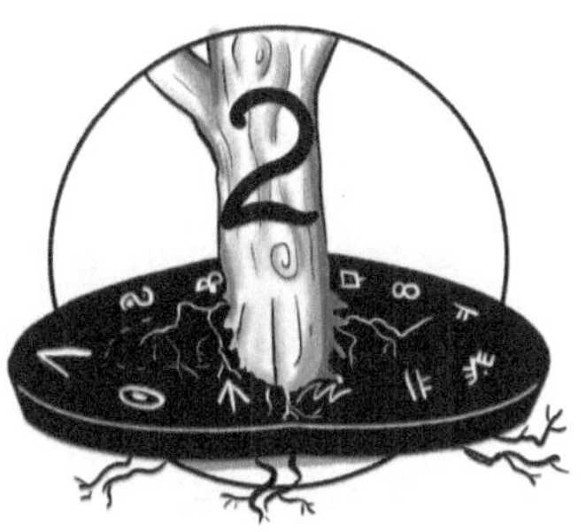

ALCHEMY IN COBALT SQUARE

Rowan gripped his burlap sack and shakily walked up the steps and onto the stage. His heart beat loudly in his chest, a hush forming around Cobalt Square's stone buildings. The memory of his last attempt—the fungus, the screaming, the shame—threatened to overwhelm him. But this time would be different. It had to be.

He approached the slab, averting his eyes from the crowd and the dean, though he couldn't miss how Dean Vayu stepped back, no doubt wincing from the odor emanating from the manure sack. The sharp scent of ammonia mixed with earth didn't exactly inspire confidence, but Rowan knew what he was doing. At least, he hoped he did.

Rowan breathed in and focused only on the slab, ignoring the sea of people watching him. He reached inside, pulling out a wad of wet, grimy manure.

As expected, the crowd groaned. There weren't many botanical alchemists for a reason, and the people of Neosilica were looking for a spectacle. Rowan had been expecting this.

He started on the sigil, using the manure to craft a large square representing earth. He moved with precision, his hand well practiced despite his tremble. While chalk was the standard medium for most alchemical sigils, bigger or experimental feats often called for the components to be used in the sigil instead of piled nearby. The manure would forge a stronger connection—assuming he didn't mess up the proportions.

For this sigil, the stronger the connection to earth, the better the result. Wavy lines intersected two opposing edges of the square. Each wave represented water, life-giving and essential. Triangles pointed outward from the other two edges, sharp and decisive—the power of fire. Spirals tailed inward, representing aether as they formed the inner circle, the mystical force that bound all elements together.

The crowd's whispers grew louder as he worked. He caught fragments of their discussions—speculation about what the strange botanical alchemist was attempting, whether this would be another disaster like last time. He pushed their voices away, focusing only on his work.

When it was done, he stepped back, running the sigil over in his head one more time. This was the culmination of years of study. It had to be precise, right down to which portion was drawn first. He looked back at the dean, who frowned at the slab, slowly taking notes.

Rowan pulled the last component from his pocket, carefully extracting the tiny metallic blue seed from its jar and placing it in the center of the sigil. He took his position, kneeling down and placing his palms on the edges of the square. He focused, green magic pouring out of him like cold liquid, seamlessly tracing along his drawn lines. His mind stretched and followed, coursing through a labyrinth of turns and curves until it reached the seed. Fractals filled his mind, unending patterns and possibilities flashing. He was the sigil, and the sigil was him. He was the lines, the curves, the manure, and the seed. Magic vibrated in his heart, and energy pulsed from the slab. The sensation filled him, a familiar buzz of life.

First, he heard the crack of stone, which sent murmurs rippling through the crowd. Then came a rush of air as the seed burst.

The connection between him and the sigil broke with an audible snap, and Rowan fell back as roots drilled into the ground.

They spread like lightning through the stone, cracking and drilling into it. A trunk twisted up toward the sky, its bark a strange metallic blue that shone in the late morning light.

One moment, the sun looked down on him, and the next, branches covered his view, spreading like fingers. Thin, blue leaves sprouted in waves, their sharp, serrated edges stretching long like willow leaves. Each one created a kaleidoscope of blue that painted the ground, and the crowd grew silent.

Then, as quick as it had grown, the leaves trembled. They came clattering to the ground like metallic rain, and the tree—his beautiful, impossible tree—crumbled into dust. His heart sank. He hoped the tree would stay a little longer to take in its beauty. But there was still a chance he passed. There had to be.

Rowan looked up at the dean, who sighed and scribbled a note on the paper. Rowan had to move quickly, before the dean announced his failure.

He reached into the pile of dust, feeling the edge of a leaf cut into his skin. He pulled it out and held it up. "This," Rowan shouted, "is the final."

Dean Vayu raised an eyebrow.

"They named Cobalt Square after the rich deposits of cobalt that have since been mined. However, plants have a way of absorbing trace minerals and metals. I've been working on a project that can dredge up and deposit them in the leaves. The process is still unstable and time-consuming, but I believe we can bring botanical alchemy back to Neosilica."

The crowd burst into laughter, but as Rowan stared out at them, he found several people carefully kicking aside the dust and inspecting the leaves.

He turned to Dean Vayu, who pursed his lips. "You broke my slab," he grumbled.

"Sorry, Dean Vayu. I didn't—"

The dean cut him off, quickly drawing a purple sigil in the air and shouting to the crowd, "Rowan Mosswood, you have demonstrated your... abilities in your selected discipline. I hereby grant you this seal of approval, denoting you as an Alchemist of the Botanical Arts of Flamel University. May you remember the excellence and expectation of all graduates of Flamel University as you step into the world beyond these halls."

Rowan pocketed his cobalt leaf and wiped his hands before grabbing his certificate. He'd finally done it; he'd finally passed. Before he could take the certificate, Dean Vayu leaned in and spoke in a smooth, almost paternal voice. "Rowan, about your loans, I may have a solution that could benefit us both."

"Right," Rowan said, biting his lip. "I can pay them back. I promise."

"Actually, the university has an opportunity," Dean Vayu said. "We'd like to put you out on assignment. A small place, a week's travel north by train. Consider it your...

postgraduate research."

Rowan's eyes widened. "Assignment? And my debts?"

"Paid in full after you report back to us in a year." The dean's voice dropped lower. "There are... peculiarities up there that need investigation. Things that might interest a botanical alchemist."

"A year?" Rowan asked. "But that far north? Does magic even work there?"

"That is for you to find out, but I need an answer now," Dean Vayu said, his grip tight on the certificate.

This paper was everything Rowan wanted. Everything his mother wanted for him. He ran the offer through his head, looking over to Marley, who was laughing as she spoke with a businesswoman with a long red braid. Her joy was infectious, even from this distance. She'd made these years bearable, giving him friendship when he needed it most. And now he was considering leaving—not just the city, but everything he knew.

It was only a year away from Neosilica. From the constant hum of automatons and the shine of metal towers. No new silly inventions to try out at the weekend market. And away from Marley and all her unwavering support.

But away from all this, far up in the northern countryside, maybe he could find what his mother had always talked about. People still need healers and botanical alchemy, a place untamed by city walls and mechanical progress. Maybe he could finally become the alchemist she'd believed he could be there.

"I-I," Rowan stuttered. Then, stronger, he said, "I'll take it."

Botanical Alchemist Essentials: Dirt

"I swear," Marley heaved, sweat dripping down her face. "If you only packed books and no clothes, I'm going to kill you."

Rowan's heart pounded in his chest as he waddled up the marbled steps of Argentum Station backward—named for Marley's great-grandmother Millie, one of the legendary alchemists who forged the nation's railways—in a sweat-covered button-down and slightly oversized pants only held up by a pair of suspenders. His fingers ached as he clutched onto his one and only suitcase that would accompany him on his journey.

"There's dirt in it too," he said.

"Dirt?!" Marley shouted, slamming her end of the suitcase down on the stairs. She adjusted her grease-covered overalls and pulled back her purple locs into a ponytail. "Who the hell packs dirt?"

A tinny voice echoed next to them, sounding from one of the many tall metallic automatons lining the stairwell. "Please, do not hinder the flow of traffic. Proceed up the stairs."

Argentum Station was packed, and even though they kept closer to the line of automatons than the rest of the crowd, their momentary stop on the stairwell had already resulted in three shoulder checks from passing people.

"Yeah, yeah, yeah," Marley grumbled, yanking up the suitcase and begrudgingly walking up the stairs.

"It's a botanical thing," Rowan said, finding purchase on the last step up onto the platform.

"What?" Marley asked, pushing through the last few steps. Immediately, she let go of her end, and the wheels bounced on the solid stone with a loud clunk.

They paused for a moment, catching their breath before weaving through the crowd of people in various forms of dress. Although newly built, Argentum Station quickly became the hub of Neosilica, providing the fastest transportation to some of the farther-reaching cities and villages. All that meant to Rowan was more people in his way as the two of them settled under the sign for Platform 3, the exact spot Dean Vayu had instructed him to wait.

"It makes alchemy easier," Rowan said, holding the stitch that had formed in his side. "Botanical alchemists get accustomed to local dirt. For all I know, they're sending me off to the coast, and I doubt they considered the time it takes to acclimate to a region's soil composition. So, I brought dirt."

Marley elbowed him before leaning up against the smooth marble wall. "You better take care of yourself. You hear me? If it's two months in and I'm not hearing about some boy you're chasing after, then don't come whining to me because you only have two pairs of dirt-covered clothes."

"What?" Rowan said, spreading his arms wide, showing off the various lines of dirt that had already found their way into his clothes. "The rustic plant-daddy vibes don't do it for you?"

Marley snorted, "Plant daddy? More like sprout twink, if you're asking me."

"Hey, who are you calling a sprout twink, my little grease mommy?" Rowan retorted, falling into a fit of laughs.

"I'm going to miss this," Marley said after the laughter died down. "You got your ticket?"

"No," Rowan said. "The dean said he was sending someone to meet me." Rowan watched people pass by, eyeing people with significantly smaller luggage hopping onto a large two-story train, crafted by the finest metallurgical alchemists to travel up to the far north. A knot formed in his stomach, and he looked down.

Marley bumped shoulders with him. "It'll be fine. You said it's a week north of here, right? I mean, I'm visiting, obviously. As soon as I get a break from this internship."

"Hold up," Rowan said, a smile stretching across his face. "It's official?"

Marley stood straighter and cleared her throat. "Yep. You're looking at the newest employee of Titanium Innovations, the shinier and better version of Steelwright Industries."

"When were you going to tell me? Congratulations!" Rowan dove in, wrapping arms around her, taking in the acrid scent of burnt metal and grease.

Marley grunted and wriggled free from his bear hug. "I just found out this morning. You were caught up in—"

"Rowan Mosswood?" a gruff voice said behind him, cutting Marley off.

Rowan turned and came face to chest with a tall, broad-shouldered man adorned in a deep blue uniform with gold cording and the crest of Flamel University embroidered on the chest.

"Uh, yes?" Rowan said.

The man held out a train ticket and a sealed, cream-colored envelope. "Courtesy of Dean Vayu." He nodded to the double-decker train. "Better board, they're leaving soon."

"Uh, thanks," Rowan said, taking the ticket and envelope from the man. "What's in the—" he started, but before he could finish, the man turned and vanished into the sea of people.

"Well, bye," Marley shouted after the man. She turned and pulled the ticket from Rowan's hands. "So, where is it? Are they putting you on some beach?" After a long pause, she looked up. "Frostfern Valley?"

"Where the hell is Frostfern Valley?"

"Second to last stop," Marley said, squinting at the ticket. "Somewhere in the Ferra Mountains."

Rowan spun around, eyeing a large map with a red line trailing up and into the coast. On it was one tiny dot way up in the mountains, spread far apart from the other stops. "That's the middle of nowhere! Are you serious?"

Marley handed him back the ticket. "Yep, and they put you up front. Better get some earplugs."

A horn sounded, echoing loudly onto the platform.

Rowan looked over at the train, then back at Marley. "Well. I guess this is goodbye?"

"Don't make it weird," Marley said, diving in for a hug. "It's just a year. And I'll come visit. I promise. Even if it's a five-day ride."

"You're right, it's just a year," he squeezed her back.

"You'll do great, Mosswood," she said, grabbing him

by the shoulders. "And if you don't, and you destroy Frostfern Valley with another one of your sentient fungus stunts, I'll be sure to make you look good in your biography."

Rowan laughed. "Thanks for the vote of confidence."

"Any time."

He gripped his suitcase, giving Marley a last wave before starting toward the train.

It loomed over him, the fine, dark, metallic train glimmering in the sunlight. A conductor automaton, dressed in full garb with a deep red woolen three-piece suit, took his ticket and helped him heft his suitcase onto the train. Inside, the floor was carpeted with the same deep red, and the corridors were lined with rich mahogany paneling, contrasting the cold metallic exterior.

Rowan navigated through a few cars until he reached the front, stopping at sleeper car 1A tucked right at the front of the car. As he slid the door open, he saw just how small the room was, with a bunk that would cause him to sleep in the fetal position across from a small drop-down wooden table that would only work if he sat hunched over on the bed.

The sharp scent of burning coal wafted into his room, a strong undertone that intertwined with the pleasant woody smell of a newly furnished train that Rowan could get used to.

Atop his bed were two packaged earplugs, which

Rowan promptly stuffed into his ears as the churning engine rumbled his room. He tucked his suitcase underneath his bed and leaned in toward the small window, looking over heads until he spotted the purple hair in the crowd. He waved, eventually catching Marley's gaze, and she waved back, sending him a kiss in the air.

The train whistle blew one last time, and the train started its slow churn away from the station.

Rowan's chest tightened, and his neck grew hot. This was really happening, and this would be his home for the next five days. Then what? Frostfern Valley? What would even be there waiting for him? Would he fit in?

He slowed his breathing, and his eyes fell on the envelope, still sealed with a wax imprint and the crest of Flamel University.

He cracked it open and dumped the contents out onto the table. Aside from a letter, a few stacks of crisp banknotes and an ornate brass key with an intricate leaf design clattered onto the desk.

He'd packed everything he had in his suitcase, including what little money he had to hold him over until he found himself a job. But now, with the money in front of him, he wouldn't need one. At least, not for a while.

He quickly stuffed the banknotes into the envelope and wedged it beside his suitcase. Something for him to worry about later.

He looked over the letter and read:

Dear Mr. Rowan Mosswood,

I trust this letter finds you earnest and prepared as you embark on your postgraduate studies. First and foremost, I must reiterate that you are traveling as a representative of Flamel University, and all future certifications and degrees for your studies will depend on how you represent our fine establishment.

We have assigned you to study the depletion of magic in the northern expanse, in the small town of Frostfern Valley. We at the university have been aware of this depletion, even studying it a decade prior, but funding for the previous research halted. Anonymous donors have provided the funding for the research due to Neosilica's industry's interest in expanding infrastructure and connectivity. Enclosed in this envelope is your first quarterly stipend for your year-long study. Additional payments will follow, pending your monthly reports. You will also find a brass key. The previous researcher in Frostfern Valley owned a greenhouse and laboratory just outside the city. While the town has honored our agreement to preserve the property's ownership, the building has stood vacant for a decade. Though we've allocated funds for basic maintenance over the years, I cannot speak to the current state of the structure—I suspect you may need to dedicate some of your stipends to necessary repairs.

We expect updates on the status of your research on a monthly basis. We would like to know if there is any biological correlation between the natural ebb and flow of magic in the north and how to predict, leverage, or potentially restore balance. All tests, methods, procedures, new alchemical discoveries, and field notes will be returned to the university for review.

At the end of your studies, we will grant you an opportunity to publish your findings in the Journal of Alchemical Arts.

Mr. Mosswood, I have the utmost confidence in your abilities and look forward to your findings. May your work in Frostfern Valley be a testament to the profound relevance of botanical alchemy in our world today.

With warm regards,
Dean Vayu

Flamel University
Grand Alchemist of the Ethereal Arts

Rowan leaned back in his chair. Publication in the Journal of Alchemical Arts? He could hardly believe it. His mind wandered to the great alchemists whose work filled those pages—masters who chose their own paths, who pursued whatever called to them rather than chasing after whatever paid the bills. Maybe someday he could have that kind of freedom, choosing his own research like Dean Vayu instead of scrambling for whatever would take a botanical alchemist.

He looked out the window, his heart racing as the city melted into the countryside.

The Art of Alchemical
Transportation

Two days in, and the ceiling of Rowan's train roomette was practically mocking him. How could days in this room overlooking gorgeous rolling hills and forests be so mind-numbingly dull? If he read another page from his books, he was going to gouge his eyes out—he'd never felt this desperate for distraction before, even during his longest study sessions. He'd spent years locked away in college. Still, nothing compared to the torment of stuffing cotton into your ears and locking yourself in a room where you could touch both opposing walls with outstretched hands. He craved escape.

The last time he freed himself from his self-dubbed "broom closet," the train was packed with other travelers. Granted, since then, more and more people left the train than stepped on. But the memory of grouchy glares because of his mostly dirt-covered apparel as he squeezed his way through the filled observation deck and sleeping cars to a locked car five cars down was enough to keep him secluded in cabin 1A.

Finally, his restlessness winning out over caution, he let out a hefty sigh and pushed himself up to his feet, gingerly stepping out onto the carpeted floor of the hall. As he'd hoped, the hall was nearly empty, with only one woman, with a wrinkled and pinched face, waddling back into her roomette. The observation deck was more occupied than he'd hoped, with a scattering of passengers, but he could at least pause and look up through the glass and see a gray-covered sky.

All the booths were still taken with people far too focused on their mugs of coffee or newspapers to truly enjoy anything beyond the glass. However, there was one table in particular that caught his eye. A young woman, a little younger than himself, hunched over a makeshift fort constructed of books atop the table. As he approached, he saw a tiny pinprick of wavering light hiding between the books, casting a slight glow on her blue eyes, soft, freckled face, and blond, braided hair.

Rowan cleared his throat. "Mind if I join you?"

Doing exactly the opposite of what Rowan had intended, she jumped, sending a tower of books cascading down. A green tome fell right into the light, and it hovered in the air for a moment while the other books clattered onto the table. Then, it collapsed in on itself, vanishing along with the light.

"Oh shit! Shit! Shit! Shit!" she shouted, drawing disapproving glances from the other occupants.

Rowan looked down at the table, noting the unmistakable markings of an alchemy sigil written in chalk. While many people in Neosilica revered alchemy in all its glory, the farther north you got, the less supportive people were. Especially when it was done near them, on a train, where they couldn't escape if something were to go wrong.

Acting on instinct, he slipped into the booth, shielding her exposed sigil work from the prying eyes of the few passengers present.

"What was that?" Rowan whispered, his gaze fixed on the fading symbols. The complexity was mesmerizing, especially the recurrent elemental symbols intertwining in an intricate dance.

"It's... nothing," she mumbled, a little too quickly, clearly flustered. "Professor Valeria warned me about practicing on the train. I'm dead if she finds out I lost her copy of Aether to Quanta."

Rowan picked up a few of the books, reading titles like Quantum Alchemic Paradigms and From Cauldrons to Quarks: An Alchemical Guide to Improbability. "Name's Rowan," he said, smiling up at her. "Recent grad from Flamel."

She sighed, looking around the room as she pushed the books aside. "Oh, good. Flamel? Me too, second year. Elara Frost."

Rowan held up a paperback with a rather lewd image on the front and the title Briefs and Bosons: The Story of My Quantum Entangled Underwear. "Quantum, I take it?"

Elara's cheeks flushed, and she snatched the book from his hand. "Dr. Phomen writes some... questionable books, but he has some real practical uses in them. I mean, his personal life is a mess too, cheated on his partners after that came out."

"Really? Well, I, for one, am shocked," Rowan said, exaggerating as he clutched his chest.

Elara laughed, shoving some of her books into her bag. She looked out at the rolling green hills. "Just six more months, then I'll be back in class. Back where I can actually make a simple space fold without making everyone panic." She looked back at him and frowned. "You graduated, right? What are you doing going north?"

"Postgrad study," Rowan said. "Dean Vayu has me checking on some greenhouse in Frostfern. Ever heard of it?"

"You could say that." Elara looked down and smiled. "My mom's the mayor."

"Oh!" Rowan said, a little louder than he intended, based on the grumbles from the other patrons in the car. He leaned in close and whispered. "Wait, how does a kid from Frostfern get into Flamel? I mean—" He stumbled over his words, seeing the look on Elara's face. "I mean, this far north, with the magic and all, how?"

Elara looked away and shifted in her seat. "I wish I could say it was talent, but my mom got me in. Hard to say no when a mayor, even a small one, from the north is willing to send her daughter to school at a magic academy."

Rowan nodded to the stack of books. "But quantum? You've got to be a genius to get any of that stuff."

For a moment, she smiled. "Try telling that to my mom. Quantum alchemy? Might as well tell her I'm throwing my education away. We northerners aren't stupid. We know about alchemy. We just care more about the practical ones. Ores, electrical, heck, even automaton studies would have been better than quantum." She looked him up and down, her eyes stopping on a few stains on his shirt. "What'd you study?"

"Botanical."

Elara leaned back and grinned. "Ah, you'll fit right in then. Better watch out for Mr. Tiller; he'll talk your ear off if you can help his crops."

Rowan smirked, running a hand through his

unkempt hair. "That might be a nice change of pace."

"What's that supposed to mean?" Elara said.

"Botanical alchemy is a dead art. Even after my final, the scouts walked right past me. Not that I expected anything different, but I mean you're in quantum for a reason, right? Maybe the people up here won't roll their eyes when they find out what I studied."

Elara smirked. "Oh, they'll still do that. They don't love alchemy but help them out here and there, and you'll turn them around. You're moving into that old greenhouse, right?"

"I am," Rowan nodded. "Why?"

"Because the last guy who was there got the crops to grow out of season. I don't remember it much when it happened, but people now complain that we ran the alchemist out of town when things were getting good."

"Well," Rowan said, laughing to himself. "They better watch out if they try to run me out of town."

Elara frowned.

"Remember the sentient fungus?"

"That was you?!" Elara shouted.

A man behind her turned around and glared. "Keep it down," he hissed.

Elara crouched low to the table. "That was you?" she whispered.

Rowan nodded, rubbing the back of his neck. "The one and only. Took a whole year to get it all."

"Remind me to stay on your good side. I remember Professor Berms was stuck working out of a closet for four months because of that."

"It wasn't my finest moment," he admitted.

A giggle escaped Elara, which quickly turned into laughter. "Oh gods, I remember seeing the boy running all over campus. And that was you! " She wiped away a tear, still chuckling. "Well, it was nice finally meeting you, Rowan. Just don't make yourself a stranger. I might lose my mind if I can't talk alchemy to someone."

Rowan grinned. "As long as you don't collapse me into some space fold."

She smirked, gathering her books. "Deal. And in return, no sentient fungi."

"Deal."

Hours turned into days as Rowan and Elara took up residence on the observation deck. Others slowly filtered away, and soon enough, it was just the two of them. Rolling hills turned into mountains, and the train slithered up and through stony corridors, until all Rowan could see were snow-covered mountains and dark green blotches of a valley forest below.

"We're almost there," Elara said as they settled into the booth early in the morning on their last day. She sat across from him, holding a steaming mug of hot chocolate.

"Is it always this cold?" Rowan asked, clutching onto his two layers of button-down shirts.

Elara chuckled. "Up here, yeah, but Frostfern is down in a valley." She looked out the window and straightened up. "You should see it in a second."

Rowan leaned in close to the window as the train rounded another corner. Below them, between jagged mountains and snow, was a valley that looked like it was taken straight out of a fairy tale. Clusters of homes, each topped with a smoking stone chimney and sharply pointed roofs covered in moss and splotches of lingering snow, huddled together between cobbled streets. Even from this distance, Rowan could see the buildings were colored in pale pastels, and lights flickered from within as the town woke.

Following the streets with his eyes, Rowan could make out the heart of town, where buildings gathered around what appeared to be a central square. However, the details were lost to the morning mist flowing in from the river.

Surrounding the town, creeping up the sides of the mountain, were farms, slightly browned but mingling among the dense trees that cascaded up the stone.

A massive waterfall streamed down on the other side of the valley, crafting a river that cut the landscape in half before vanishing out into the forest.

"It's... beautiful," Rowan breathed.

"It's Frostfern," Elara said, sipping from her mug. "Home, sweet home."

PLANT PROPAGATION AND ROOTING TECHNIQUES

A polished maple carriage drawn by two dappled gray horses awaited them at the station, its brass fittings gleaming against the wood. Rowan watched as porters and travelers bustled around them with handcarts and simple wooden wagons, unloading supplies from the train. When Elara approached her waiting transport, the uniformed driver bowed slightly and opened the door.

"Come on," she said, gesturing to Rowan. "There's plenty of room."

Rowan hesitated, clutching his dirt-filled suitcase. "Are you sure?"

"Of course. Better than trying to find space with the market deliveries."

Even this fine carriage differed drastically from the automated metal carriages that had overrun Neosilica. As they wound down the mountain path, Rowan pressed against the window. Frostfern drew closer—a picturesque valley town already alive with activity as vendors erected colorful stalls on nearly every street. Fresh bread and sweet cinnamon wafted through the window, making his mouth water.

He jostled in his seat, noting how the buildings grew more densely packed, their pastel colors growing brighter in the morning light as they approached the town center. They passed by stalls, and Rowan noticed how the vendors stopped to look, all eyeing him. Eventually, they stopped in front of a huge home, and their driver helped Elara step out as Rowan nearly stumbled out and fell flat on his face.

Adjusting his clothes, he eyed another carriage pass and asked, "Busy day?"

"Just take my things inside," Elara said to the driver. "I'm going to help my friend find someone who can take him to the greenhouse. Mind grabbing one of the handcarts? He really shouldn't be lugging that around."

The driver grunted, lifting her suitcase and trailing inside without a word.

"What did you ask?" Elara asked.

"Oh, just, the carriages. Busier than I thought it'd be." The driver came back out, pulling a small metal cart behind him. He and Rowan maneuvered the suitcase on top of it. "Thanks," he said to the driver, who grunted again and skulked off toward the house.

"Well, you're lucky," Elara said, starting down the road. "The spring shipments just came in. Merchants and traders from all over bring goods from the south, and families from nearly fifty miles away come to Frostfern for the market festival. Some are already trickling in, but by week's end, the town will be bursting." She quickened her pace. "If we go now, I might be able to get you to the greenhouse before the early crowds arrive."

They headed toward the town center, which was a kaleidoscope of color. Not only were homes painted in lilac, mint green, and buttercup yellow hues, but people were also constructing colorful stalls and decorations along the roads.

"This is... amazing!" Rowan said, following behind as the handcart rattled over the cobblestones. He paused at a table filled with white flowers, their petals almost translucent in the morning light. Though slightly dull and misshapen, they held a peculiar beauty.

The vendor, an elderly woman with weathered hands, eyed him warily. "Completely free of any alchemical tampering," she said.

"We call those frostblooms up here," Elara said, cutting off the vendor. "They're the first signs that our frost season is almost over."

He approached the table, studying the blooms. Their petals were thicker than any lily he'd seen, with a waxy coating that caught the light, and their leaves grew in spiraling patterns up unusually sturdy stems. "They're like lilies but hardier. Built to survive the cold, I'd guess."

They walked deeper through the square, dodging a table filled with wilted turnips and another of somewhat questionable apples. Regardless of their looks, much like the flowers, everywhere he could see, people were smiling and eyeing up the tables.

"My mom told me the crops were struggling this season," Elara whispered as they passed another stall of lackluster produce. "She's been trying everything we can think of, but nothing's working."

"Good thing you've got a resident green thumb now," he smirked. "You all could do with a few healthy medicinal herbs growing too."

"As long as you don't introduce yourself to everyone like you did me, then you might get a few of them on your side."

"For the record, I was quiet. You're just jumpy," Rowan said.

Elara smirked and tutted her tongue. "Well, for the record, you owe me a copy of Aether to Quanta then."

They turned down another street, this one less crowded. "So, uh, where are we going?" Rowan asked.

"To Nevs's carpentry shop. My cousin's an apprentice there, and he lives out by your greenhouse," Elara said. "I'm guessing he came here early to skip out on farm work."

"Does this cousin have a name?"

"Jimson. He's really good, too. You'll see."

As they turned a corner, Rowan caught sight of a quaint little shop nestled between two bright blue-painted buildings. The scent of slightly burnt pine wafted out from the partially cracked sliding door, somewhat minty and earthy all at once.

"Jimson, I hope you're decent!" Elara shouted, sliding the door open the rest of the way, revealing a treasure trove of masterfully crafted wooden wonders. From furniture with smooth clawed feet to delicate figurines that looked so real, Rowan had to do a double take on some of them.

"Holy hell. Is this all his?" Rowan breathed, unable to tear his eyes away from a red wooden statue of a man draped in fabric. Somehow, the fabric, which was also carved, looked like it could slip off any second. "It's amazing."

"That one is," Elara said. "But mostly, it's all Nevs's."

"Is that a Lars I hear?" A tall figure emerged from the back of the shop, wearing a thick apron and wiping sawdust off his large belly and bushy reddish beard with thick, muscled arms. He grinned from ear to ear when his dark eyes met Elara's, and Rowan's heart skipped. "Hey, little cuz. I didn't know you'd be back so soon. Finally, drop out of school and start shadowing Aunt Willow?" Jimson asked.

"Ha. Ha. You and she wish. I'm on summer holiday," Elara said, sticking her tongue out.

Jimson's eyes met Rowan's, and all Rowan could think about was how warm and squishy those arms would be wrapped around him, holding him close and running his hand through that short-cut hair—

"Who's your friend here?" he asked.

"Uh-hi. Uh, I'm Rowan. Rowan Mosswood," he stuttered, the words tumbling out. He shook Jimson's hand, feeling the rough warmth of his calloused grip. As he looked around the room again, his gaze fell upon a set of simple cabinets just behind Jimson. Around the edges of the doors were delicate etchings of leaves and vines, curling around the wood as if they were growing right before his eyes.

"Is that—is that what you're working on?" Rowan stammered.

"Yep," Jimson said, looking back at his work. "Couldn't do it without Nevs—"

"Couldn't do what without me?" a voice called from the back of the workshop. A tall woman emerged from behind a partition, her muscular arms covered in light sawdust that stood out against her dark skin. As she approached, she wiped her hands on her work apron, her bright red braided hair wrapped into a large bun on her head.

"Speaking of," Jimson grinned. "Nevs, this is Rowan. He's, uh—Lars's friend?"

"Alchemist," Rowan said. "Here from the college to help."

Nevs's eyes lit up as she studied Rowan, her gaze sharp and considering. "Botanical, right?" When Rowan nodded, she smiled. "Good. This town could use someone who can help with the farms." She ran her hand along the cabinet's etched vines.

"These works are so detailed. Did you—" Rowan started, then stopped.

"Use magic?" Nevs laughed. A warm sound filled the workshop. "Nope, just years of practice. Though some people might call it magic, I guess. So, you'll be living out of that old greenhouse then?"

Rowan nodded. "Yep, the college said it might not be in great condition, though."

Nevs turned to Jimson. "Let's show our new alchemist some Frostfern hospitality. Help him get settled—those repairs won't be quick."

"That place has been abandoned for years," Jimson said. "It's not bad, but uh, you might be better off shacking up at the inn."

A buzzing hum traveled through Rowan as he looked at Jimson, one he couldn't quite put his finger on, but something that made his heart beat hard in his chest.

"I'll finish up the Tiller order," Nevs said, heading back to her work. "Take what time you need."

"Great. See? I brought a friend for you, cousin." Elara smiled. "Now don't pick on him, you hear me? Mom will kill me if we get letters from the college that the townsfolk of Frostfern are harassing students."

"As will I," Nevs said, heading back to her workstation. "You won't be giving us carpenters a bad name."

Jimson pinched Elara's cheek hard and said, "The only one I'd pick on is you." He turned to Rowan and clapped his hands together. "I'll grab some tools and help you take a crack at it. No guarantees, but better start fixing up the place now."

"Uh, yeah, that'd be great. Thank you," Rowan replied.

"And I'll leave you both to it," Elara said, grinning from ear to ear as she turned on her heel. "I'm sure Mother Mayor would be mad if I didn't stop in and say hi."

As Elara left, Jimson turned back to a bench and started gathering tools. Rowan ran a finger along one of the wooden figurines and cut through the silence. "So, what got you into woodworking?"

Jimson pulled off the apron and hung it up on the wall. "Well, I used to get in trouble for hanging out near the woods when I was younger. Always making wooden swords and shields to fight off the monsters. And it's this or farming, and my brothers seem to do that just fine."

"The talent, though. I've never seen anything like it. Neosilica is too focused on industry to make anything like this."

"I think that's why Elara loves it down there. You said your discipline was botanical, right?" Jimson asked.

"Yeah. Not quite the industry-driving discipline."

"Ha, maybe not there!" Jimson laughed, dimples showing on his close-shaved face. "But up here, we could use a little magic. What you do is what I try doing here every day. Taking nature and exposing its beauty."

Heat flushed through Rowan's cheeks, and he looked down at the floor. "Yeah, I guess so."

"Well, Mr. Rowan. Shall we get you settled in?" Jimson hefted a bag of tools.

"Sounds good to me," Rowan agreed, following behind Jimson as he closed the shop.

Rowan pulled the metal handcart holding his suitcase behind him as they strolled through the cobblestone streets of Frostfern, the air perfumed with the scent of wildflowers and freshly baked bread. Rowan's throat stayed dry as his mind raced. Buildings dwindled, and homes spread farther and farther apart. Once they reached the outskirts of the town, Rowan couldn't help but notice the stark contrast between the dense forest filled with greenery and budding leaves that trailed off beyond the valley and the struggling yellowed farms.

"So, uh, Jimson?" Rowan asked.

"Yes?"

"Is it just me, or do the farms around here look... well, off?"

Jimson slowed his pace and stared out at the wilted crops. "It's been a tough start to the year. The snow didn't want to melt, and now we're fighting against weak soil. All I've heard from my dad and brothers is that nothing wants to grow, no matter how hard they try."

"Any idea why?" Rowan asked.

"Nope. But if this keeps up, we're gonna need more supply trains," Jimson said.

They continued toward the edge of the woods, cresting over a small hill, and the once majestic structure came into view. Rowan's heart sank like a stone. The greenhouse was worse off than he'd imagined; many broken windows stared back at him like empty eye sockets, and ivy had wrapped itself around the rusted metal and wood frames. It seemed to groan beneath the weight of years of neglect.

"This is it, isn't it?" Rowan asked, not ready for the answer.

"Yup," Jimson replied. "We've got an extra bed out on the farm. We could probably get you all set up there if you didn't want to walk back into town."

Rowan's heart raced at the thought. "No. That's fine. I

can do this. It can't be all that bad. I mean, half the building is still standing, and looks like the living quarters have all four walls and a roof."

Rowan fished around in his pockets for the small brass key as he tried to quell the doubt gnawing at him. He could be back in Neosilica right now, sharing an apartment with Marley. Maybe even setting up a small shop of specially crafted metal plants. Instead, he was pretty sure some animal had made a home of half this building, and he'd have plenty of manure to contend with.

"Well, uh," Jimson said softly. "I'm here to help. We'll start with the living quarters. Get the windows patched up. Clean out the debris. I can get some glass this week and we can get you some proper windows. Sound good?"

"Yeah, I mean. If you—" Rowan took a deep breath, filling his lungs with the crisp forest air. "Yes, I would love the help."

Jimson smiled, "Great! Let's do this."

Bonding Sigils 101

Rowan inserted the key into the arched chestnut door and twisted the lock, the heavy door groaning in response. Instead of swinging open smoothly, the door lurched forward, wobbling in its frame before succumbing to gravity. It fell, crashing into the ground with a thud, raising a cloud of dust.

"Well, uh..." Rowan stared at the fallen door. "That's a great sign."

A deep, rumbling laugh erupted from Jimson's chest. The sound filled the space between them, and Rowan couldn't help but be drawn in by its infectious nature. His smile grew as Jimson's shoulders shook, and his eyes crinkled at the corners.

"You could say that." Jimson wiped tears from his eyes, still chuckling. "First on the list, repair the door."

"Hope you don't have any plans for the rest of the day," Rowan replied, laughing to mask the dread of what else could go wrong.

He stepped inside and wafted away dust as he peered into the living quarters. Before he could even focus on one thing, he heard scurrying little feet racing off into nooks and crannies. Once the dust cleared, his eyes fell on a heap of broken furniture and torn fabrics.

"Oh, this is bad," Rowan muttered under his breath.

Jimson stepped in behind him and hefted up the door, leaning it up against the wall. "We'll do what we can today and get this place fixed up in no time." He patted Rowan on the shoulder, giving it a slight squeeze that made Rowan shiver. "If it makes you feel better, I've seen worse."

"Really?" Rowan raised an eyebrow.

"Maybe." Jimson looked past him and toward the heap of furniture. "Maybe not." He grabbed his tools and worked on the door. He moved quick, inspecting the frame and the door and pulling loose nails. Rowan did his best to peel his eyes away from watching the man work and instead focused on the rest of the room. There was a broom in the corner, which proved invaluable in sweeping up the nests and other questionable debris from the floor.

"Looks like some of this stuff is pretty far gone," Rowan said a while later, after clearing the floor and finally mustering the will to inspect the furniture closely. Some of the wood fell apart in his hand and rotted away.

Jimson tested the door, now properly reattached, and looked at Rowan. "That bed of yours doesn't look too good either. You'd be better off with a new one."

"And I don't suppose I'll be able to just pick one up in town?" Rowan asked.

Jimson tilted his head side to side. "No? Not a good one, at least. We've got space back at the farm. I could have a new one for you in a few days."

Heat surged up the back of Rowan's neck. "Uh. No. I-I can manage here."

"Really? What are you going to do, sleep on the floor?" Jimson asked. "Offer still stands. We've got blankets and beds that actually work."

Rowan eyed his suitcase. He didn't want to use it already, but he wasn't about to be more of a burden than he'd already become. "No, I can fix it. I think."

"You think? How?"

Now, it was time for Rowan to shine. He puffed up his chest and grinned. "With a little alchemy. I'm not sure how well it will react here, but it's worth a shot."

He pulled the broken bed frame out into the center of the room and grabbed a stick of chalk out from his suitcase.

He started with the outer element ring, focusing primarily on square shapes representing earth, intermixed with waves of water and spirals of aether. Other shapes could represent these elements too, but he found these were the best for his mind to trace. As he closed the outer ring, he stepped back and eyed the broken frame. "What kind of wood is that?"

"Mountain hemlock. Bit of a softer wood than I'd go with."

Rowan nodded and started in on the botanical matrix, defining the conifer and how the pieces of wood could revitalize and fuse back into the shape they once were. There was also the mattress to contend with, which was a mix of cotton and down feathers, he suspected. He drew out the weavings that should hold it together and then finished the matrix, defining the entire bed and how it would be used.

It wasn't perfect since much of his studies were on living plant matter and definitely not construction, but once he was done, he stepped back and nodded. "That should do it. Just need to add in a little bit of dirt."

"Dirt?" Jimson asked as Rowan scooped up a handful of dirt from his bag, placing it in little piles around the edges of the sigil.

"Yep, dirt. Here goes nothing." Rowan dropped to his knees and placed his hands on the edge of the matrix. His mind seeped into the chalk, tracing along the elemental symbols as a buzz formed in the back of his neck. He struggled to fill the matrix as the green energy popped and sizzled. It was as if it argued with him, refusing to fill in the simple sigil to revitalize and bond the wood and fabrics.

The bed frame shuddered before the pieces jumped and stood on end. The wood twisted and snapped as the new wood grew and warped. Rowan frowned, opened his eyes, and watched tiny sprouts of green needle-like leaves grow from the wood. "That's not supposed to happen," he muttered.

"Uh, Rowan, should we—" Jimson started, but the bed frame rushed together, fusing as the growth twisted and braided. The mattress seemed to breathe as little tufts of cotton formed and weaved into each other, patching up holes and filling in the lost stuffing. In seconds, a fully sturdy bed sat before him as if grown from a tree that had spent decades meticulously shaped.

"Well, that looks... cozy," Jimson said, chuckling.

Rowan stared down at the fading sigil. "That shouldn't have happened like that. I had dirt I was familiar with that should have helped connect me to the wood. But it should have mended, not... grow from nothing."

"Think you can do that on the rest of this?" Jimson asked, nodding to the piles of wood.

Rowan crouched beside the bed, running a hand along the wood, now full of scaled bark and twigs with pointy leaves. It was warm to the touch, inviting, and vibrating with magic. "They said it was depleting," he whispered.

"What was that?"

Rowan straightened up from his crouch, dropping his hand. "Nothing. Just didn't expect that to happen. I don't think I should. This is different. Wilder."

Jimson walked over and tested the frame. "Way better than I could have done. Really went for the all-natural look."

Looking at the remaining work to be done, Rowan rested his hands on his hips. "I think I'd rather hold off on the magic. Would you help me with the rest?"

Time passed as they cleared out the fireplace and wiped down a small iron oven that appeared in good condition. The last remnants of daylight filtered through the windows that they hadn't boarded up, casting a warm glow on Jimson. Rowan looked down at the floor and smiled just as his stomach let out an audible rumble.

"I don't suspect you packed any food in that dirt-filled suitcase of yours?" Jimson asked.

"I did not," Rowan said. "Any chance the market is still open? I should've stocked up before we left."

"Maybe, but do you really want to walk all the way back there? Tonight? You could join me and my family for dinner at the farm," Jimson suggested. "Best home-cooked meals in all of Frostfern."

"No, I couldn't—" Rowan hesitated, his heart rate picking up as panic clawed its way up his chest.

"Seriously, they wouldn't mind," Jimson said, nudging Rowan's shoulder. "I can't have you wasting away in this greenhouse. Not after Elara trusted me to not pick on you."

Rowan smirked. "I'd just hate to impose—"

"You're not imposing, and now I won't take no for an answer."

"Okay, fine then," Rowan said, crossing his arms. "I would love to go to a stranger's farm and eat their food."

"Perfect," Jimson said, patting his stomach. "That's more like it."

Jimson pulled open the door, now perfectly gliding on sturdy hinges, and held it as they both stepped outside into the last remaining light.

Farmsteading for
Botanical Alchemists

T he two of them walked along a small dirt path that separated the forest from a large farm filled with slightly yellowed plants.

"You said your farm was right next to the greenhouse. Is this all yours?" Rowan asked.

"Yep, Evergreen Farm. Not the best year for crops, but this is the best farm for fresh produce in nearly forty miles."

They crested a hill, and Rowan spotted a large farmhouse with a high peaked roof, bright yellow pastel-painted sides, a massive front porch, and a barn painted the same bright yellow.

Three men emerged from the barn as they approached, waving down Jimson.

"Hey, Dad," Jimson said as they got closer. The man was a spitting image of his son but with a smattering of gray that peppered his hair and beard. "I brought a friend over for dinner. This is Rowan. Rowan, this is Hawthorn, but most people call him Thorn. And those two are Alder and Sorrel," Jimson said, nodding to his two brothers, who were both older. Alder looked to be the oldest, with broad shoulders and muscles packed onto each other, while Sorrel was much thinner than even Rowan.

"Nice to meet you," Jimson's father said, extending a calloused hand. "You here for the festival?"

"No, actually," Rowan replied, shaking the man's hand. "I came in with Elara from Neosilica."

"Wait, Neosilica?" Alder asked. "Does that mean..."

Hawthorn's face paled for a second, and he let go of Rowan's hand. He glared at Alder and Sorrel, then, as if nothing had happened, he smiled wide and gripped onto Rowan's shoulder. "Well, a friend of Elara and my son is always welcome here. Why don't you show him around while I let Mari know we have a guest?"

Jimson nodded and waved. "Come on, let me show you around the farm."

He led Rowan along a gravel path that snaked

around the property, giving them a full view of the crops, mountains, and village in the distance. They came full circle, stepping onto the front porch and staring off toward Frostfern.

"It's really gorgeous. Better than the sea of metal and skyscrapers," Rowan marveled as he took in the sight. Frostfern was such a natural beauty, surrounded by snowy mountaintops and a river cutting through the picturesque town. He turned and spotted a beautifully crafted porch swing, wide enough for two people to sit comfortably, its honey-colored wood gleaming in the late light. The armrests were carved with delicate leaf patterns that caught the sun. "This is your handiwork?"

"It is," Jimson said, his cheeks flushing as he ran a hand along the smooth wood. "I might not be a farmer, but I do what I can to help make this place better. Thought it'd be nice to have somewhere to watch the sunset."

Rowan settled into his chair as he breathed in the roasted chicken, flavored with garlic and rosemary. Plates passed around the table, and soon enough, his plate was filled with potatoes, chicken, and wilted greens.

"Rowan, dear, could you pass the butter?" Jimson's mother asked, her voice warm and melodic.

"Sure thing, Mrs. Evergreen," Rowan replied, sliding

the dish across to her. She sat tall at the head of the table, silvery hair wrapped in a tight bun.

"Please, call me Marigold," she insisted with a smile.

"Uh, yeah, of course, Mrs. Marigold," Rowan said, shifting in his seat.

Marigold deftly scooped up a bit of butter and spread it across a piece of sourdough bread as she said, "Thorn mentioned you came with Elara from Neosilica? Are you a student?"

"I was. Just graduated," he said.

"Congratulations," Thorn said, raising his glass before taking a drink. "What did you study?"

"Botanical Alchemy at Flamel University."

The clatter of cutlery all seemed to stop at once, and there was a momentary pause in conversation. Rowan felt the weight of their stares—he'd seen that look before, the mix of fear and distrust that came with mentioning alchemy.

Sorrel cleared his throat. "You're not here to replace the last guy, are you? We've had some... troubles with crops since he left."

"Troubles?" Alder laughed. "More like dying crops."

"Alder," Thorn grunted.

"He is here as his replacement," Jimson chimed in, casting Rowan a smile. "And I'm sure he could use all the hospitality from us he could get. Besides, did you two forget we have a cousin in Flamel?"

Sorrel and Alder looked down at their plates. Thorn waited a moment before clearing his throat. "So, are you down at the greenhouse, then?"

Rowan nodded. "Yeah, the university sent me here on a postgraduate research project."

"Oh, that's lovely," Marigold said. "But the greenhouse? That place has seen better days."

"Actually," Rowan started. "That's what Jimson and I were working on before coming here. Needs some more work, but at least it's livable now."

Marigold offered Rowan a warm smile. "Well, I think we could use another alchemist around here, if not to set things straight again."

"I couldn't agree more," Thorn said.

"So, uh," Sorrel said, picking at his food. "Did you grow up in Neosilica then?"

Rowan finished chewing on the last of his chicken and said, "Just outside it, actually. We weren't a farm, per se, but we grew a ton of different plants. My mom had a knack for it."

Marigold excused herself from the table, returning with a freshly baked apple pie. Marigold passed out dessert as Thorn poured out glasses of a dark brown liquid. Rowan took a sip, and it tasted like vanilla and cloves before burning all the way down. He nearly choked, and all Thorn and the others could do was laugh.

Thorn took a swig from his own glass and smiled.

"Famous Frost whisky. One of the cousins makes it up in the mountains. Strong stuff."

The evening died down, devolving into yawns between fits of laughter. The family worked together, clearing the table and insisting Rowan stay put as they cleaned up. Moments later, there was a neatly wrapped parcel sitting in front of him.

"Consider it our welcome gift," Marigold said. "Should keep for a few days until you stock up in town."

"Thank you," Rowan said, too weary to argue against the gift.

Thorn handed him a small metal flashlight. "I'll need that back, but there's no electricity over there, so keep it until you get a lantern or something."

"Thanks," Rowan said. He looked over to Marigold, noting her rubbing her wrist. "Everything alright?" he asked.

"Yes, dear," she said. "Just my joints acting up. I'll be fine."

Rowan reached into his pocket, pulling a small tin from it. "Here, this might help. Chamomile and arnica, nothing magical. My knuckles sometimes act up."

Marigold shook her head. "Oh, no, I couldn't—"

"Please, I insist. I make it all the time. I'll bring you more in a few weeks if it works for you," he said.

A smile formed on Marigold's face as she accepted the tin. "Why, thank you, Rowan."

"Well, need a guide back?" Jimson asked, stifling a yawn.

Rowan shook his head and stood. "No, I'll manage. Thank you. For everything."

His soul buzzed as he stepped out into the crisp night air. Coming to Frostfern had been the right choice, he knew that now. The warmth of the Evergreen family and their acceptance made the uncertainty of leaving Neosilica worth it.

The moon was nearly bright enough to walk comfortably back to the greenhouse without a flashlight. The woods next to him seemed to loom over the path, watching him and waiting. He kept the flashlight tucked away, as he didn't want to draw attention to himself in case something was lurking in the darkness between the trees. His imagination ran wild, and he thought he saw a pair of glowing blue eyes out between the trees for a moment.

"Get it together, Rowan," he muttered under his breath.

He reached the greenhouse and pushed open the door. The darkness inside seemed almost alive, and he quickly turned on the flashlight, chasing away the shadows.

He set his things down and knelt beside the fireplace, filling it with wood.

Movement caught the corner of his eye. His heart skipped a beat, and he whipped his head around.

"Who's there?" he called out, voice wavering slightly.

No answer came.

He swept the room with his flashlight, and in the center of the room was a ball of shadows that didn't seem impacted by the light.

It moved and uncoiled into a ferret-like creature but looked to be made of smoke or shadow, with little wisps of darkness wafting off it as it absorbed the light. It opened its eyes, and they glowed a bright blue. The creature tilted its head, curiosity peering back at him.

"Uh, hi there, little one," Rowan said softly, his fear giving way to fascination. He crouched down, extending a tentative hand toward it.

The creature stepped forward carefully, looking at his hand and back up at Rowan several times before sniffing the outstretched fingers. And then, without warning, it darted toward him, jumping into his shadow and vanishing altogether.

Rowan jumped up and spun around, his flashlight circling the room. "Wait! Come back!" Rowan called out, his heart racing.

Rapid-Growth Matrix

Rowan dumped out another pot of old dried soil into a large bucket and wiped down the pot.

The past few days had been a whirlwind as Jimson periodically stopped by with more and more furniture to fill the space. He'd even come with a wagon full of glass, which Rowan insisted he pay for, to help replace the broken glass in the greenhouse. Despite his first stipend running low, Rowan had splurged on a shiny red bike during his first visit back to town—a purchase he made after realizing how far he was from town. But the price was worth it, even if he had to be careful with his money until his next payment came through.

He appreciated all of Jimson's help, and company, over the past few days, which made it easier for him to finally start the research he was sent to do. His first monthly report to Dean Vayu was nearly due, and he needed something substantial to show for his time here.

Rowan emptied the last pot and stacked it against the wall before taking the bucket of dirt over to the water spigot and filling it, hoping to bring some life back into the soil.

As that filled, he walked over to the workbench, which had a large flat surface, several glass bottles, and an assortment of chalk. It would take him some time to figure out what was in those bottles, or to clean them out, but all he needed now was space to craft a growth sigil.

Rowan scooped up a heap of dampened soil, a mixture of local and his own dirt, and filled a small pot, placing it in the center of the workspace. He then went to work, crafting a sigil of all five elements and then a detailed matrix depicting stable, rapid growth. This was botanical alchemy 101, speeding up the growth process. Granted, it took a lot of components, and depending on the speed, the produce was rather lackluster. It did, however, help with finding the best seeds to grow over a season, picking only from crops that could withstand rapid growth the best.

He placed a small, shriveled pea, which Jimson had given him, among other seeds from the farm, to test on, inside the pot, covering it with the wet soil.

"Okay, let's see what happens," Rowan muttered, placing his hands on the sigil. He squeezed his eyes shut as the energy fought him to fill the lines. Once his green energy reluctantly filled the familiar etchings, he could feel the pot at the center, the wet soil within, and the pea waiting for instruction.

"Come on, buddy," he muttered. "Grow."

His energy sparked in his hands, and something shifted within the dirt. Rowan opened his eyes to see a tiny sprout shoot up from the soil, absorbing the water within the dirt and stretching up. It wrapped around the small wooden post in the pot as yellowed leaves sprouted and little flowers turned into withered pods.

"Huh," Rowan huffed, noting the results in a small notebook. "I wonder," he said as he looked outside, eyeing the wildflowers just outside his window. They were unaffected by the browning effects of the crops.

He stepped outside and gathered some seeds, placing them in a second pot and preparing another sigil at the workbench. The wildflower seeds responded instantly to his crackling energy, stretching out from the soil, bright blossoms unfurling and stretching toward the sky like living fireworks.

"Wow, okay," he breathed, stepping back from the flowers. "This and the bed suggest the magic isn't depleted. But..."

He scrawled more notes down before standing and stepping out into the cool air. He leaned down and picked at the soil, rubbing it between his fingers. It was richer than the dry dirt from the fields next to him. He stood and eyed the woods, which seemed to lean in conspiratorially, knowing that he was on to them.

The deeper into the woods he looked, the better off the plants seemed to be. He stepped forward, past the tree line, and immediately felt a change in the air. As if he walked inside a cloud, it was suddenly more humid than it had been a second ago, the air thick.

"Strange," Rowan mused, jotting down more notes. He looked at the ground, seeing nothing but mossy earth. "I wonder what's causing this."

He ventured deeper into the woods, the sun dappling through a canopy of green leaves and speckling the ground like golden freckles. Rich soil filled his nose, hearty and ancient, stronger than anything he'd smelled before.

His eyes fell upon a cluster of ferns, larger and broader than anything he'd seen before. They were thriving here, almost breathing as he passed by them. He crouched down and snipped a cutting, packing it away for later.

Soon enough, his pack was nearly full of samples, from fungi to flowers and bark as well. The deeper into the woods he got, the bigger and brighter things became. It was like a microcosm of botanical wonders that surpassed anything he'd ever seen or learned about in his years of study.

His notebook was filling up fast, from sketches of what he saw to notes and hypotheses. His head was down, buried deep in his book as he trudged on. This had to be some kind of magic. A remnant of alchemy from years ago, but what? A siphoning of resources? But even then, how could the magic still be running its course? That just wasn't possible. Unless—

Something flitted by his ear and thwacked hard into the tree next to him. It was an arrow nestled deep into the wood. Something else squealed and ran off behind him, hiding in the underbrush.

"Oi! Watch it!" a voice shouted off to his left.

Rowan crouched down low, dropping his book and scanning the area.

Someone stepped out from the trees, covered head to toe in ferns. They pulled off their hood and revealed a tanned bald head with tattooed markings trailing up their neck. "What the hell are you doing out here?" they yelled, stomping forward and yanking the arrow from the tree.

"Uh, sorry," Rowan said, scooping up his book and stepping back from the person. "I didn't-I-"

The person eyed Rowan and sighed. "You must be new around here. I'm Tamsin, and these woods are off-limits."

"Off limits? Why?"

"Because I hunt here. And no one in town is stupid

enough to walk around in these woods. You could end up killed. Or worse."

"Worse? Okay," Rowan said. "Look, I just wanted to see the plants. They're all... so alive."

Tamsin hesitated, eyeing Rowan. "And who are you, exactly?"

"Rowan Mosswood, resident alchemist here on research," he replied, standing up tall.

"Should've known," Tamsin scoffed, crossing their arms. "Here to fix all our problems?"

Rowan shrugged. "I don't know, but you can't ignore the fact that it's a little strange how alive everything is in here and how bad it is for the farmers."

Tamsin nodded. "Fine. Alchemist. Do your research, but tell me the next time you plan on going through here, okay? Can't be dragging you out of here with an arrow in your chest."

"Deal," Rowan agreed.

Rowan carefully arranged the samples he'd collected from the forest on one of the worktables, laying out the various seedlings, cuttings, fungi, and clumps of dirt. He pulled out some of his own dirt and mixed it with the rich soil from the woods before placing it in a pot. Then he grabbed another withered pea and pushed it into the dirt.

Tracing another regrowth matrix and placing his fingertips against the chalk, he mentally filled the sigil. The edges burned, but his green energy raced to fill the sigil, nearly forcing him to lose his grasp on it. It pulled against him, and he strained while focusing on the pea.

Something took over, a surge of energy and strength, and the pea plant shot up from the dirt, wrapping tight around the stick. Massive leaves sprouted out from the plant, followed by large flowers that dropped as pea pods the size of Rowan's hand burst forth. Then, the soil in the pot dried up, and the plant turned yellow and brown before crumbling away.

"Huh, would you look at that," Rowan breathed, racing to scrawl down his notes. "Dirt from the woods is full of something. Magic maybe? The fields are missing it."

He was one step closer. He just needed more dirt. And perhaps the trust of Tamsin, the self-appointed denizen of the woods.

PROPER WORKSHOPS AND CRAFTING

Rolled-up sketches filled Rowan's arms as he approached Nevs's workshop in the late afternoon. Flecks of sawdust caught the light, dancing in the air like little stars. The workshop quickly became one of his favorite places in Frostfern—so different from the cold metal and steam workshops he passed by in Neosilica. The rich scent of fresh-cut wood mingled with a sharp oil while hand tools hung on the walls in careful arrangements.

"You gonna stand there all day letting the heat out, or

are you coming in?" Nevs called.

"Just admiring the view," Rowan said as he stepped inside. "With all the metal shops and labs in Neosilica, I never see a proper crafting shop like this."

Nevs looked up from her workbench, her dark skin gleaming with sweat. Her red braids were tied back, though a few strands had escaped to frame her face. In front of her was an intricately carved cabinet door with leaf patterns so delicate they seemed almost impossible. "Some things can't be rushed," she said, running her calloused fingers along one of the carved vines. "Down south, they've forgotten that craft takes time and patience."

Rowan stepped closer, marveling at her work. The leaves curled off the doors like they were draped on top instead of carved from it. "That's incredible," he said. "I've never seen anything like it."

Nevs chuckled, her braids swaying as she shook her head. "Flattery will get you everywhere here, alchemist." She gestured to his arms. "What are those, sketches for a new project?"

"Yeah, I need a workbench for my experiments," Rowan said, carefully spreading his drawings across an empty worktable. "Something sturdy with a wide surface for preparing components and testing soil samples. And drawers—lots of them—for storing herbs and materials. The last workbench fully rotted out."

"Are you fine with Jimson doing this?" Nevs asked,

studying Rowan's reaction.

"Yes, of course," Rowan said a little too quickly. He paused, heat filling his cheeks. "I mean, if you're okay with it."

Nevs laughed, a gleam in her eye. "It'll suit him well. That young man needs a project he can sink his teeth into. All this work around your greenhouse is good, practical work, so any big projects to show off what he can really do will help." She smiled. "You should have seen him when he started—all eagerness, no patience. Now, he's learning to listen to the wood and letting it guide his hands. He's going to be better than me someday, mark my words. Good thing, too, since I have my travels soon."

"Travels?"

"Mhmm. When the weather warms, I make my rounds to the other villages. Someone needs to keep an eye on the craftwork up here," she said. "That's why I'm glad to finally have someone like Jimson to take over the workshop when I'm gone." She grinned. "He's come a long way from that first chair he made."

"How so?" Rowan smiled.

"He did his best, but that book chair was so wobbly I thought anyone who sat in it would end up on the floor."

A sudden clatter from the corner of the shop made Rowan whirl around. He saw a shadowy form darting behind a stack of lumber—the little shadow ferret. It was only the third time he'd seen it, each appearance briefer than the last, but those blue eyes seemed to study him with an unsettling intelligence.

"Little jumpy there?" Nevs asked.

"Yeah," Rowan said. "Must have been a mouse or something."

The workshop door swung open, and Jimson strode in, his arms wrapped around some wooden planks and a bag of tools. Rowan's breath caught as Jimson's face lit up at seeing him. "Hey! I wasn't expecting to see you here."

Nevs smiled and grabbed a cloth, draping it over her project. "Well, I need to head out for some deliveries. Rowan here has a project for you, something a bit more practical."

Jimson smiled. "Nice, I'll take a look."

As Nevs headed out, she said, "Don't work too hard now!" Jimson smiled, studying the floorboards intently.

Rowan cleared his throat. "So, uh, I was thinking of a workbench for the greenhouse. I'm happy to help, I mean if you want to work on it now."

Jimson looked over the drawings, then at their stock of wood. "I think we can get something started."

They fell into an easy rhythm as Jimson worked. However, Rowan became increasingly distracted by how Jimson moved as he shaped the wood. Despite his size, the man had such a gentle touch, carefully treating each piece of wood. Rowan nearly dropped a measuring tool when Jimson looked up and caught his eye.

"So," Jimson said, a slight smile playing at his lips as he carefully smoothed a rough edge, "tell me about Flamel. What's it like being an alchemist?"

Stories bubbled to the surface that he wanted to tell this man. "Well, there was this one time I tried to create a sentient fungus—"

"Wait," Jimson cut him off, eyes sparkling with amusement. "A what?"

"Yeah," Rowan laughed, enjoying how Jimson's whole face lit up when he smiled. "I thought it could help relay information about soil health and root diseases. But then it sort of took over an automaton, and that was the end of that."

Jimson's deep laugh made Rowan's heart skip. "Too bad," he said, still chuckling. "We could probably use something like that up here. You know, if it actually listened."

A knock sounded near the entrance to the workshop, startling them both.

"Oh, hello, Jimson," a voice called out. A short, plump woman peeked her head in, her long, silvery hair pulled into a tight braid that draped over her shoulder. She wore a long green petticoat and carried a basket of fresh bread on her arm, the warm scent filling the workshop.

"Miss Juniper, hello! How's that stool treating you?" Jimson asked.

She stepped inside, finding a small bench to settle into,

wincing as she adjusted her petticoat. "Very nicely. Helps a lot after a full day at the market," she said, then turned to Rowan. "And you must be that new alchemist, yes? I've seen you passing by my produce stall."

Rowan's stomach flipped a little as he met her gaze, worried how she might look at him after knowing he was the alchemist. "Ye-yeah, that's me," he said. "Jimson here is helping me get that old greenhouse back up and running."

Miss Juniper's face softened into a warm, motherly smile. "Oh, that's lovely, dear. The greenhouse has been so lonely these past years." She leaned in. "And between you and me, Petal, we've needed someone with your talents. These old bones aren't what they used to be, and the farmers..." She shook her head. "Well, they're too proud to admit it, but they need an alchemist around here."

Rowan smiled, trying his best to hide his excitement over another person in Frostfern who didn't hold some hesitation to an alchemist from Flamel.

Miss Juniper rubbed her knee. "I don't suppose you know how to help aching joints, do you? The last alchemist tried helping my arthritis, but it wasn't quite in his wheelhouse."

Rowan's eyes lit up. "Actually, my mother was an herbalist. I could make you a salve. It's got arnica and peppermint and a little alchemy to boost the effects. I could bring some in a few days if you'd like."

Miss Juniper smiled a wide grin. "I knew I'd like you,"

she patted her basket of bread. "I got some leftovers from the market I have for Nevs. Be sure to take a few things before leaving."

Miss Juniper slowly stood, leaving the basket behind as she waddled out of the workshop, mumbling something about the townsfolk being foolish for not trusting the new alchemist.

They went back to work, Jimson preparing more wood for cutting when a small group of people came to the door, peering inside.

"Can I help you?" Jimson asked.

"Yeah," one of the older men asked. "Miss Juniper said the new alchemist is here. I've got this bunion that's killing me."

"And I have a bad back," someone shouted behind him.

Soon enough, Rowan was fielding questions and making a mental list of all the herbs and salves he'd need.

"I'll do my best," Rowan said, "but with the poor growth around here, some of this stuff will need to be ordered from the south."

Soon, Rowan was standing in the street, offering advice to strangers he barely knew how to help with their ailments.

The sun dipped below the buildings of Frostfern, long shadows stretching across the workshop floor. The crowd had finally petered out, leaving behind the peaceful quiet of early evening. Before stepping back inside, Rowan could see the first stars appearing in the purple sky while a lamp-lighter made their rounds through the cobblestone street.

The workshop felt different now—more intimate—with just the two of them and the soft glow of the oil lamps Jimson had lit.

"Sorry about that," Rowan said.

Jimson shrugged, looking over the base of the workbench he'd put together. Joints were put into place seamlessly as if the entire base of the workbench were one solid piece. "I think I made pretty good headway. Now, I just need to clean up and call it a day."

"Here, let me help," Rowan said, finding a broom and getting to work. In the close quarters, he was very aware of Jimson's presence—the sound of his breathing, the warmth radiating from him whenever they passed each other.

As Rowan reached to put the broom away, Jimson turned at the same moment. They collided, and Jimson's hands came up instinctively to steady him. Those strong fingers were gentle against Rowan's arms. For a moment, they stood there, faces close enough that Rowan could see the flecks of gold in Jimson's eyes. His heart pounded in his chest as he looked at the man, the air humming around them.

Then Jimson stepped back, looking away quickly. "Whoops, sorry about that."

Rowan cleared his throat, hanging up the broom. "No worries."

Jimson placed his hands on his hips and looked around the workshop. "I think this is the cleanest I've seen this place."

"I bet Nevs will be happy," Rowan said.

Jimson laughed. "Bet she will. Well, I've got another project I wanted to finish up here. See you around?"

"Yeah," Rowan headed to the door. "Have a good night."

The walk back to the greenhouse seemed to take an eternity, his mind replaying that moment in the workshop over and over. He tried to focus on his plans for tomorrow's experiments, but his thoughts kept drifting back to the feel of Jimson's hands on his arms, the warmth in his eyes when he looked at Rowan.

A rustling in the shadows caught his eye as he approached the greenhouse. The ferret emerged, blue eyes glowing in the dusk. It dipped in and out of the shadows just ahead of him.

Rowan looked down at the creature, a wry smile tugging at his lips. "You know," he said softly, "one of these days, you're going to have to trust me. Maybe come a little closer so I can have a good look at you."

The ferret stared back at him for a moment as if processing his words before vanishing completely in shadow.

Harmonious Elixirs and Meditations

Rowan tossed a tiny bit of crisped potato on the floor, at the edge of the shadow drawn by the morning light streaming in through the window. He sat down in one of the mismatched chairs Jimson had given him and eyed the steaming potato as he shoveled some into his mouth. Smashed, crisped, and seasoned with flaky salt, just the way his mother made for him.

The edge of the shadow quivered, and a pair of bright blue eyes peered out, focused intently on his plate. The tiny little shadow ferret dove out and snatched up the potato before it ducked back into the shadows.

"Oh, so that's how it is," Rowan said, leaning forward with a grin. He tossed another bit of potato, and the creature darted out, nabbing it mid-air with surprising agility. It paused just long enough to eye him, whiskers twitching as if calculating its next move.

He extended his fingers, holding out a piece of bacon, and spoke softly. "It's okay. I'm not going to hurt you. Look, something even better than potatoes."

The ferret creature cautiously stepped forward, more of its long body coalescing. It looked solid enough as it sniffed his fingers and promptly gagged, giving him a look that could only be described as deeply offended.

"What? You hate bacon? Who hates bacon?"

The ferret made a slight chittering sound almost like laughter, its eyes now locked on the remaining potato on Rowan's plate. Before he could react, it dove into the shadow like it was water and popped back out on the table, snatching the whole potato in one fluid motion.

"Hey!" Rowan shouted, reaching for his breakfast, but he was too late as the ferret vanished beneath the shadows, leaving only wisps of dark smoke behind. "You little thief!"

A knock came at the door, followed by Jimson's voice. "Rowan! You better be decent." He peered in through the window, a huge smile on his face. "Come on, we're going to town."

"Town? But I need to—"

"Nope. It's festival day, and you don't need to do anything," Jimson insisted, leaning his muscular arms on the windowsill and running a hand through his scraggly beard. "You've been cooped up here for days. When was the last time you even went to town?"

"I went yesterday."

"Doesn't count. Come on," Jimson walked around to the door and pushed it open. He eyed the remaining bacon on Rowan's plate and bit his lip. "You gonna finish that?"

"I was," Rowan said, handing the plate to Jimson. "I'm sure they'll have plenty of food in town."

"Oh yeah," Jimson said between bites. "Seriously, you don't want to miss it."

Rowan's chest fluttered as he shut his notebook and stood up. Jimson had come by unannounced a couple times this week, checking in on him and dropping off new furniture, and Rowan struggled to find his words every time. His tongue seemed to be completely tied when he was around the man, but he couldn't be more grateful that he kept stopping by.

"Al... Alright," Rowan said, heat rising from his neck. He adjusted his overalls, failing to brush off a dirt stain. "Lead the way."

They traveled down the familiar path and onto the cobbled streets of Frostfern, entering a crowd of people as the roads were more filled than he'd seen them. The town had somehow become even brighter overnight, with streamers and balloons lining the streets as even more vendors crammed into every inch of space available. Music from fiddles and flutes filled the air, followed by a rhythmic beat and claps.

"Wow," Rowan breathed. "Neosilica had their festivals, but nothing like this. It feels so... cozy."

"Well, bring villagers from dozens of miles away, who usually stick to their farms, and this is what you get," Jimson grinned, playfully tugging Rowan deeper into the celebration.

The bustle of the crowd enveloped them, and soon enough, he was shoving a flaky apple pie topped with a sweet and salty caramel sauce into his mouth as they passed by vendors crafting a myriad of foods with spices and ingredients Rowan had never seen. He was fairly certain one of them used green pinecones, and he noted that he would come back to that one later. Booths with handmade crafts clustered next, with practical goods from baskets, clothes, and hand tools selling left and right.

"And there is the ever-wonderful cousin!" Jimson shouted, peering over the crowd at Elara, whose hair glinted in the sunlight.

"Oh, good!" Elara said, stepping out from the stall. "I was worried you two were about to stand me up."

"Rowan was going to," Jimson said, nudging his side. "If I didn't come and pull him away from whatever research he was buried in."

Elara smiled and stepped between them, hooking her arms between the two. "Hope you two are ready."

"For?" Rowan asked, finishing the last of his apple pie.

"Dancing," Elara said as she pulled them along. "Frostfern festival requirement."

Rowan tried to stop in his tracks, but Elara pulled him along. "Uh. Dancing? I can't dance."

"Neither can I," Jimson said, laughing, "but she's going to make you. Mayor's daughter duties and all."

Elara pulled them both into the center square, where others gathered and looked at her. She started slowly, grabbing Rowan's hand and pulling him in, guiding his hands where they were supposed to go before gracefully pulling him along the square. Others followed suit, and the dance picked up the pace. Soon enough, Rowan was dancing and whirling around in Elara's hands in a blur, and all he did was try not to step on her.

"You know, you're not half bad," she said.

"Bet you say that to everyone," Rowan said, tripping and catching himself.

"Ready to switch?"

"Switch? Wait, I—"

She used his momentum against him and spun him around. The square blurred around him, and a massive hand slid around his waist, pulling him in.

Rowan's eyes met Jimson's as he fell into his large

chest before steadying himself. It was warm, and he could hear Jimson's heart pounding. Cozy. Everything he wanted. Everything he—

"You're lucky you lasted as long as you did," Jimson said, holding up Rowan's other hand as he maneuvered him easily around the square.

Elara slipped by them in someone else's hands, grinning and winking at Rowan.

"She," Rowan started, his breath catching in his chest. "She did this on purpose."

"What was that?" Jimson asked, looking down at him.

"Nothing."

Jimson grinned and squeezed Rowan's hand. "You're doing great. A real Frostfern natural."

Neither switched in the two times the rest of the crowd did. Either Jimson hadn't noticed, or...

The song came to an end, and Jimson broke away, clapping toward the musicians.

Elara waved the two of them over to an empty table as she chugged half a glass of water. "Mayoral daughter duties are done," she breathed, resting her elbows on the table.

"That was fun," Rowan said.

"I'd rather be home all day buried in my books. Wouldn't you? I mean, how's the research going?" Elara asked.

Rowan perked up with the mention of his work, and his words tumbled out of him. "The soil here is different.

I've almost acclimated to the soils around the greenhouse, but the forest dirt is strange. Not just the nutrients, but something else I can't quite put my finger on."

"That reminds me. If you need more land to test, my dad said you could use the patch of land just over the fence," Jimson said.

"Oh, good. Yeah, I'll need that soon." Rowan hesitated, biting his lip. "But he shouldn't have his hopes up just yet. Nothing's been working. I can get plants to grow in pots, but they still grow sick."

Jimson shrugged. "Nothing grows well there, anyway. Might as well give you the space to try out some things."

"At least your alchemy is working," Elara said. "I'm losing it up here. I can barely get a quantum sigil to work without sparking out. I knew it was bad, but come on, there is no reason a simple entanglement sigil should be so hard."

"Probably a good thing you aren't making wormholes in your bedroom," Jimson muttered.

"Quantum entanglement is not a wormhole. It's perfectly safe," Elara said.

"But that's weird, right?" Rowan asked. "Some of mine work too well and get out of control. But then I can focus for forty minutes on another and barely get the energy to move."

"You know," Jimson said, staring between the two. "You two could work together. Maybe figure something out?"

Elara laughed. "Would if that made sense. But he's botanical, and I'm quantum. That's like putting an art history major with a theoretical mathematician."

Rowan frowned and thought for a moment before saying, "He's not wrong. I mean, a lot of the sigils you used on the train looked familiar. We could exchange notes. See if there is anything in common between the two."

"I'll give anything a shot at this point," Elara shrugged. "Maybe once you get that cabinet stocked, we can try a few things."

"Cabinet?" Rowan asked.

Jimson glared and cleared his throat. "That was meant to be a surprise."

Elara's face blushed. "Sorry. I thought you told him."

"What cabinet?" Rowan asked.

Jimson pushed himself up from the table. "Alright, come on. Might as well show the both of you."

"Show what?"

"A little gift I was working on. After you gave me the designs for the bench, I thought I could surprise you with something more."

They weaved through the crowds, the sounds of music fading behind them as they turned down cobbled alleys and to the workshop.

"Okay, okay," Jimson said, rubbing the back of his neck nervously. "Remember, it's not finished, so don't be too hard on it." He led them into the back room, and in the center sat a stunning wooden cabinet with dozens of little cubbies and drawers.

Rowan gasped, following the intricately carved floral designs that wound around the deep cherry wood. Each drawer had a differently shaped metal leaf or flower knob.

"Jimson... What? I... It's beautiful," Rowan stammered.

"Consider it a gift from the people of Frostfern. Got the funds from the city, and a few elders chipped in with the common or medicinal plants you'd probably want. Miss Juniper saw to that. I figured a drawer for each one made sense," Jimson replied. "Though you could use it for whatever you want."

"I think this is the best work I've seen from you," Elara said, tracing a finger across the carvings.

"Thanks," Jimson said. "Should be done in a few weeks. I've got to stain everything and finish up a few things here and there. And then schedule to get it moved."

"I..." Rowan started, struggling to find the words. "Thank you."

Observation Locking
Matrices

Rowan stood outside the large green home bordering the town square, eyeing the city's emblem painted right across the tall wooden doors.

"Are... are you sure she wants to see me?" Rowan asked. "I mean, she's the mayor. She's got to be busy with other things."

"Ah, yeah, the mayor of Frostfern is going to ask Neosilica to send someone to study our failing crops and then just never meet them." Elara rolled her eyes. "Hope you're ready. She can be a lot."

"Ready as I'll ever be. I guess."

As they stepped inside, Rowan's jaw dropped. The foyer led down a hall with floor-to-ceiling shelves filled with tiny trinkets and little statues. After removing his shoes in the small, tiled mud room, his feet bounced on various plush rugs, all different colors and textures. Down the hall and into a large circular room was a winding staircase and a domed skylight that streamed in light from outside. On the floor, in the center of the circular room, was a massive, thick, round rug depicting an elaborate map of Frostfern and the surrounding mountains.

"Told you," Elara said, picking up a small brass statue of a bear. "A few years ago, someone gifted her this, and she said she'd put it on display. At this point, I think some people send them as a joke, and I think she actually likes all this junk."

Elara set the statue down, walked up to a set of closed double doors, pressed her ear against them, and then rolled her eyes. "Let's go hang out in my room. I can hear Hank in there, and trust me, you do not want to be out here when he comes out. Unless you want to talk about how the taxes are different in the Iridian Coasts."

Rowan smiled, peeling his eyes away from a particular wooden statue of a burly four-armed man. "Sure, lead the way."

He followed as she led him down one hall and into

a room that looked more like a library than a bedroom. Whereas the shelves in the rest of the house contained trinkets and statues, this room was floor-to-ceiling covered in books and tomes, some with golden inlay on the spine and others that looked more like a sewed-up stack of papers. Several books lay stacked on a sturdy wooden desk, and beyond that was a four-poster bed with books piled up into some haphazard nightstand.

"This is—wow," Rowan said. "I could get lost in here for weeks."

"Me too," Elara said. "It used to be the library, but my mom said she kept finding me asleep in one of the chairs here when I was younger. Instead of fighting it, she just moved me in. Honestly, I get more peace and quiet in here than anywhere else in the house."

Rowan inspected the table, noting several drawn sigils, all with similar symbols on the inside but as foreign to him as another language. "What are you working on?"

"Wormhole retrieval." She gave a slight laugh, plopping onto her bed. "Not like I can accurately cast it up here, but if I can figure it out before the end of summer, maybe that will be what I work on for graduation. I've got another copy of that book on order. Just in case."

"Sorry."

"Hey, it gives me something to work on while I'm here," Elara said. "What about you, though? Any luck?"

"Maybe? I think so," Rowan said as he looked up from

the desk. "It's obviously something with the soil, especially around the farms. It's like the nutrients are vanishing. Maybe going into the woods? I mean, how else is there so much abundance in there?"

Elara sat up. "Yeah, sounds like what my mom was talking about. They tried carting soil in from the woods once, but that didn't work."

"Yeah, I don't think that would work. If only Tamsin would let me go further."

Elara hopped up off her bed. "Of course they would get in your way. I think the whole soil retrieval irked them. They protested it, saying that doing that would kill the forest."

"Well, they might be right," Rowan said. "I'd need to take some samples, but they might kill me if I go in there again."

"Leave that to me," Elara said, standing up straight.

"To you? What are you going to do?"

"It means that I'm the mayor's daughter. Tamsin may not like my mom, but unless they want to deal with the city, they will let me go into those woods with anyone I please."

"You sure that won't just piss them off more?"

Elara laughed. "Oh, it will, but they'll get over it. We don't tax them for living up there. Mostly because no one wants to go in and get it, but they owe us."

"Why? I got pretty far into those woods and didn't see anything. The only thing scary in there was Tamsin when they jumped out of nowhere."

"Oh, I know. Don't get me started, but everyone still thinks those woods are full of monsters or evil spirits or something."

"Or little shadow-dwelling ferrets?"

"What?"

"Nothing," Rowan said, pausing and rubbing the back of his neck. "I mean, I guess you should know. I came across something weird back at the greenhouse. It was like a ferret or something, but it could slip inside the shadows."

"And I'm assuming you're not thick enough to mean a weasel hiding in the shadows?"

"Obviously. No, it could teleport from one shadow to another. It dove into one and appeared on my table in seconds. I've got it to come out once with a little food."

Elara looked past Rowan and onto the floor. "Is it here now? Do you know what it looks like?"

"I don't know. It's a black ferret," Rowan shrugged.

"I was just reading about this. Like a couple weeks ago," Elara said, pulling her backpack open and fishing out one of the books. "I thought it was all just fairy tales, but the shadows. The shadow thing makes sense."

"What? How do the shadows make sense?"

"Quantum alchemy," she said, flipping open a book as she placed it down on the table. "Here, 'with so many tales regarding the translocation within shadows, there is no doubt in my mind that shadows are the simplest form of quantum alchemy, allowing for the loss of observation to enact a primitive form of quantum physics.' I thought he was just talking nonsense, but that might explain it. He even had a theory on how to hold observation temporarily, but the sigil was off."

"So, are you saying the ferret was doing alchemy? I don't think I saw a little piece of chalk in their hand," Rowan said.

"No, obviously not. But this far north, there are tons of tales of weird things happening in the woods; there are these tales about shadow beasts hiding in the woods. It wouldn't shock me to learn that some animals can use simple alchemy when threatened." Elara pulled a bit of chalk and plopped down on the ground, hastily drawing a spiraling spirit outer ring with triangles for fire and air followed by an internal matrix of a few simple geometric patterns disrupted by lightning-like lines on the floor. "Let's see if this works. Stand over there. Get your shadow to line up in the middle of this."

"Are you sure this is a good idea?" Rowan asked. "With the sparking and all?"

"No," Elara said. "But it's worth a try. Just a couple tweaks. If it works, then we know it's using alchemy, right?"

"Okay, sure," Rowan said, positioning himself. "I mean, it might not even be in my—"

Elara dipped down and placed her hands on the sigil, squeezing her eyes shut as Rowan's shadow passed into the circle. Sparks of bright violet light cracked high into the air, singeing the floor before a small black ferret with shadowy tendrils popped up from the floorboards and landed on the ground.

"It worked," Elara said, eyes wide. "Shit, it worked!"

The little ferret flipped over and stood up, looked at Elara, then Rowan, and then bolted off toward the nearest shadow. It leaped up into the air and dove headfirst. However, instead of slipping into the shadows, violet electricity sparked all around it, and there was an audible thud as the little creature's head rammed into the ground.

It stood back up, wobbling and shaking its head before darting out of the room.

"Dammit!" Elara shouted. "Quick! We have to grab it before it wears off!"

Rowan sprang into action, racing out the door, his arms outstretched. The ferret zigzagged across the floor. Rowan was inches away from its slinking body before it slipped between the shelved trinkets on the wall.

"No, you don't," Rowan shouted as the ferret knocked over several small statues and little metal trophies.

"Rowan!" Elara hissed behind him. "Wait!"

But it was too late. Rowan was too focused on the shelves to notice the change in rugs under his feet. His toe caught, and he tripped forward, hands wrapping around the furry body of the ferret as he turned and collided with the shelf.

Wooden statues, metal trinkets, and mechanical knickknacks fell down around him like rain, and he shielded the little creature from harm.

"What in the ancestors is going on in here?" a woman said, stepping out of the office. She looked like the spitting image of Elara, with a little more wisdom and streaks of silver in her hair.

"I. Uh. Ow!" Rowan started as the ferret bit his hand.

"Mom. I mean Mayor Frost," Elara said. "I brought Rowan. The botanical alchemist you called for?"

A spark of violet energy crackled around the ferret in Rowan's hands, and he instinctively let go. The streak of black fur raced out of his reach and slipped right into a small shadow cast by one of the trinkets.

"Dammit," Rowan muttered.

"Well. You certainly know how to make an entrance," the mayor of Frostfern said. "Well, come on in. I have a few things I'd like to discuss."

As she turned around, a tiny little ferret head popped up out of the floor near her feet, staring at Rowan, eyes squinted.

SALVES FOR SORE ARMS

R owan pedaled down the cobblestone streets of Frostfern, taking in the early morning summer air. He shivered, realizing that his light linen button-up shirt was not the wisest of choices for a bike ride this early in the day. The streets were now nearly empty, only a couple weeks after the festival. As he pulled into the shaded market square, he noted only the permanent produce shop and fish stands were still standing.

He parked his bike and detached the basket, making his way to the produce stands, which were being stocked from the early train from the south.

"Well, if it isn't the alchemist. Haven't seen you in a while," Miss Juniper called out, her familiar silvery braid swinging as she wrestled with a crate of onions from behind the stall. In the weeks since he'd first met her, she'd become one of his regular visitors, always insisting on trading produce for his remedies. "I'll be open in a bit. Just waiting for the last of it to come in."

"Morning, Miss Juniper. How have you been holding up since the festival?" Rowan asked, eyeing over the display of tomatoes, bright carrots, and a hefty supply of red potatoes.

"Been all but dead," she said. "Lucky we got this shipment when we did, with the farms struggling and all." She looked up from her crate and frowned. "Dear me, you've been withering away up there, petal. Have you been eating?"

"Fast metabolism," he said, giving her a slight smile, wondering if he might have also skipped a meal or two by accident. "How, uh, how's Sir Brutus?"

Miss Juniper pursed her lips. "He's been fine. Probably down by the river competing against the fishers. If he brings one back, maybe you should take it. Get some more meat on those bones if you don't mind the little bite marks."

"Maybe," he said, imagining Miss Juniper's decades-old patchy gray cat with one eye lugging a fish back to her as he looked over the tray filled with beets. "Any chance I might be able to stock up before you open? We're headed out of town today, and you might be all out when we get back."

She eyed him, raised a finger, and said, "I'll allow it this one time since you need some meat on those bones. But you better keep your pantries stocked. Understand? You can't be hiding away in that greenhouse of yours all the time."

He grabbed a tomato and placed it in his basket. "I... I've just been working hard. Lost track of time." That wasn't entirely true. Since he'd made a fool of himself at the mayor's house, he'd definitely avoided coming into town, even though Mayor Frost was completely accommodating and welcoming after the debacle with the shadow ferret.

Miss Juniper eyed him for a minute, then picked up a crate full of cabbages. "Well, stock up for a few days. Storms should be coming in later this week. If you end up withering away because you bought one tomato from me, I'll be beside myself. Ah!" she shouted, letting go of the crate and dropping the cabbages as she held her elbow.

Rowan raced to gather up the rolling cabbages. "Sit, please. I got it. Are you okay?"

"Yeah, just my darned elbow," Miss Juniper said, pulling her arm out of her coat and massaging it. "That last batch of salve helped wonderfully, but I'm about due for more with this morning cold."

Setting down the crate, he paused and looked at her

arm. "It's in the joint, right?"

She nodded. "Been like that since Oliver died 'bout fifteen years ago."

"I have some curing now. I could probably bring it over tomorrow. Should help."

"That's very kind, but no. I shouldn't be taking salve that wasn't made for little old me."

"Oh, I'm not taking no for an answer," Rowan said.

Miss Juniper eyed him for a moment, smiled, then stood. "Fine, hand over your basket, then. If you insist, then your produce is on me today."

"No, wait. I-I—"

"Hospitality feels uncomfortable, doesn't it, petal?" Miss Juniper said, snatching the basket and filling it with potatoes and onions. "I suppose you'll just need to get used to it, dear." She shoved it toward him and let go, forcing him to take it from her or else let it fall to the ground.

"But I—"

"If it isn't Rowan Mosswood," a voice called out behind him.

He turned and spotted Marley, of all people, pulling a cart behind her filled with several boxes of produce. Her vibrant purple hair and oil-stained overalls stuck out between the muted pastel homes around her. "Marley? What are you—"

Marley walked past him, parking the cart next to Miss Juniper. "That's the last of them."

"What are you doing here?"

"Helping Miss Juniper here with her crates," Marley said, smirking at Miss Juniper. "He can be a bit dense sometimes, but I promise you're in excellent hands."

"No, you dork," Rowan said, setting down his basket and wrapping his arms around her in a tight squeeze. "You didn't say anything about coming."

"Dying," Marley struggled to say. "Can't. Breathe."

"Oh, whatever," Rowan said, giving her one last squeeze before pulling away.

The sun peeked over the mountains, and people flooded into the square as if on cue, lining up in front of the produce shop. Rowan picked up his basket and nodded to Miss Juniper. "I'll be back tomorrow with a salve."

She gave him a quick wave and turned to her first customer.

"Okay," Rowan said, attaching the basket to his bike and wheeling it beside him. "How are you here right now?"

Marley straightened up and grinned. "Official work business. I might have volunteered when they said they needed someone to come up here."

"Work business?" Rowan's eyebrows shot up. "For what?"

"Top secret metallurgy study." She wagged her finger at him. "Apparently, your reports piqued their interest."

"What? How? I didn't even understand the reports when I sent them out. They wanted weird ratings and samples. I barely had space for my own notes," Rowan said.

Marley shrugged. "I think the soil leaching grabbed their attention. I've got a list of checks to report back on. But, more importantly, I get to see how my hopeless romantic is doing."

"Of course that's why you volunteered," Rowan teased, slipping past a crowd of sleepy fishers carrying buckets only partially full with the day's catch. "Not to see me, but to hear if I had any gossip."

"I mean, obviously," she retorted. "Your letters are the worst. I mean, you could have a league of suitors after you, and I'd still get letters about some ivy you found outside."

"Hey, that ivy could be a whole new species," he said.

"So, no secret romances?"

"Well—"

"Wait, really?" she paused, turning toward him, her eyes wide. "Tell me!"

"There's this guy—"

"Yes?"

"And. I mean. I think it's going well. I don't know."

"Where? When can I meet him? Tell me everything about him," Marley said.

"Actually, I'm headed out to the woods with them today," he nodded at the basket of produce. "Just needed to grab this before Miss Juniper sells out."

"Them?"

"Jimson and his cousin, Elara. She's an alchemist too,

quantum."

Marley stopped in her tracks. "You don't mean Elara Frost, do you?"

"I do," Rowan frowned. "She's the mayor's daughter."

"Of course she is," Marley said, taking a cautious step forward. "Maybe I... Maybe I shouldn't—"

"Maybe you shouldn't what?"

"Nothing. It's fine." She slowed her walk. "Where are they meeting you?"

They walked down the cobbled paths until they reached the double doors of the workshop. The doors were wide open, revealing Jimson and Elara standing inside. Rowan instantly took notice of Jimson, who wore a tight shirt that accentuated his massive arms and curvy midsection along with brown suspenders that held up a pair of slacks. Peeling his eyes away so he didn't gawk, he noted that Elara was just as fashionable, wearing slacks and a long blue coat.

Rowan pulled at the basket on his bike, but it stuck for some reason, and he nearly lost his balance trying to jostle it free. Jimson raced over to Rowan's side, moving gracefully for a broad-shouldered man in the middle of a woodworking shop. He grabbed the basket, his fingers brushing against Rowan's. "Here, I got it," he said, pulling it free from the bike. "We've got a cellar downstairs; it'll keep just fine until we get back." He looked up at Marley and smiled. "Who's this?"

"Marley. She's a friend from down south," Rowan said, turning to find Marley standing behind him as if hiding.

"Wait, Marley?" Elara said, stepping outside. "What? What are you—?"

"Hey, Elara," Marley said, stepping out from behind Rowan.

"You two know each other?" Rowan asked.

"Yeah," Marley said, rubbing the back of her neck as she stepped out from behind Rowan. "I might have... uh..."

"Dated me for a couple weeks before sabotaging my roommate's final and almost burning our dorm room down?"

Rowan looked over at Jimson, who held back a smile as he slowly backed away, basket in hand. Rowan mouthed, "Don't you leave me," but Jimson vanished into the back.

"Okay. Okay. Hold on," Marley said. "The fire was her fault, not mine. And she really should have been testing that outside. I mean, any metallurgical alchemist with an iota of common sense would know that heat displacement matrices are finicky at best. And she was trying to do it with an iron base. I mean, come on. Honestly, she's lucky I swapped it out."

"That doesn't explain you ignoring me for weeks," Elara said, her face unreadable.

"I figured the accusations of attempted murder covered that," Marley said.

"Wait," Rowan cut in. "The fire was you? I knew you were in trouble, but you never said it was because of the fire."

Marley didn't respond, and then Elara cut the silence with a roar of laughter, nearly doubling over.

"Not the response I was expecting," Marley said.

Elara gained her composure and wiped a tear from her eye. "Honestly, you saved me. I heard she was sent off to one of the islands after her last failed pre-exam."

"Doesn't surprise me," Marley let out a breath and chuckled. "During one of our labs, she somehow made a beryllium isotope. Even the professor was stumped. Had to abandon the lab for a week after that."

"So, it wasn't anything I did?" Elara asked, crossing her arms.

"No," Marley said. "It was all me. Just worried you'd be mad."

"Good," Elara said, dropping her hands to her hips. "Because, no offense, Rowan, but I need someone with a little more inorganic chemistry to help me with a sigil I've been working on."

Jimson emerged from the cellar and grinned at Rowan before clapping his hands together. "So, the four of us are going then?"

"Yep," Rowan said as Elara and Marley continued to talk.

Jimson came up to Rowan's side and wrapped an arm

around Rowan, giving him a tight squeeze. "Good. Lars could use another friend."

Heat filled Rowan's cheeks as his mind raced. Jimson's arm was still around him, and he was pressed against his side, only fabric separating the two. He gulped and pulled back. "Yeah, Marley will talk her ear off if she lets her."

"Perfect, then I have you all to myself." Jimson grinned, picking up a backpack and heading to the door. "Alright, everyone, you coming or what?"

WALKING THE GREEN PATH

Early morning fog billowed out from the trees, shielding the sun above, as Rowan and the others trekked from the city to the forest's edge. Here, away from the town and farms, the scent of rich, old earth filled Rowan's senses.

"What about Professor Ironstone?" Marley asked Elara, walking close to her side. "Do you remember him?"

An image of a squat man with a balding head came to Rowan's mind.

"Yeah," Elara said. "He subbed for Artie once, but he

was a jerk, so they didn't ask him to come back."

"Didn't he try to expel you?" Rowan asked, joining the two of them along the stony path.

Marley nodded. "He did. All because I told him if he tweaked his energy a little when he crystallized his titania, then the nanobot he was showing us in class would perform better."

"We're almost there," Jimson said, nodding to the small stone basin with a brass lid on top.

"What's that all about?" Marley asked.

"Tamsin is very adamant about people going into their forest," Elara said, pulling a box of matches from her pocket. "If we want anything from them, we're supposed to light it."

She pulled off the lid and dropped a lit match into a small pool of liquid. It instantly burst into flames as she stepped back, turning the brass cover in her hands.

"What now?" Rowan asked.

"We wait," Jimson said. "They usually show up pretty quick."

As he spoke, leaves rustled in the woods. A person, dressed head to toe in green and brown with a bow and quiver on their back, eyed them through a slit in their balaclava.

"What?" they asked.

Elara dropped the lid on the basin, snuffing out the fire. "I've brought the alchemists. They need to—"

"No," Tamsin said, turning back toward the woods.

"No?" Marley said. "They can just say no and walk away?"

"Yep," Tamsin called back, entering the tree line.

"It's official alchemy business," Elara called out. "These two need in for their research."

"I know," Tamsin said, turning back and eyeing Rowan. "Which is why I said no."

Jimson crossed his arms and let out a sigh. "Look, if you don't let these two in now, then they'll just send more. I don't think anyone in Frostfern wants more southerners poking around."

Tamsin paused. "The woods aren't safe."

"And?" Marley said, glaring at him. "I think three alchemists and this bull over here can handle ourselves."

"Marley," Rowan hissed. "You're not helping."

"What? They're being a jerk."

Tamsin frowned. "Fine. What do you need?"

"Soil samples," Rowan said, pulling out a small set of vials from his pockets. "As far in as you'll take us."

"Please," Elara added.

Tamsin eyed the four of them, then nodded. "Fine, but stay close. Follow me and stay on the path. These woods don't take kindly to strangers poking around."

Rowan followed behind Tamsin, Jimson by his side as Marley and Elara walked behind, whispering to each other. Tamsin moved quickly, and Rowan and the others struggled to keep up as the brush grew dense. The leaves seemed to expand to massive sizes the deeper in they went. Rowan slowed, pausing in front of one particular moss-covered tree with a collection of mushrooms growing at the base.

"Look at this," Rowan said, kneeling and eyeing a mushroom the size of his head. With the massive leaves blotting out the sun above, he saw a faint glow of blue emanating from it. "The amount of energy that small mushrooms take to glow, and this one is nearly a hundred times that? This shouldn't exist."

Jimson knelt by his side and trailed a finger along the top of the cap, blue light trailing behind where his finger went. "Couldn't you make one of these, though? With alchemy?"

"Not one that would last longer than ten minutes. But if I studied it. Maybe I could learn something."

"Well, a small sample wouldn't hurt," Jimson said, pulling out a knife.

Tamsin grabbed his wrist before he could bring it down on the mushroom. He glared at Rowan. "You said soil samples."

Rowan stood up and brushed his knees. "I did. Sorry."

Tamsin deftly pulled the knife from Jimson's hand and turned, leading them deeper into the woods. "Little bit farther. There's a fallen tree up ahead that you can dig around."

A few more turns in the path and down a sloping hill was a massive tree, fallen and half decomposed and covered with vines. At the base was fresh earth, intermixed with torn roots.

Rowan frowned, approaching the roots and placing a hand on the damp earth. He scooped up some, filling one of the vials. "This looks like the tree only fell this morning, or maybe only a couple of days." He stood and walked around the base, eyeing the vines. "But that looks like weeks' worth of growth."

"Hurry up with your samples and keep your voices down," Tamsin called. "Those vines cover quick and attract all sorts of things."

Rowan reached out a hand, feeling at the little tendril, which gently wrapped around his finger and squeezed.

"That's odd," Jimson said, looking out toward the vines. "Do you see that?"

Rowan followed his gaze, noting how the leaves seemed to ripple out from the tendril around his finger, like a sea of green matching his heartbeat. He pulled away, breaking the connection that had made its way up his hand, and the leaves stopped.

"Come on," Tamsin said. "Those vines will trap you if you let them."

"Score!" Marley shouted, holding up a chunk of metallic rock from the base of the tree.

A low, rumbling growl sounded from beyond the

trees.

"Dammit," Tamsin said, pulling out a machete. "Stand behind me."

The ground trembled, leaves popping free from the canopy above and gliding down around them. Another low growl echoed, pulling all the other sounds of birds and bugs into silence.

Another tremble and a massive beast crawled up and onto the vine-covered tree. It was a bear covered in lichen and moss and easily four times larger than any bear Rowan had seen before.

"No sudden movements," Jimson whispered.

Rowan's heart beat heavily in his chest. He needed to do something. Needed to run before that thing—then, as his panic rose, the shadow ferret leaped out from his chest, expanding as it jumped onto the tree, meeting the bear, now half the bear's size and chittering loudly as it puffed its back high.

"What the—?" Jimson shouted, frowning at Rowan, then the ferret.

"Run!" Tamsin yelled, grabbing onto Marley and Elara as they spun on their heels.

Rowan and Jimson followed behind as the ground shook and the two beasts clashed behind them. They traveled deeper into the woods, following a thin trail that quickly turned into brush.

They broke out into a clearing, with the sun beating

down on them as Rowan spun around, his heart pounding as he eyed the tree line.

Tamsin stepped in front of them, bow at the ready. "Stay behind me."

A streak of black zipped out from the trees and appeared next to Rowan, limping a few inches before dipping into his shadow.

In no time, the bear broke free from the trees, and Tamsin didn't hesitate. They launched an arrow that nestled deep in its shoulder. The beast roared, biting at the arrow and yanking it free.

Elara pulled her satchel free and withdrew a small bag from within, pouring what looked like black sand on the ground.

"What are you doing?" Rowan hissed.

She moved quickly, drawing out an outer elemental ring of curvy spirit lines followed by a complex set of intersecting spirals and crude drawings of a person and a bear.

"Helping," she said, dropping to her knees and laying her hands on her sigil. Her brows knitted together as bright violet energy sparked and fizzled on the surface of the sigil. She squeezed her eyes shut, and sparks of light exploded from the ring, first encircling her and then shooting off toward the bear.

The massive beast froze as the lights swirled around its head and then legs before vanishing into the creature's fur.

"What was that?" Jimson asked.

Elara fell to her knees, straining to say the words. "Entanglement. It won't move unless I move."

Tamsin looked back at Elara and glared. "And do you plan on being stuck here unless I kill it?"

"I don't know," Elara struggled to say.

Sparks flew off the bear and it lifted a leg, then another as it growled. Elara groaned as her body followed suit.

"The entanglement goes both ways," Rowan muttered, eyes wide.

Marley stepped forward, pulling a plate of metal out from her pocket, blue light trailing from her fingertips as she flung it like a frisbee at the creature's feet. Spidery metal stretched out from the plate, wrapping around the creature, imprisoning it.

"Where the hell did you get that?" Rowan asked.

"Work," Marley said. "They sell those to enforcement agencies to detain people safely. Should hold."

Marley swiped her foot through Elara's sigil, breaking the connection. Elara collapsed, little violet sparks flitting off her and fizzling away. "Good," she breathed. "Cause I don't think I can do that again."

The bear roared, and the metal groaned.

"That won't hold," Tamsin said. "We need to—"

The cage snapped.

"Run!" Jimson shouted.

The five of them turned and raced back into the tree

line, the sound of metal snapping behind them.

Rowan followed behind Jimson, weaving in and out of the brush, his heart pounding in his ears, and something heavy thudded behind him.

Jimson looked back at Rowan, then stopped, nodding to a hollowed-out tree. "In there," he whispered.

Both of them slipped inside, stifling their breaths. Thudding raced past them, trailing off until Rowan couldn't hear it anymore. Jimson took a slow breath, and Rowan realized his face was pressed against the man's chest, and he could hear his heart quickening.

Rowan leaned away, controlling his own breath. "I... I think it's gone."

Jimson stared at him for a moment as he worked his jaw. "Yeah," he breathed. "I think we're safe."

Rowan's heart felt like it was about to burst out of his chest, and being pressed this close to Jimson wasn't doing him any favors. "Yeah. I... I guess we should." He attempted to shimmy toward the exit in the tree, but his foot caught. He stumbled, catching Jimson around the waist as the tree cracked, and the two of them broke free, tumbling onto the ground, surrounded by debris.

Rowan lay on something surprisingly warm and squishy, and—he jerked his head up, recognizing the chest he was lying on and the dazed look on Jimson's face as he stared up at the sky.

"I'm—I'm sorry," Rowan said, attempting to push

himself up, but his hand slipped, and he fell face-first into Jimson, headbutting him.

"Ow," Jimson said, holding his head as Rowan sat up and blinked away stars.

"I'm sorry. My hand. It slipped."

"If you wanted to kiss me, all you had to do was ask," Jimson laughed.

"No. I. My hand. It. Wait. You—what?"

Jimson looked up at him, his cheeks blushed. "I was just—I mean, we should probably get to the others. But. I mean. If you wanted—"

Rowan dipped down, his heart racing in his chest as his lips pressed against Jimson's.

He could feel the brush of the man's beard on his chin and smell the sweet scent of sandalwood mixed with the sharp, earthy scent of pine. Jimson kissed back, his calloused hand grabbing the back of Rowan's neck while the other gripped the small of his back.

Rowan let up for air, and his senses came back to him. They were in the middle of the woods. Their friends were nowhere to be seen, and a bear was chasing them. Even though he could dive in for seconds, he pulled away, rolling off Jimson and eyeing the surrounding trees. "We—We need to get out of here."

Jimson rolled up to his feet and rubbed the back of his head. "Yeah," he shook his head. "Let's hope they're okay."

The two of them started back toward the path, and

not long after, branches cracked behind them. They spun around, readying to face another attack. Instead, Marley burst through the underbrush, leaves tangled in her purple hair.

"There you are!" she hissed. Elara appeared close behind her. "We've been running in circles looking for you two."

"Where's the bear?" Jimson asked.

"Lost it near the river," Elara said, holding her side. "Tamsin led it away."

Rowan's cheeks flushed when he noticed Marley looking at him and Jimson and how close they were to each other. "We should get out of here," he said quickly. "Before it circles back."

DOUBLE-DISCIPLINE MATRIX

"So while the rest of us were about to die, you two were making out?" Marley asked, spooning porridge topped with blueberries into her mouth. She pointed her spoon at him and glared. "I'll remember that next time you're screaming for help."

"This is why I didn't want to tell you," Rowan said, prodding his own porridge. He recounted the events from yesterday and what transpired after. "It happened so fast. It was an accident. And now—ugh, I just feel so stupid. Why did I rush things?"

"Woah, calm down. Don't spiral now that we've got to the juicy bits. How was it?"

"It was fine," Rowan replayed the kiss in the woods. Jimson's massive hands on the back of his neck, and the softness of his lips. His cheeks felt hot as he mumbled, "More than fine. Yeah. I wouldn't be upset if he did it again. I mean, after we got out of the woods, he didn't say anything and left so quick."

"You both rushed off," Marley said, gulping down a glass of fresh apple juice. "At least that explains why you were both so weird. You missed out on all the fun." She let out a big yawn and leaned back in her chair.

"Fun?"

"Elara and I were up all night until the fishers started their day."

"Doing what?" Rowan grinned and scooped up his porridge.

"Not that, you dingus." She pulled the metallic stone from her pocket. "We got caught up with this. I did a couple of tests on it, but we couldn't determine what it was. But the alchemy worked really well on it. Like the stone wanted the energy or something. So, we tested one of Elara's wormhole sigils with her holding the stone, and the portal held open way longer than she's been able to make it up here."

Rowan reached out a hand and took the metal from her, turning it over in his hands. It was warm to the touch, and even without performing alchemy, he felt something strange emanating from it. "Weird. I wonder why it—"

"Oh, and check this out." Marley pulled out a vial of soil and held it close to the metal. Clusters of dirt slipped up the sides of the glass like they were somehow magnetized to the stone. "There's no iron in that dirt, but when we tried this on some of the dirt from outside the mayor's house, it barely moved."

Rowan eyed the clumps of dirt as they clung to the side of the glass. Then it clicked. Of all the things that might leach nutrients from the earth, he hadn't imagined it would be as obvious as this. "Marley. You're a genius!"

"I mean, I know, but why?"

"Magnetism!" he shouted, pushing his chair back with an audible screech. "This metal is what's doing it. We just need to—but the polarity—Marley, come with me!"

His heart hammered in his chest as he grabbed his bag and raced out the door.

"Rowan! Wait up!" Marley shouted behind him.

Warm summer air hit his face as he darted down the cobblestone roads and out to the greenhouse with record speed, his mind racing as he burst into his greenhouse and grabbed a metal box, pulling the sides off and laying them flat on his workbench. "It has to be metal," he muttered.

"What are you doing?" Marley asked a few moments later, leaning against the frame of the greenhouse, catching her breath.

"I need your help," he said, grabbing a rusty nail from his workbench and starting to scratch a sigil into the metal slats. "Your trap made me think of it, but you'll have to help me with the metallurgical part."

"For what? Rowan, you're not making sense."

He paused and looked up. "If that metal is pulling nutrients into the woods, then what if we do the same? We have some of that strange ore, and if we make some kind of cage—"

"A cage that blocked the pull from the woods," Marley nodded. "It could work, but they'll want a sample of this to send back to Neosilica."

"We just need a little bit. Here," Rowan pulled a hammer off the workbench and handed it to her. "Chip off a bit of this. Trust me, if this works, then they'll want this in your report."

She took the hammer and set the chunk of metal down on a slab of stone, slamming the hammer into it and splitting it in two. She eyed the slats on Rowan's workbench as she handed him back the hammer. "And those are—"

"The cage. We put these at the cardinal points." He turned back to them and etched into one of them a square and rigid outline for earth, followed by intersecting waves of water. "We need to start simple. Two classic elements. Then I can put something inside about soil composition and retention, but I need you to put in something about repelling the polarity."

"Like a double-discipline matrix? I've never done one of those."

"They're easy. I had to do a couple in botanical. If you just focus on making a ring for repelling and leave me space in the middle, we'll be fine." He handed over the hook, but she pulled a small knife from her pocket, using the point to craft fine lines inside the ring.

Rowan worked on another side of the disassembled metal box, crafting an elemental ring before swapping with Marley. She hadn't left him much space, but he etched in a crude rapid-growth sigil with a rooted plant taking nutrients and intertwined arrows for growth and support.

"I told mine to use the metal of the box after our initial spark," Marley said, pocketing her knife. "It might last a couple days. If it works, I'll need to think up a more stable one."

"Uh, hey," a deep voice said from behind Rowan.

Rowan jumped and slowly turned around, spotting Jimson stepping inside the greenhouse.

"I, uh," Jimson started.

Rowan's shoulders relaxed, and he smiled. "Good! You're here." He turned back to the slates of metal. "That should be enough. The rapid-growth isn't perfect, so it'll probably take a bit."

"What are you two up to?" Jimson asked, peering over Rowan's shoulder. "I saw you two running up here like the place was on fire."

"Oh, you know," Marley started, flipping the metal slate in her hands. "Just crafting reverse polarity matrices to determine if the ground is being affected by a magnetizing nutrient field. And you, why did you race over here?"

Jimson's face reddened, and he looked at Rowan.

"Marley, be nice," Rowan said, nodding to Jimson. "Can you help me get some supplies? I need a pail of water from the well. I've got a sack of manure and some seeds, and Marley, you've got the slabs and metal." He looked over everything once again and nodded. "Yeah. This should work."

"Sure," Jimson said, heading out the door.

Marley and Rowan grabbed their supplies and walked to the field, plopping them down on a dry patch of land. Nothing had grown in this patch since Rowan had moved in. Closer to Jimson's parents, there were a few sprouted plants, mostly wilted and yellow.

Jimson joined them at the field, carrying a pail of fresh water as Rowan picked up the burlap sack of dirt he'd brought from Neosilica and began loosely drawing a sigil on the ground.

When the dirt sigil reached the north, south, east, and west points, Rowan dug his heel into the ground. As he finished, he nodded to Marley. "Okay. Hand me the metal. You bury those slabs one by one in the dirt while I go over this with water. Jimson, mind spreading those seeds out?"

Marley kneeled at her first section as Rowan poured

water over the dirt lines, splashing mud onto her clothes. "Hey, watch it. These are my nice clothes," she mumbled as she placed the first slab in the dirt.

"Nice clothes?" Rowan smirked, nodding to the constellation of oil stains decorating her overalls. "I'm pretty sure those clothes haven't been clean since Flamel."

"Hey, these are my professional grease stains, thank you very much. There's a difference between an engineered mess and..." she gestured at the mud now coating her knees, "this."

A blueish energy flowed from her into the ground, sparking as it dipped into the dirt and filled the metal.

Rowan knelt in the center, burying the metal and placing his hands around it as he let the energy flow from him. His greenish energy flowed freely, quickly filling his crude sigil and holding it clear in his mind. As his energy touched Marley's blue energy, the fizzles and sparks stopped instantly, the metal glowing a bright white.

"Okay, do the next one," he said, his eyes shut as Marley buried the next sigil slab, then the next, his energy linking on and holding until all four were buried. He felt the white energy between the slabs linking, creating a barrier. Then, the interior sigil sunk into the ground, grabbing onto the seeds and water and pulling them into the soil. He let the energy go and stumbled to his feet, backing away from the plot of land.

As his eyes adjusted, he could see little bits of green

popping up from the ground, bright and lively. He grinned and muttered, "It worked," as the sigil settled.

"Woah," Jimson's voice cut through as he crouched beside the sprouting plants. He ran a finger along one leaf, which grew big and bulky as he did. "It isn't yellowing."

He let out a loud gust of laughter and jumped up. "They aren't yellowing!" He wrapped his massive arms around Rowan in a bear hug that lifted him off the ground. "You did it!"

"Well, I—" Rowan strained to say.

Jimson pulled away, both hands gripping Rowan's shoulders as he said, "You really did it!" The plants were already knee-high and still growing strong. "You have no idea what this means!"

And then, before Rowan could process, Jimson pulled him in and brushed his lips against Rowan's. Then he did it again, and again before his hands slipped to the small of Rowan's back, and he pulled their bodies in close for one last long kiss. His bristly chin tickled Rowan's as his lips worked and parted.

Rowan could be in this moment forever. He lifted his hands and squeezed Jimson back.

As they parted, a sigh slipped from Rowan's lips. He wanted more, and he could see the same in Jimson's eyes. He frowned, struggling to find the words. "Does this mean? In the woods? You wanted—?"

"I did. And if you want, it could be something more,"

Jimson smiled. He looked down at Rowan's shirt and laughed. "Maybe with less manure."

"Yeah," Rowan laughed. "I... I do. I would like that."

"Um, hello?" Marley said, waving her arms. "As much as I don't want to break up whatever that is, we need to start the reports on the plants."

Rowan cleared his throat and stepped back. "Right. Uh, right."

"Tomorrow night," Jimson said, backing away. "Dinner? And we can pick up where we left off?"

Rowan nodded. "Yes. Yes, I'd like that."

AURUMBELLS

Frostfern was in full bloom as Rowan strolled through the sun-dappled streets, a spring in his step as he adjusted his suspenders. Vibrant flowers spilled out from window boxes, red and orange poppies, bright blue forget-me-nots, and clusters of white and purple alyssums carrying the distinct scent of honey in the air.

They weren't perfect by any means, many showing signs of wilt and yellowing, and they probably wouldn't last much longer. Still, Rowan had never seen anything like this in Neosilica. Sure, there were gardens and parks, but streets were rarely filled with flowers now that everyone was more preoccupied with automatons and metal fixtures that could cut anyone who got too close.

A child with long braids and floral trousers raced by him, leading a group of kids. They all giggled, and she shouted, "You can't catch me!"

A smaller kid with short, buzzed hair stopped beside Rowan and huffed. "Sadie, come back! We don't have to play tag anymore."

Rowan laughed, seeing the kid pause their breathing and look up for a second before pretending to be out of breath again. "Think that will work on them?"

The kid grinned. "Always does," he said before racing forward, chasing the other kids into the partly crowded town square.

Rowan shook his head, smiling as he carried on, making his way past the town square and toward the riverbank. The sound of rushing water grew louder, echoing off the stone walls as he wandered through the winding alleys until he emerged onto an open plaza that descended into a grassy riverside. Yellowed wildflowers fought to grow, presenting their deep orange and yellows to a rather large bumblebee lazily bobbing between flowers.

White-barked aspens towered up high beside the river, their leaves casting a dappled shade where a checkered blanket lay in the grass. Jimson sat there, fidgeting with a small basket. When he spotted Rowan, he jumped up and adjusted his shirt before opening and closing his hands.

"Hey there, stranger," Jimson smirked as Rowan approached. "I was starting to think you'd gotten lost. Have a seat."

Rowan sat down and said, "And miss out on all this? Not a chance." He looked out into the river, which stretched wide with massive boulders, forcing the water to weave and flow around them. The other side was the edge of the woods, which wrapped around the town and filled the rest of the valley before sloping up into the mountains. He watched the trees sway as if they were waving at him, beckoning him to cross the waters. "I haven't been out here. It's gorgeous."

Jimson opened the basket and started pulling out small rolls of crispy sourdough bread, cheeses, and a small assortment of fruits. "I hope you're hungry. I went a little overboard this morning at the market. Miss Juniper still had some fruits left from the train, but they might be a little too ripe."

"And is that pie?" Rowan asked, eyeing the inside of the basket and spotting a flaky golden lattice-work crust. "You made pie?"

"Well," Jimson said, rubbing the back of his head. "I got help. Mom's recipe. She takes a trip with her sisters out to Mosshollow every year and collects bilberries to preserve."

Rowan could tell Jimson's mother was on to

something based on the sweet but earthy scent coming from the basket. He leaned back and smiled. "This is incredible."

Jimson picked up a piece of cheese and broke off two bits, handing one to Rowan. "This is from a town just south of here. Willowbrook. Takes a long time to make, which is probably why they send us so much of it." He popped it into his mouth and closed his eyes. "A little grainy, but worth it."

Even outside, the scent of the cheese was pungent yet pleasant. He popped it into his mouth, and his taste buds were filled with a sharp, soured flavor that smoothed out into a rich and nutty one the more he chewed. He grabbed a bit of bread and tore it off, popping it into his mouth and adding a welcomed tang and crunch.

Jimson nodded to one aspen. "I got stuck up there when I was five."

"How?" Rowan asked, holding back a laugh.

"Sir Brutus. He got chased up there when he stole a fish from the fishers. Miss Juniper was all out of sorts, and I thought I was helping. Needless to say, Sir Brutus got down just fine, and I was stuck up there above the river until Nevs came with the ladder. Even with all her help, I fell in the river."

Rowan choked and let out a laugh. "I'm sorry," he said between fits. "Just imagining the whole town here. And you—and—"

Jimson laughed. "That's not the worst of it. After I moved into town above Nevs's shop, I once forgot the key and locked myself out in nothing but my underwear. Had to sneak down the alleys to find someone to let me in."

"That happened to me too!" Rowan laughed. "But we were skinny dipping in the lake. Of course, someone stole our clothes. So there were just five college students streaking through Neosilica before the sun came up."

They both fell into fits of laughter, grabbing more food and chewing between laughs.

"I haven't laughed this much in ages," Rowan said, wiping away a tear.

"Me either," Jimson said, leaning back and bumping shoulders with Rowan while he looked out into the woods.

"I didn't know the forest came all the way over here," Rowan said, catching something moving just beyond the trees.

"Yeah," Jimson said, his voice lowering. "Speaking of the forest. I've been meaning to ask. That shadow ferret? What was that?"

"Oh, yeah. It just sort of appeared that night I had dinner with your parents. Been hanging out in my shadow ever since."

Jimson looked around. "And now? It's still there."

Rowan frowned and thought for a moment. He could feel something attached to him, something just beyond his reach. "It is. But I think it's hurt after what happened in the woods."

"Do you think it will be okay?" Jimson asked.

"It was pretty banged up after the fight, but I think so," He shut his eyes, and the image of the ferret filled his mind. "It just needs time."

People gathered close to the river's edge, and Jimson straightened up. "Oh, it's happening."

"What?"

"Aurumbells flower once a year," he said, standing up and grabbing Rowan's hand. "And when they do—"

Rowan looked out to the waters, spotting streaks of shimmering gold and purples trailing through the water. He traced the color upstream, finding deep purple flowers half dipped in the river, with rich purples and gold streaking off them like they were bleeding ink. He knelt at the edge of the water and dipped his hand in as the pollen passed by. When he did, it left behind a bright purple stain.

Jimson laughed and nodded to a bunch of kids lining up near the river. "If you want to join them, you can be one of the purple brigade."

"Ha. ha. No, I think I'm good," He frowned. "But that doesn't make sense. If all the pollen goes downstream..."

"Salmon," Jimson said. "When they come up here later this year, they'll have a few whole seeds in their bellies."

Rowan stood up, leaning closer to Jimson as the entire river turned a rich purple with flecks of shimmering gold. "It's beautiful."

Jimson smiled and wrapped his massive arm around Rowan. "Is this okay?"

"More than okay," Rowan said as he reciprocated, wrapping his smaller arm around Jimson's back and resting his head against Jimson's chest.

They stood there, watching the river along with others from Frostfern, the late spring warmth finally strong enough for children to leap in and splash each other. Nearly two months had passed since he'd arrived in the northern town. For the first time since leaving Neosilica, Rowan felt like he was finally somewhere he could call home.

Automaton Behavior Analysis

Rowan made the trek up to the train station, sweat on his brow as the heat from summer already took its toll. He wasn't too thrilled to be wheeling a hundred pounds or more of metal back to his workshop, but better now than later.

And it would all be worth it.

In the past weeks, after his wonderful evening with Jimson by the river, he'd been expanding on the original design he and Marley had crafted. He'd been able to cover a sixth of the Evergreen farm, and they'd already harvested and made the market look a little less like a free-for-all whenever shipments came in from the south.

The other farmers had already come to him, knocking on his door and asking when he'd be working on their farms. Now, with some stable metals from Neosilica, already infused by Marley and the others, he could get to work on those plots without burning himself out.

He reached the platform, navigating past a small crowd of people with empty carts lined up for the morning shipment. He spotted Elara leaning against a wooden bench, her nose deep in a thick book.

"Didn't expect to see you here," Rowan said, plopping down beside her on the bench.

Elara marked her page and looked up at him with a slight smile. "Just waiting on the morning train. Letters and shipments from Neosilica usually come in on this one."

"Oh yeah, speaking of letters," Rowan chuckled and rubbed the back of his neck. "I really need to send Marley one. I barely remember to send out the updates on the farms."

"How is the project going?" Elara asked, tucking her book away as more people wheeled their carts into position. "I know Uncle Thorn's been raving about you to my mom. But that much alchemy has to be taking a toll."

Rowan slouched in his seat. "It is. The new plates coming in should help, though. They're imbuing them beforehand, so I just need to do the final anchoring magic. In theory. Other than maintaining the metals and replacing them when they decay, it's been holding. I'm actually surprised you haven't come up and tried your hand at the alchemy. I know it's not your discipline, but better than nothing, right?"

"Actually," Elara started, "I convinced Tamsin to get me another piece of that metal. They weren't too happy, but now that I have it, I've been able to work through a couple of sigils of my own."

"Nice. Didn't think they'd do that."

"They didn't want to, but they'd rather do it than have me traipsing through their woods."

"Well, I'd love to see you in action sometime. I never had time to check out quantum back at Flamel."

"Are you sure you'll have time? I mean, if this frees you up, then I know a certain someone who would probably want to spend more time with you."

"You mean Jimson?" Rowan asked, his cheeks growing hot.

"I mean Jimson," Elara said matter-of-factly. "How's that been?"

"It's fine," Rowan smiled. "I mean, he stops by a lot and helps. Things are... really good." Images of them pausing work for a couple minutes of kissing flashed in his mind. It was nothing more than stolen kisses for the past few weeks, but butterflies fluttered in Rowan's stomach at the thought of what the two of them might look like when Rowan wasn't spending every waking moment trying to revitalize the farms.

Elara laughed and elbowed Rowan. "Look at you, all smitten. Adorable."

Rowan looked down at the cobblestone platform, hearing the faint horn of the train. "What can I say? He makes me happy."

"And I know for a fact he feels the same way," Elara said, putting her book aside and standing up from the bench. She adjusted her clothes.

Rowan frowned. "What's got you all excited?"

"Nothing," Elara said, opening and closing her hands as the train rounded the corner and came rolling into the train station.

Rowan stood, ready to ask more questions as the screech of metal on metal tore through the station until the train came to a complete halt. Then he saw it, the reason Elara was here and looked so nervous. Familiar purple hair stepped onto the platform.

"Marley? You're back?" Rowan called out, a smile stretching across his face.

She turned and helped the train attendant with her luggage as two men started pulling crates of produce off the train and placing them on handcarts. Marley rushed over and pulled Elara in for a kiss that nearly toppled the two of them over. Then she leaped onto Rowan, squeezing him as she jabbed at his side. "No letters?!"

"Sorry!" he shouted, trying to peel away from her. "Been... ow.... busy. Why are you here?"

Marley pulled away and turned back as the two men hefted a small crate, straining to walk, before dropping it into the cart with a loud thud.

"Because of that," Marley said. "Bosses are really interested in what we made, so I signed up to come back for an extended stay."

Rowan looked down at her bag, spotting the small sprigs of green sticking out. "And you got what I asked for?"

Marley held up her bag. "Got everything but the water lilies."

"That's fine. Got some milk thistle growing now, so I should be able to get Mr. Fernfield his tincture soon."

"So I take it you aren't slowing down on that front either?" Marley asked.

"He's got half the town lined up outside his door every week," Elara jumped in. "Not that I'm complaining. Lots of happy customers."

Rowan's face lit up. "Should have seen it when Thorn showed everyone he could swing his axe again without throwing out his elbow. They haven't had an herbalist up here in decades. Basics go a long way when you haven't had anything."

"Then good thing you're here. Any chance they need a mechanic, too?" Marley laughed.

"We've got a few wagons in disrepair if you want to check them out," Elara grinned. "That is if the trip didn't already take its toll on you."

Marley returned the smile, shaking her head. "Nah, you want me to get my hands dirty, then I'll do it."

Rowan turned, snickering at her enthusiasm. His laughter was cut short as he spotted a sudden flit of movement in his shadow. His ferret pulled itself free, slipping behind a nearby bench, its bright blue eyes fixed on Marley.

"Oh, hey, little one," Rowan said softly, squatting down to get a better look at the ferret. "Haven't seen you since the woods."

The ferret chittered, its gaze on Marley intense and unwavering.

Rowan followed its gaze to Marley. "Seems pretty interested in you."

The ferret took a tentative step closer to Marley, its nose twitching as it sniffed the air. Marley crouched beside Rowan and slowly extended a hand, palm up. "It's okay. I have a friend for you."

"A friend?"

Marley reached into her coat pocket and pulled out something metallic. She set it down in front of her, a small metallic ferret automaton.

"Is that...?" Rowan trailed off.

"Yep. I made some improvements from when I made

it at the final," Marley said, placing a finger on the small etching at the nape of its neck. "Just needs a little jolt, and Sir Gearington here will come to life."

"You named it Sir Gearington?"

"Sure did," Marley grinned.

It flashed blue energy and shook its head, its tiny metal paws clicking against the wooden planks as it scampered around in a circle. The shadow ferret's eyes widened, and it crouched down, its tail twitching in excitement.

Sir Gearington loped over to the shadow ferret, tail twitching back and forth. The shadow ferret inched its way out from the bench and sniffed the automaton before hopping on it and running away, turning back as if inviting Sir Gearington to chase it.

"How'd you know they'd get along?" Elara asked.

"I didn't," Marley said, "But I did some more research on ferret behavior and made some improvements to his design. He's stronger now, more responsive. Figure if we run into trouble again, having two magic ferrets watching our backs is better than one."

Rowan shook his head in amazement. "Genius."

Marley shrugged, a smile tugging at her lips. "I know."

As the ferrets darted around their feet, Rowan helped Marley gather her bags, his mind already racing with ideas for the next phase of their project. He glanced over at Elara, who was watching Marley as she bit her lip.

"So, where are you staying?" Rowan asked.

Marley paused, her face flushing red as she glanced over at Elara.

"With me," Elara said.

"Oh. Oh! Excellent." Rowan said, heading over to the handcart containing the crate of metals. "Well, when you two have settled in, why don't you come by the greenhouse? I'd love to get one of these up and running tonight if possible."

"Sounds like a plan," Marley said, slipping her hand into Elara's and squeezing.

ALCHEMICAL CONTRACTS AND CONSEQUENCES

Rowan dug into the wet mud at the edge of a field lush with tall green stalks of corn. With all the rain they'd been having the past few days, it was easy to find the small metal plate and feel around its edges.

"We're going to be late if you keep checking each one," Jimson said, holding an enormous umbrella over both of them.

Rowan stood and brushed off the mud on his pants. "Fine. It's just weird that they are barely degrading. I suspect one of them is getting the brunt of it, and the last thing we want is for that one to go before we catch it."

Jimson held out his hand, waiting for Rowan to reciprocate, which he did. He felt his rough, calloused skin as Jimson squeezed and pulled Rowan away from the fields. They walked hand in hand along the rain-soaked dirt path that wound down the valley. The pastel buildings of Frostfern spread out below them, their usual bright colors muted under the gray sky. As they passed the outer farms and onto the cobbled streets, the grand ivy-covered arch marking the entrance to the town square came into view, its weathered stone glistening with rain.

"Big puddle up ahead," Jimson said.

"Oh, you mean this one," Rowan ran forward and jumped right in the center, spraying Jimson.

Jimson chuckled as he wiped the water from his face and beard before grinning and dropping his shoulders. "Well, I hope you're ready to go in the river."

Rowan turned on his heel and ran, hearing Jimson barreling behind him.

He didn't stand a chance; even though he was much smaller than Jimson, Jimson seemed able to race forward with such haste that in three bounds, he wrapped his massive arms around Rowan and lifted him up from the ground.

"No! Okay, okay! I... won't... splash." Rowan strained, squirming around in Jimson's arms until he faced him.

Jimson planted a kiss on Rowan. Their lips danced and explored each other as the rain bucketed down on them.

"You are adorable," Jimson whispered.

Rowan melted into Jimson's embrace, his kisses trailing down the taller man's neck before nuzzling into his shoulder. A warmth bloomed in his chest, the kind that made the rain and cold fade away.

Jimson breathed deeply, then let Rowan go, picking up the umbrella and shaking it off before holding it overhead. "I win," he said.

"You win," Rowan agreed, leaning in as Jimson wrapped an arm around him.

At the entrance to the town square, they spotted Elara and Marley waiting beneath the ivy-covered arch.

"Any idea what this is about?" Rowan asked, ducking out from the rain.

Elara shook her head. "My mom just said there was a developer in town who wanted to talk to the alchemists."

"If it was anyone from Titanium Innovations, they would have told me," Marley said.

"Well, as long as they leave our research alone, then I don't care," Rowan said.

Elara nodded. "Agreed. Well, shall we?"

Jimson and Rowan did their best to wring out their clothes before stepping inside. The array of rugs that filled the floor inside the mayor's house instantly consumed the pattering sound. Elara led them down the hall and to the right, opposite the library and toward a set of large wooden doors.

Inside, they found themselves at the back of the large meeting room. Old Man Thistle sat near the front, Miss Juniper and several of the farmers whose fields Rowan had helped sat in chairs scattered throughout the room, along with Nevs, who stood against the far wall, her arms crossed. At the front of the room, Mayor Frost stood beside two people Rowan had hoped to never see again—Mr. Steelwright and his son Calder. Both wore pristine dark suits that contrasted the light pastels of everyone else in the room.

Ice formed in Rowan's veins. His hands clenched as memories surged forward. That slick-backed blond hair and shark smile were still the same as when Calder pressured him to help finish assignments. Of course, he blamed his dad, claiming he was pressuring him. He'd nearly ruined Rowan's relationship with Marley when she tried to warn him about Calder. He'd used Rowan, and almost sabotaged Marley's final.

Jimson nudged him and whispered, "Everything alright?"

"That's Calder," Rowan said, his voice tight. "My ex from university."

"What is he doing here?" Marley hissed.

Jimson's hand found Rowan's, intertwining his

fingers with Rowan's. Rowan squeezed back, drawing strength from the man next to him. He steadied his breath, reminding himself he wasn't that insecure student anymore. He had friends... and love.

"You okay?" Jimson asked.

"Yeah," Rowan sighed. "Yeah, I'll be fine."

Mayor Frost turned toward the rest of the sitting crowd and smiled, her gaze commanding the room into silence. The meeting chamber was packed, with nearly thirty of Frostfern's residents filling the rows of chairs. "Thank you all for coming to this on such short notice. The Steelwrights have approached us with a proposal that could greatly affect our town. I believe it's important that we hear them out and consider the potential benefits and risks. Mr. Steelwright, if you would?"

"We don't want none of your business," Old Man Thistle shouted.

Mayor Frost shot him a look. "We need to hear the proposal first, Gregg."

Mr. Steelwright stepped forward, his focus on the front rows. Behind him, Calder's shoulders tensed at Rowan's presence, but he kept his eyes fixed straight ahead. With a gleaming white smile, Mr. Steelwright spoke with a booming voice that filled the chamber. "Imagine your town bustling with visitors far and wide. Travelers eager to stay in your inns, visit your farms, and patronize your businesses. Not only that, but an economic boom like nothing you've seen before."

"What are you getting at?" Gregg grumbled. Several others leaned forward in their chairs, either intrigued by what Mr. Steelwright was saying or interested in where this was all going.

"We've been reading the reports from the graduate alchemist—reports that belong to Flamel University and its investors, mind you—and we wanted to act first before some other corporation came in and pushed out you farmers. We want to work with you and develop a sustainable business to optimize the rich soil from the forest and your farmlands."

Mr. Steelwright's eyes fell on Rowan, and he felt the weight of that look, a pressure that seemed to squeeze the air from his lungs.

"Why should we let you fancy business people come muck with our way of life?" one farmer shouted.

"Mr. Mosswood and Ms. Argentum have already provided you with vast improvements, but if you want that to sustain, then you'll need refinement of the forest soil and sigil plates."

"Wait," Elara said, frowning. "Forest soil refinements? You'd be taking soils from the woods? That's dangerous. Mom—I mean Mayor Frost—have you talked to Tamsin about this?"

"Tamsin chose not to come," another farmer shouted. "Why should we care about their woods when our farms suffer?"

Calder stepped in front of his father, a smile on his face. "We've read the incident reports. However, some of the finest metallurgical alchemists are engineering our automatons to excavate safely, risking no one's life."

"Automatons? Up here? They wouldn't last fifty feet inside those woods," Marley scoffed.

"That is why the Steelwrights will need you overseeing the project," Mayor Frost said. "They've at least promised to work with the three of you, unlike the other offers I've been getting."

Calder's face paled slightly. "Father, maybe we should consider a different approach. After what happened in the Azure Islands—"

"The Azure Islands were a trial," Mr. Steelwright cut in sharply, his smile never wavering though his eyes hardened. "Those automatons were prototypes. Unstable, yes, but we learned valuable lessons."

Calder's shoulders tensed, but he said nothing more. Rowan noticed his hands trembling slightly before he shoved them into his pockets.

"Frostfern doesn't need to be forgotten," Calder said, his gaze swept out toward the farmers. "With the great findings from our alchemists, you're no longer a city dependent on others. Now is the time to bring Frostfern forward and show the rest of the world that this can be the farming capital it should have always been."

Old Man Thistle leaned against his chair, rubbing his face. "I would like to see that."

Others nodded along.

"But what's in it for you?" Jimson asked. "My family is just getting back up off the ground, and you all come in. I don't buy it."

"And the woods," Elara added. "Tamsin protects those woods for a reason."

Mr. Steelwright grinned. "Mayor Frost mentioned the other offers," he started. "These are from developers who haven't even come here to meet you all face-to-face. If they aren't willing to give you a moment of their time now, then what sort of time and opportunity do you think they'll give once they sink their claws into Frostfern? Today, I am offering any farmer who signs up to work with us sixty percent of the profits made on their land. I promise there won't be a better offer than that, and once they patent those plates of Mr. Mosswood and Ms. Argentum, you will pay a fortune to keep them on your land."

"Patented?" Rowan asked. "No one's mentioned a patent."

"To you," Calder said, finally looking at Rowan longer than two seconds. His eyes shifted to Jimson, and Rowan saw a slight reddening in Calder's ears. "But the patent is already pending."

"Them two youngins don't answer to no patent," Old Man Thistle said.

"Yet," Mr. Steelwright said. "Those two work for investors like me. All the work they have done here is the property of people back in Neosilica." He paused and stood tall. "Without our backing, the cost of these alchemical plates would be astronomical. The government regulators and other corporations would demand fees that would bankrupt any farmer trying to use this technology. But with the Steelwrights, you keep more than half your earnings."

"Then where do we sign?" Farmer Tiller shouted from the back. "Better to band together with Steelwright than let those vultures from Neosilica's government come take everything!"

Several other farmers nodded in agreement.

"Before we do that," Calder said, pulling a piece of paper from his coat. "We'll need approval to break ground from both Mr. Mosswood and Ms. Argentum. The council in Neosilica will not agree unless their proxies sign. Today."

Rowan looked at Marley and frowned. This had Steelwright manipulation written all over it.

"Now, hold on a minute," Marley said. "We're not signing anything without reviewing the contract."

"Then I fear your farmers will suffer when someone else comes up here with a lesser offer, or worse—eminent domain," Mr. Steelwright said.

"They wouldn't," Mayor Frost gasped.

"They would," Mr. Steelwright said. "The courts take longer than investors, Mayor Frost, but if you don't sign with someone, then the judges at Neosilica will swoop in. I don't think you understand how... interesting... these woods are to the people down south."

"You two better sign them damn papers," Old Man Thistle shouted.

"I don't know," Marley whispered to Rowan. "Steelwrights aren't known for their generosity."

"But are any of the others?" Rowan asked.

"Titanium Innovations—"

"Titanium Innovations is more interested in your double-discipline matrices than field work up here," Mr. Steelwright said. "They've settled a non-compete with us and withdrew their bid. One of the few places to agree."

"So what?" Elara asked. "Rowan and Marley sign off on this, and you break ground? Where?"

"My son Calder will oversee much of the work in the following weeks," Mr. Steelwright said. "We need to survey a refinery for the soils in the forests, a facility for production storage and transport, and finalize land agreements with the farmers. The three of you will enter an agreement with Steelwright as temporary hires to assist my son as needed as I return to Neosilica and prepare the construction materials and automatons for transport."

"Sign the papers!" one farmer shouted.

"Your call," Marley muttered.

Rowan studied the paper in Calder's hand, then looked at the farmers who had welcomed and trusted him.

He knew this day would come—that their work would draw attention. The Steelwrights were manipulative, but they were also thorough. If Rowan and his friends could keep them close, monitor their actions...

Rowan glanced at Marley, then back at the farmers. He took a deep breath and said, "We can't sign without fully understanding what we're agreeing to." He lifted his hands as grumbles sounded from the farmers. "However," he paused, looking at Calder, "we will agree to sign a temporary trial agreement and assist with the initial surveys while we review the terms. That should be enough paperwork to tie up anyone else long enough."

Mr. Steelwright stared at Rowan for a moment, then nodded. "Then we have an agreement." He held out a hand and approached.

Rowan took his hand and squeezed, a weight forming in the pit of his stomach as he saw the toothy grin on Mr. Steelwright.

"Good thing you agreed," Mr. Steelwright said. "Had you refused, the council agreed to appoint a replacement better suited to assist us. Someone with a more... compatible skillset."

The pit in Rowan's stomach grew heavier as he took a copy of the contract from Mr. Steelwright. "Then let's hope this contract is worth it. For both of us."

Field Notes: Shadow Expansion

"When did he say he'd get here?" Marley said, stifling a yawn as she leaned against a tree at the edge of the forest. Her ferret automaton weaved back and forth between her feet, a sleek glint of silver metal.

"Dawn," Elara said, crossing her arms as the sun crested over the mountains. She turned and looked back at Rowan. "You sure you're up for this?"

"Yeah," Rowan said, shifting his stance and peering down the path back toward Frostfern. Two days had passed since Mr. Steelwright departed for Neosilica, leaving Calder to oversee their interests. He chewed on his lip, tension building in his shoulders. Dealing with Calder was like walking on a dangerous line—one wrong move and the Steelwrights would have everything Rowan and the others had built here.

Memories threatened to creep in again—helping Calder pass an exam he barely understood, the need to sneak around Mr. Steelwright. Couldn't have his perfect son in a relationship with someone studying the botanical arts. But now Rowan had real love and support and people worth protecting.

Gravel crunched ahead, and platinum blond hair crested the hill as Calder appeared, wearing a black suit, a small capelet, and brightly polished shoes that gleamed in contrast to the rugged forest.

"Rowan, Marley, Elara," Calder greeted them, his smile wide as he looked at them. "Thank you for coming."

Rowan nodded curtly, swallowing before saying, "Why did you call us out here so early?"

Calder's eyes widened, and he pulled a small notebook from his pocket. "I need to survey the perimeter of the forest since that Tamsin of yours won't let us in before the train heads south for the day. My father wants a report for the development plans."

Marley pushed herself off the tree, frowning. "Development plans? But we haven't signed the contracts."

Calder waved his hand dismissively. "It's all part of the process. This is just an assessment before we secure the council's permits and funding. Can't break ground without Neosilica's stamp of approval."

Rowan exchanged knowing looks with Marley and Elara. The Steelwrights' tactics hadn't changed since their time in Neosilica, collecting nearly any promising student from Flamel before anyone else could. Surely, this was no different, but if they wanted to help Frostfern, they had to comply with Calder.

"Shall we?" Calder asked, breaking the silence as he eyed the metallic ferret.

Rowan stepped back and gestured toward a small path that carried on along the edge of the woods. "Lead the way."

They set off along the forest's edge. Rowan carefully watched as Calder stopped to examine a rather large plant or vibrant flora. The trees pulsed with life here, the leaves casting dappled shadows on the mossy ground.

Calder strode ahead, scrawling something in his notebook before holding a thumb up to the woods and walking heel-to-toe for several paces.

Rowan fell into step beside him, peering over his shoulder long enough to see the words "entrance" and "cut down" before asking, "What exactly are you surveying for?"

Calder pulled back his notebook and glared at Rowan. "Potential building locations, access points, anything that could be useful for development. We'll need service roads, too."

"Tamsin's never going to let you build inside the woods," Elara said.

Calder turned back to Elara. "Well, Tamsin doesn't own the woods. Frostfern does. Tamsin can take it up with the farmers who've already signed. Along with your mother."

Marley caught Rowan's eye, appearing ready to speak her mind, but Rowan shook his head. As much as he'd love to see what she had to say, there was no point in arguing. Not yet. They needed to be strategic about this.

"Are we done?" Marley asked instead.

"Not quite," Calder said, continuing down the path. He paused again, running a hand along one leaf. He looked back at Rowan. "This must be killing you."

"What?"

"I may not know plants like you do, Rowan Mosswood, but I know that nothing in these woods is normal. Your reports indicated as much, but not to the extent I see here." He spun on his heel and met Rowan face-to-face. "I know you. You've always had a keen eye. I bet you've discovered something incredible here, and you're holding back."

Rowan stood his ground and squared his shoulders. "It's still ongoing. I want all the facts straight before I report it. It's too delicate, the ecosystem here. If anything gets rushed, it could get misinterpreted. Just like now."

Calder backed up and nodded. "I wouldn't want to rush you, but I would like to see those notes." He paused, thinking about his next words. "We could help each other, you know. If I knew what you were working on, I could help."

"They're not ready," Rowan said, trying his best to mask the churn in his stomach.

Calder started down the path, scrawling some more notes into his notebook. "Very well, but know that if this venture continues, your work here will depend on your cooperation with Steelwright Industries."

Elara fell into step beside Rowan, her voice low. "I don't like this. He's up to something."

"Let me get my hands on him," Marley whispered.

Rowan shook his head. "We just need him out of here. Before he sees something in the woods he shouldn't."

Calder held up his hand, revealing a gleaming piece of metal. "You mean something like this?"

It caught the sunlight, casting a kaleidoscope of colors across his palm. Rowan's breath hitched.

Marley frowned. "Where did you get that?"

Calder smiled and turned the metal over. "Your friends at Titanium Innovations gave it to us. They say it has properties unlike anything they've ever seen."

"More like you stole it," Marley scoffed.

"Hmm," Calder said, frowning. "Do any of you hear that?"

A low, guttural growl emanated from the woods, shaking the trees and setting birds loose into the sky. Cold sweat formed on Rowan's brow as the hairs on his arm stood on end.

The metal automaton raced up Marley's legs and burrowed into her jacket.

Something in Rowan's chest shifted, and the shadow ferret burst forth from his shadow, tail flicking as it faced the woods.

"What the hell is that?" Calder stumbled back.

The metal in his hand glowed a faint blue, and the shadow ferret grew in size, nearly as large as a small bear cub, eyes blazing with wispy blue light. Its hackles raised as it bared its teeth. It made a chittering sound that turned into a low and echoing growl that echoed deep into the woods.

Moments passed, and the growl from the woods faded. The ferret's fur smoothed, and it relaxed, shoulders dropping. It turned to Rowan, eyes shining as it playfully cocked its head.

"What... what?" Calder asked, his eyes wide.

Marley stepped forward with a smirk as she wagged her finger at Calder. "If you breathe a word about this, you'll regret it."

Calder's gaze darted between Marley and the shadow ferret. "I... I don't understand. What is that?"

Rowan met Calder's eyes with steel in his own. "It's part of the forest's magic. And if you want any chance of working here peacefully, you'll keep this to yourself until we understand it better." His voice carried authority he didn't know he had. "Think carefully about your next move, Calder."

Calder hesitated, his eyes flicking between the ferret and the glowing metal in his hand. He straightened, his jaw set. "Fine. But you three need to figure this out before my father gets involved."

He turned, his eyes still locked on the ferret as he pocketed the metal and stomped past them down the path and toward the town.

The shadow ferret shook its head and let out a whine. Wisps of smoke rolled off it, and it shrank until it was back to its normal size. The metal automaton climbed slowly out from Marley's jacket. It crept forward, sniffing the air before nudging the shadow ferret with its nose. The shadow ferret froze for a moment, haunches raised, then sprang sideways with an excited hop, arching its back in invitation to play. The two devolved into wrestling and chasing, racing through leaves and underbrush while Rowan looked up at Elara and Marley.

Elara looked back down the path, then back at the ferret. "The metal did that. Somehow."

"What are we gonna do about him?" Marley asked. "If he tells anyone—"

"He won't," Rowan said, starting back toward town.

Tonics, Salves, Potions, & Lotions

"Got you another one, Miss Juniper," Rowan said as he reached into his basket, pulled out a small jar of salve, and handed it over with a smile.

The sun bore down on the town square as summer was in full force, but that didn't stop the townsfolk from filling the cobblestone streets with the scent of fresh herbs and baked bread for another market day.

"Why thank you, petal," Miss Juniper said, grinning as she placed the jar behind her produce stand. "Here's hoping those Steelwright automatons come soon."

Rowan's smile faltered. "Soon?"

"Oh yes. That young Mr. Steelwright promised nearly everyone their own automaton. Free of charge. Soon enough, I'll have my own helper doing all the heavy lifting for me so these creaky joints can rest."

Rowan pushed down his disgust. The contract wasn't even signed yet, and Calder Steelwright was making promises left and right. "That sounds really generous of them, Miss Juniper."

Before she could respond, Rowan was swallowed up by the other patrons, eager to get their hands on Miss Juniper's produce.

He navigated through the crowd, locating others to whom he'd offered his carefully crafted potions and salves, overhearing the conversations that bubbled around him.

"I heard those Steelwright contraptions can plow a field in half the time," Mr. Tiller said, his sun-weathered face lit up with a wide, toothy smile. "Can you imagine the crops we could grow?"

"We wouldn't need to wait weeks for repairs from Jimson," another farmer said. "That Evergreen boy may be a skilled crafter, but these automatons could do the work in minutes."

Nausea washed over Rowan. The excitement in their eyes was all he needed to see to know that standing up against the Steelwrights was a losing battle.

Yet, what would that mean for Jimson?

Old Man Thistle stepped out in front of Rowan and eyed the basket in his hands. Rowan pulled out a small hawthorn berry tonic, good for his heart, and handed it over.

The old man leaned in close, his voice low and gravelly. "You might want to charge for these while you still can, lad. Steelwrights will run you out of business quicker than a rabbit from a fox."

Rowan shook his head. "Health over wealth, that's what my mother always told me. I'll never say no to a basket of your finest carrots, but I'd rather save the charging for when you need help with your crops."

"You're too generous for your own good." Old Man Thistle smiled, pocketing the tonic. "But I'll keep in mind that you've got a hankering for my carrots."

Rowan wound his way through the square, his basket getting lighter as his heart grew heavy. Calder's name was on the tongue of every person he walked by, and it would seem he made promises to nearly everyone in town.

Doubt weaseled into the back of his mind as he took in the vendors who had traveled from miles away to sell their goods, from specialty produce to new tools and one-of-a-kind artwork. If the Steelwrights could really deliver on their promises, then would markets like these even matter anymore?

Squaring his shoulders, Rowan glanced at the last few

items in his basket. No, he thought, I won't let them ruin this.

He doled out the last of his products and marched out from the market as his mind spiraled. Down the cobbled streets, turning left and right, until he stopped at Jimson's workshop. He closed his eyes and breathed deeply as the comforting scent of sandalwood and pine filled his nose and melted the tension that had built in his neck.

He opened his eyes and focused on Jimson, hunched over his workbench, his large hands wrapped around delicate tools that were intricately carving away at a filigreed wooden box. Rowan leaned against the doorframe, admiring Jimson's skill and perhaps how his arms flexed beneath his fitted shirt.

"Rowan? Everything alright?"

Rowan blinked a few times, so completely lost in thought that he hadn't noticed Jimson had been looking back at him.

Jimson set his tools down and wiped his hands on his apron. Flecks of sawdust speckled his beard like glitter, and Rowan's heart fluttered at the sight.

"It's the Steelwrights," Rowan finally said, pushing off from the doorframe. "They're making a ton of promises to everyone in town. Nearly everyone at the market claims they're getting their own personal automaton. We don't even have that in Neosilica, but they don't know that or seem to notice how much it will hurt them in the long run."

"Hurt them? How?" Jimson asked.

"You don't see it either?" Rowan paced inside the shop. "If an automaton can till a field in half the time Mr. Tiller can, or cart Miss Juniper's crates, or water the fields, or anything else, then what use does anyone have for carts or tools? Give it long enough, and nearly anyone in that market will be out of business. Right when Marley and I breathed life into the farmlands, the Steelwrights came in and pulled the rug out from everyone."

Jimson's calloused fingers found Rowan's hand and squeezed. "Hey, it'll be okay. Just breathe. The town is just caught up in the excitement."

Rowan shook his head. "But what about you? This place? Your livelihood!"

"I'm not going anywhere," Jimson said. "They're excited over the novelty of it all, but give it time and they'll be back. You don't think those engineers from Neosilica want to deal with farmer automatons, do you? They need someone here. Marley's been showing me some metalwork. It might not be woodworking, but if I can bash one of those things back to life, they'll be lining up outside my door."

"She... What?"

Jimson caressed the back of Rowan's hand. "I adapted. That's what we do in Frostfern. Weather the winter and come out stronger."

Rowan leaned into Jimson's touch. "I just can't shake this feeling that Calder and his father are up to something."

"Oh, they most certainly are," Jimson said, then he paused, frowned, and added, "But is this about more than just the Steelwrights? I know Calder was a big part of your life... before."

Rowan's heart lodged in his throat as he cupped Jimson's face, his thumb brushing away the sawdust clinging to his beard. "Calder is my past. And a past I'd rather forget. But you, Jimson Evergreen? You are my present."

Jimson's shoulders loosened, and he sighed as he leaned into Rowan's touch.

Rowan nuzzled into the crook of Jimson's neck, inhaling the mix of freshly cut cedar and Jimson's musky scent.

"I feel the same," Jimson said, resting his head on top of Rowan's head.

A muffled laugh escaped Rowan's lips. "Looks like you're stuck with me, then."

The air between them shifted, and the grip on Rowan softened. Rowan wrapped a hand around Jimson's waist, pressing himself closer as he looked up and found Jimson's lips.

Their kiss was deep and hungry, and at that moment, Rowan wanted nothing but to explore every inch of Jimson.

Strong fingers threaded through Rowan's hair, holding him as their lips danced. A soft moan escaped

Jimson's throat as Rowan's teeth grazed his bottom lip.

Before Rowan knew it, rough, calloused hands slipped under his shirt, and the feeling threw him into a frenzy.

They stumbled back toward the upper loft where Rowan often slept, still entwined. They bumped against a wall, and Rowan pulled back, gripping Jimson's shirt and pulling it up over his head, revealing a belly covered in ginger fur.

"Are you sure?" Jimson asked as he breathed heavily.

"Very," Rowan said, finger slipping beneath Jimson's waistband.

Jimson pocketed a small jar off the bench near the stairs, grabbed Rowan's hand, and pulled him up the stairs into a hot loft.

He deftly unbuttoned Rowan's shirt between kisses, their heads spinning with desire as the heavy, hot air of the attic trapped the scents of pine and cedar.

When his knees hit the edge of the makeshift bed, Jimson lowered him down gently and crawled on top of him. A resonating growl escaped his lover's throat as Rowan's hands explored the broad chest above him.

"Are you still sure about this?" Jimson murmured against his ear.

"I've never been more sure of anything in my life," Rowan breathed hungrily.

Rowan's head rose and fell under Jimson's heavy breathing as he listened to Jimson's slowing heart. The air was thick, and the two of them lay covered in sweat, but Rowan couldn't imagine any other place he'd rather be. He traced his fingers up and down Jimson's chest, toying with the man's springy hair as he felt Jimson's fingers tickling the small of his back.

"We'll be alright, right?" Rowan finally asked, thoughts of Steelwright's promises to the town creeping back into his mind.

"We'll figure it out. You, me, Elara, and Marley. Steelwrights won't know what's coming."

Rowan paused, looking up to see Jimson's face. "I... I love you."

Jimson pulled Rowan in for a kiss, gentle but deep. As their lips parted, he whispered, "I love you too."

OLD TALES OF FAMILIARS

Rowan looked up at the sky, tracing the vibrant oranges and pastel pinks that painted it as the sun set over Frostfern's snowcapped mountains. He, Marley, and Elara stood near the forest edge just outside his greenhouse, taking in the cool night air. It carried the scent of pine and wildflowers, tickling Rowan's senses and tugging at memories of the past few nights he'd spent with Jimson.

"Okay," he said to the others, pushing aside his thoughts. "I'm ready." He closed his eyes and inhaled, bringing his attention to the shadow ferret, which sat like a foreign thing in the back of his mind.

He reached out mentally, grasping at a thread that connected them. The creature responded, emerging from the darkness. Tendrils of black smoke coalesced, weaving into pitch-black fur. As Rowan opened his eyes, sapphire eyes gleamed back at him with a slight tilt on the ferret's head, awaiting Rowan's command.

"Okay, so you can summon it now?" Elara asked.

Rowan nodded. "It was like pulling a string in my mind."

"What now? Do you still feel connected to it?" Marley asked, pulling the automaton ferret from her pocket and setting it down on the ground.

"I think so," Rowan murmured, feeling at the thread between them. "Let's see what we can do."

Marley's automaton sprang toward the ferret as if on cue, hopping excitedly to see its friend. The bond between Rowan and his ferret tugged as the shadow ferret's ears perked up. It wanted to play, and Rowan wasn't about to stop it.

He felt his mind travel with the creature, darting toward their mechanical companion, chasing it off into the woods.

He'd never explored this link between him and the ferret before, and he found himself smiling as his head filled with images of leaping after fireflies, their tiny lights flickering in the gathering dusk.

An idea sparked in Rowan's mind. He focused on the shadow ferret, mentally willing it to climb a nearby oak tree. The ferret obeyed without hesitation, swiftly scurrying up the rough bark before jumping back down to join his metal friend, Sir Gearington.

"It worked!" Rowan exclaimed as he grinned at Marley and Elara. "I just told it to climb that tree, and it did!"

"No way!" Marley shouted. "You can control it?"

Elara rested her hands on her hips, frowning. "My quantum books never mentioned anything like this. But it's almost like those old witch stories we were told when we were younger. The ones with familiars. I know we have a few in the library back home. Maybe there is some kind of entanglement happening?"

"Rowan, the forest witch," Marley grinned. "Has a nice ring to it."

"He's got all those potions, too," Elara smirked. "Just needs to scare off the children with a broom, and we'll be set."

"Ha ha," Rowan groaned. "Very funny." He paused for a moment, then added, "You know, my mom claimed she came from witches. No one believed her, but the stuff she could do with plants... I think I only learned a tenth of what she could do."

A sudden buzz coursed through Rowan, like an electric current running through his veins. The hairs on his arms stood on end as the invisible thread connecting him and the ferret thrummed with energy. He could feel a fear in the shadow ferret as its shape shifted and changed.

"Something's wrong," he muttered.

The ferret grew quadruple in size, and Rowan could see clearly through its eyes. A vibrant blue filter turned the darkening woods into a sunlit forest. The hair on the ferret's back stood on end, and it stepped in front of the mechanical ferret, ready to protect them all from some impending doom.

"Guys," Rowan said, his voice wavering as he swayed on his feet. "Something's happening. The ferret, it's—"

Leaves rustled along with snapping branches and shouts. The ferret was ready to lurch forward and bite whatever was heading their way.

But then Rowan saw it.

Calder, bursting free from the underbrush and stumbling forward, nearly losing his footing as he looked back, arms full of something shining.

The ferret lunged forward, mouth open, ready to bite.

Rowan's heart raced, and he tugged hard on the link between him and the ferret.

Calder screamed, lifting arms and dropping the objects in his arms.

The ferret instantaneously dissipated into mist inches away from him, mouth wide open.

Rowan's vision returned to his body, and he slumped to his knees.

"What's happening?" Marley asked, peering out into the underbrush.

"Calder," Rowan panted, pointing toward the trees. "Out there."

Elara and Marley raced off into the woods, only to come out moments later with a disheveled Calder, his pristine pants and button-up shirt splattered and stained with mud, and a rather springy mechanical ferret angrily hopping around Calder's legs. While the others had rushed to help him, Calder had frantically gathered the scattered stones, now clutched protectively against his chest.

"What are you doing in the woods?" Rowan asked, getting to his feet and brushing off the dirt on his overalls.

Calder adjusted his grip on the metal stones, their surfaces glinting in the fading light. "Collecting samples. I was with Tamsin, but we got... separated."

"Samples?" Elara asked.

"Yes, samples," Calder shot back. "We came to an agreement with Tamsin, and part of that agreement was collecting more of that metal."

Tamsin broke free from the woods, their face flushed with anger as they stormed over to Calder. They jabbed a finger at his chest, gripping a bow at their side. "You took more than we agreed!"

Calder shifted his weight, the metal stones clinking together in his arms. "I... I needed more."

Rowan approached, eyes narrowing as he looked

down at the collection of metal in Calder's arms. "Does this have anything to do with all the promises you've been making? An automaton for everyone, right? How's Steelwright funding that?"

"We're trying to help," Calder said, his shoulders drooping. "The metal. Even with that small amount you sent, we were able to increase production tenfold. This changes everything, but we need more of it to really understand."

"But you can't mine it," Tamsin cut in. "I won't let you."

"Yeah," Elara added. "What happens when they run out of these samples? They'll just want more and more."

Calder shook his head. "No, that's not—"

"That's exactly what they'll do," Marley said.

"That's why we came up here," Calder said, holding his chin up. "Even Titanium Innovations wanted to start mining."

"No, they didn't," Marley hissed, crossing her arms.

"What do you think they sent you up here for?" Calder asked. "We're only stopping them because we're more interested in the forest as a whole than just the metal." He looked over at Rowan. "I mean that shadow thing, for example. I know you don't want to talk about it, but there is something weird about this forest, and the more we learn about it, the more we'll find a reason to protect it."

"Or you could just leave," Tamsin said.

"Maybe," Calder said, looking down at the metal in his hands. "But Neosilica already knows about this, and if they don't get their fill now, then someone else will come."

"Fine," Rowan said. "Take them their metal. But you're either going to help us, or we are going to do everything we can to stop you."

Calder paused, his face softening, a flicker of vulnerability in his eyes. "Fine," he finally said. "You know, Rowan, I—"

"Save it," Rowan said, his heart clenching as a maelstrom of feelings attempted to resurface. He swallowed, pushing them down as he met Calder's gaze. "We've got that contract coming up soon. Show us you care, then we can talk."

Calder looked at the others and adjusted his grip on the metal stones. "I'll be gone a few weeks while I deliver this. When I come back, we'll have the contract ready."

With that, he left, fallen leaves and twigs crackling beneath his feet as he made his way toward the dirt path.

Elderflower Wine

Willow branches swayed as Rowan breathed in the sweet honeysuckle air, strolling along the river's grassy banks toward his friends. He carried a small wicker basket in his arms as he spotted the others gathered on a patchwork quilt beneath an old oak tree, its gnarled roots tracing down into the river.

Rowan savored the moment. Finally, a bit of calm now that Calder had been gone for nearly a week. Farmers stopped talking about the Steelwrights every second they could, and now they could just enjoy a warm summer afternoon before madness struck.

"Please tell me you grabbed cheese," Jimson called out, his grin widening as he nodded toward Marley. "Our friend here forgot hers, so we're stuck with dry bread and fruit."

Marley scoffed, holding up a bottle of elderflower wine. "Oh, hush. I brought the good stuff. Unless you'd rather I didn't share, you oaf."

Rowan chuckled, joining them, reaching into his basket, and pulling out a carefully wrapped package. "Never fear, I come bearing scones, jam, and, of course, the finest cheese in all of Frostfern."

Jimson nudged Rowan's shoulder. "You knew she was going to forget, didn't you?"

"I sure did," Rowan laughed, tossing the cheese to Marley with a wink. "But we mustn't forget the wine. So I think we can cut her some slack."

Marley eyed the two of them and grinned. "So, when were you going to tell us?"

"Tell you what?" Rowan asked.

"That you two were... let's say, official," Marley said.

Heat rose in Rowan's neck. "Oh. Oh! Uh, yeah, we're—"

"We're official. If that's what you call it," Jimson said, wrapping a large arm around Rowan's shoulder. "I could say the same about you and Elara."

Marley's face turned just as red as Rowan felt his own was. "Touché," she said.

Elara, who had been quietly fiddling with the knife, let out a soft curse as she struggled to slice through a loaf of crusty bread.

Marley took the knife from her, ripped off the rest of the loaf, and handed it to her. "Hey, it'll be okay."

Rowan frowned. "What happened? Was it the Steelwrights?"

"It's not that," Elara sighed, biting into the bread. "I received a letter from Flamel. I need to pick my classes for next semester."

Rowan felt a tightness in his chest. Had it already been that long? He straightened up and smiled. "That's good news, though, isn't it?"

"I guess. But it also means leaving the three of you right in the middle of all... this."

Marley shifted closer, her hand gripping onto Elara's. "None of that. We'll take care of things here, and you'll finish your degree and become the best damn quantum alchemist Neosilica has ever seen."

"Yeah. I know," Elara said.

"And if you ever need us, we're just a train ride away," Rowan added.

"I've always wanted to explore Neosilica," Jimson said. "It would be fun to visit and bug you when you're knee-deep in finals or something."

Rowan laughed. "We should make a trip of it, maybe during the Winter Festival? Jimson, you have to see the city lit up with all the lights and the horse automatons that pull you through the park."

Elara stared down at the bread. "Thanks. That means a lot."

Marley uncorked the wine and started filling their glasses. "But we're here now, in Frostfern, enjoying our time free from the Steelwrights."

"Cheers to that," Rowan said, picking up his glass and clinking it with the others.

"If only I could shake the feeling that the Steelwrights were up to something worse than what they're telling us," Marley mused, taking a swig of her wine. "All these promises... it doesn't add up."

Rowan nodded. "I know what you mean. If they followed through with everything they claim, Frostfern would become another Neosilica and push all the farmers out of work."

Jimson's hand found Rowan's, his calloused fingers intertwining with Rowan's own. "That's why we're here, to call them out if we see them doing anything that will hurt the town. And if worse comes to worst, we can always sic that ferret of yours on them."

Elara sat upright, her eyes lit with excitement. "Speaking of ferrets, Marley and I did a little something."

Rowan frowned. "What did you do?"

"You made us think of it," Marley said, reaching into her pocket. "With your double-discipline matrices. We wanted to see if there could be some kind of—what did you call it, Lars? 'Collapsable mass-displacing object?'"

Marley held up a small, intricate silver ring with two little blue gems.

"The key was making it stable," Elara said.

"Watch this," Marley said, tapping it gently. It twisted and clicked, rapidly unfolding and reshaping itself. Within seconds, the ring had turned into the automaton ferret, which tilted its head left and right, eyeing Rowan.

It hopped up and down, little paws digging at the parts of the blanket where Rowan's shadow touched. Rowan laughed and coaxed his shadow ferret free, and the two began their usual games of chasing each other and attempting to steal bread from Elara.

"I couldn't keep hiding it in my pockets all the time," Marley said. "And after seeing how you can call and dismiss yours, Elara and I put our heads together and came up with this."

"It's... amazing," Rowan beamed. "You show that off at graduation, and you are bound to get a diploma."

Elara half smiled. "It's still a work in progress, and I can't do it yet without Marley or some of that metal. But with a bit more fine-tuning, we could have all sorts of collapsible products."

"Could you imagine it?" Jimson laughed. "A whole workshop inside a wristwatch. I could be a traveling carpenter."

They continued down this trail of thought, ideas bouncing back and forth. Rowan sat back, sipping on his wine, musing at the excitement in his friend's eyes.

Marley reached into her bag, pulling out a small package wrapped in wax paper. "Chocolates?"

"Have you been hiding chocolates in your bag this whole time?" Jimson teased, snatching a small round one and popping it into his mouth.

"She hoards chocolate," Elara said. "I found a box hiding under my bed."

"Hey!" Marley laughed. "I have a sweet tooth, okay? And now these two know where my stash is."

"Miss Elara!" a voice called out. Rowan turned and spotted the dapper man who helped him with his luggage when he came to Frostfern, waving a letter in his hand as he approached. "I have a message from the mayor."

"Thank you, Bertie," she said, accepting the letter with a polite nod and a frown.

"What is it?" Marley asked as Elara tore open the envelope, her eyes scanning the contents of the letter.

"It's the Steelwrights," Elara said. "They'll be here by the end of next week, bringing the promised automatons with them. She wants us all in the office now to discuss preparations."

Marley knocked back the rest of her wine. "They're moving faster than we thought."

"We just have to be ready," Rowan said, collecting the

remaining food and placing it in his basket. "You can bet they have a contract for us to sign."

ALCHEMICAL CATALYSTS: A REFINEMENT OF TECHNIQUE

Rowan shifted on the gravel platform as the train pulled into Frostfern Station, billowing steam as it screeched to a halt. Moments later, a march of metallic clangs started before a kaleidoscope of reflections bounced from the train.

There were two types of automatons. The larger ones were at least a foot taller than a regular human. Their bodies were bulky and rectangular, with thick metal plating and intricate designs etched into their surface. The smaller automatons were sleek and slender, their bodies thinner than a child and no more than five feet high, with elongated silvery fingers. Both had a golden filigree of SWI embossed on their chests.

"Would you look at that?" Jimson said, letting out a low whistle. "They really went and did it."

Marley crossed her arms and huffed. "For now. Give them a few days and see how Steelwright craftsmanship holds up to actual work." She elbowed Jimson and smiled. "Bet you we'll get those meaty paws of yours dirty in no time."

Elara approached one of the smaller automatons. "Farm hands and caring units." She traced a finger along a panel on its arm, which showed various medical requests. "If they work, this would help so much. No more strained backs and care at all hours of the night."

Townsfolk gathered in front of the automatons, a soft murmur rippling as they anxiously waited.

A familiar figure emerged from the train, platinum hair bobbing between metal statues. Calder paused, rifling through his clipboard filled with papers.

"Alright, everyone!" he shouted, gesturing to the automatons with a broad sweep of his arm. "Who's ready to meet their new assistants?"

Excited murmurs drifted through the crowd, but before they could go on too long, Calder held up one hand. "I know some of you may be a bit... intimidated by all this." His gaze flicked over to Rowan and the others. "But I can assure you, every single automaton has been rigorously tested and approved. Safe, efficient, and at the cutting edge of modern alchemy."

He strode over to one of the larger farming models and rapped his knuckles against its broad metal chest with a dull thunk. "These farm hands are equipped with state-of-the-art soil sensors to monitor nutrient levels. They'll optimize your crop yields and alert you if the alchemical plates need replacing."

He gestured to one of the appendages, which shifted and reformed itself into an array of different tools right before their eyes. "Plowing, planting, weeding—you name it, they can do it."

Marley leaned toward Rowan and whispered, "Yeah, but what about weeding out little blond Goody Two-shoes?"

A chuckle sounded behind them before a low voice said, "I hear they have some of the finest technology to pull even the toughest of weeds."

Rowan turned and came face-to-face with a tall man in a suit with long blond hair. "Mr. Steelwright. I... we—"

"You've reviewed the revised contract we sent, yes?" Mr. Steelwright asked.

"We did," Elara said. "You approved nearly every request we made."

Rowan swallowed hard, his throat dry. They included

everything that Rowan, Marley, and Elara asked for.

Mr. Steelwright nodded. "Increased control over decisions regarding development and a more generous compensation for Rowan Mosswood's stipends." He paused before adding, "And, more importantly, we've made revisions to ensure minimal impact on your forest. Especially after that Tamsin of yours really gave my son a fright."

He peered out toward his son, handing out paperwork to the last people in the crowd.

"So," Mr. Steelwright clapped his hands together. "I believe we have an agreement, yes?"

Elara pulled a document from her satchel and handed it over. "We accept your terms. You'll find the mayor's signature along with ours in that document."

A wide grin split Mr. Steelwright's face as he plucked the papers from Elara's hands. "Excellent news!" He tucked the contract into his jacket, then stepped out in front of the four of them, announcing loudly, "With this signed, what do you say we give these good people a taste of what's to come, hmm? Mr. Mosswood, care to do the honors?"

Rowan blinked. "I... I'm sorry?"

"A simple botanical growth demonstration. I'd love for the townspeople to see what sort of revitalized alchemy we will provide."

"But, the plates. They already know. And I..." Rowan faltered, his mind racing. He needed components, tools, and preparation—not to mention soil. "I'd need components."

"No need to worry about your components," Mr. Steelwright waved dismissively. "I have everything you need."

He nodded toward the automatons, several of which broke away from formation to deposit crates and sacks on the ground before them. Rowan watched as they unpacked bags of soil, manure, and even a bundle of fresh oak seedlings.

"I've brought some nutrient-rich soil specially formulated back at our labs. And this"—he reached into his pocket, pulling out a small glass vial filled with a shimmering blue-green sand that glowed. Rowan's fingers tingled, like they could sense the power radiating off the strange substance—"is a refined sample of that metal you all discovered. This is the true test. A newly formed catalyst. That should be a spectacle for anyone to see."

Rowan stared at the vial, his heart thundering in his ears. The shimmering blue-green sand seemed to pulse with energy.

A hand on his shoulder made him start. He turned to find Jimson glaring at Mr. Steelwright.

"He shouldn't have to make a spectacle for you," Jimson said, squeezing Rowan's shoulder.

"Oh, don't get me wrong, Mr. Evergreen," Mr. Steelwright said, smiling. "With our agreement to leave the woods alone and our lack of space on the train, we need some lumber for our new facility. What better way to get it than sourcing it here?"

Rowan bit his lip. As much as he didn't want to play into the Steelwrights' game, he could feel the crowd peering at them. Staring.

Squaring his shoulders, Rowan said, "Alright. Let's get this over with."

"Excellent! Follow me," Mr. Steelwright beamed, handing Rowan the vial of shimmering liquid. Rowan suppressed a shudder as his fingers closed around the cool glass, the power humming.

Nodding to the automatons, Mr. Steelwright started a procession to the edge of town near the first of the farmlands.

Once settled, he bellowed to the crowd, "Why don't we give our friends here a bit of space? Alchemical workings can get... unpredictable, after all."

"You've got this," Jimson said, his voice low as he joined the crowd.

Rowan managed a tight smile before following Mr. Steelwright and the automatons. He trailed behind, watching as the metal figures deposited their crates and bundles on a dry patch of dirt just beyond the last of the houses.

Rowan turned his focus inward as he knelt beside the supplies. He could do this. Summoning a steadying breath, he began sketching out the first of the sigils in the hard-packed dirt.

Simple and elegant, the square represented earth. Curves weaved at two sides for water, a triangle at each opposing corner for fire. At the center was a spiral for aether, the force that gave the whole thing cohesion. Rowan worked quickly but meticulously, his movements steady as he carved a sigil nearly three times the size of his last growth sigil.

He went over the lines again with the lab soil. He placed the components within the botanical matrix, setting the seedlings apart with enough space to grow. He stepped back and looked over his work.

"Well?" Mr. Steelwright's voice cut through his concentration like a blade. "Are you ready?"

"Ready," Rowan said, carefully uncorking the vial and pouring the strange blue-green sand into a slight depression in the center of the botanical matrix. He knelt and placed his hands on top, a searing power thrumming through him.

His awareness sank into the etchings, and energy crackled, shooting bright green sparks behind his eyelids as it flowed through him and into the design.

For a moment, he felt it. A familiar resistance. The tug and pull of the forest, trying to drain his alchemical workings. He grappled with the magic beneath his fingertips, straining, coaxing it to bend to his will.

Green fire blossomed beneath Rowan's hands, racing

along every line and spiral with blinding intensity.

When he thought he couldn't take any more, the resistance pulled back, and the energy snapped like a rope.

The fire sizzled out. The power faded into nothing as Rowan slumped forward, panting hard. He blinked, eyelids heavy, and peered down at the sigil.

The soil sat undisturbed, with no extra leaf or change in the seedlings.

"I..." Rowan frowned. "I don't understand. That should have—"

A tut cut him off. He looked up to find Mr. Steelwright shaking his head. The man turned to the onlooking crowd and said, his voice booming, "Perhaps I overestimated the... qualifications of Mr. Mosswood."

Rowan bristled. There was no way Mr. Steelwright could have done anything with that catalyst. Not if Rowan couldn't. So why mock him?

"What if I just—" Rowan started, looking over the sigil once more. He closed his eyes, gently using his magic to inspect the lines.

That's when it hit him. A tug that pulled his hand under the earth, latching onto his magic while an iron fist gripped his heart and emptied the air from his lungs.

A voice tore inside his head, resonant and ancient.

"What is it you seek?"

Rowan's eyes widened, pulling at his buried hand, but it wouldn't move. He opened his mouth, but no sound came out. What was happening? That voice—he'd heard nothing like it before. It rattled inside him, aching his joints and cutting at his teeth.

The force holding him tightened. As if it wouldn't wait much longer for an answer.

"I..." Rowan thought, forcing his mind to calm. "I want to grow these trees."

"Why?" the voice pressed, rumbling through him.

Rowan blinked. Why? He scrambled for an answer, any answer that might make this thing release him. "Because they need the lumber," he thought. "What are you? Let me go!"

"Why?" it demanded again, this time pulling his arm deeper into the soil.

"Because," he thought, pulling against the force. "They'd take from the forest if I don't."

The force pulled him deeper into the ground. He felt the dampened soil moving around his fingers as his shoulder rested flush with the earth.

"Help!" he finally cried out, straining his neck to the crowd.

"Rowan?" Jimson shouted, peering through the crowd. "What's going—"

Shadows shifted and swirled around him, his mind calling on the ferret. It coalesced into a massive beast that encircled him, growling and chittering at the air.

A chorus of screams rose from the townsfolk behind

him. He spotted them through the ferret, several stumbling back, and Jimson shouldering past others, racing toward him.

"And you wish to protect the forest?" the voice asked, unfazed by the appearance of the ferret.

"I... I do," he whispered.

"And you, little one?" The voice softened. "You trust him?"

The ferret bared its teeth and let out a small bark.

"Very well, alchemist. Prove it. Finish your little spell."

The voice pulled away, taking with it the weight and force that pulled Rowan. He lifted his arm from the dirt, resting his hands on the sigil. Light burst from every line, shining high into the sky.

Power flowed back and forth, from him, into him, echoing from the ground in some kind of building resonance. The seedlings broke from their pots, rooting into the ground. But his magic didn't stop there, he could feel other seeds, dormant, now waking and ready.

He willed them to grow, and they did, bursting free from the earth and shooting high into the sky. In seconds, he sat at the center of a forest, the townspeople now lost in the foliage of a forest that appeared centuries old.

The voice spoke again in his ear, "Be wary, small one, for many eyes are upon you now."

SIGIL STRESS

Rowan stumbled, knees hitting the mossy ground as he spotted the edge of the conjured forest mere yards away. His mind swirled as Jimson found him, steadying him with his brawny arms while Elara and Marley flanked his other side.

"Easy. Don't rush yourself," Jimson said, grabbing Rowan's arm and wrapping it around his shoulder.

"Just breathe," Marley added.

Rowan inhaled, his head buzzing as he breathed the overpowering scent of earth that filled the air. He could still feel that voice in his head, resonating and rattling his bones.

Be wary, small one, for many eyes are upon you now.

He blinked a few times, trying to force the words from his thoughts, and peered up at the canopy of green above him. He'd done that. He'd summoned an entire forest in a matter of seconds. That shouldn't be able to happen, not like this.

"You alright?" Marley asked, pulling him back to reality. "You're not going to die on us now, are you? Not after you did all this."

"Ha. Ha." Rowan rolled his eyes, focusing on putting one foot in front of the other. He squeezed Jimson's shoulder, happy to have the support. "I'll be fine. Just a little shook up, that's all."

As they broke free from the newly formed woods, murmurs rose from the onlooking crowd. Most of them asked if he was alright, but all that was on Rowan's mind was getting to the bench, the world still wobbling underneath him.

"Did you see the size of that beast?" an elderly woman said, fanning herself. "It was like one of the shadow stalkers from the old tales!"

"Aye, and the way it growled?" Old Man Thistle added. "A sound to curdle yer blood, that was."

"Poor Rowan would have been a goner if it weren't for those trees."

"Do you think it's still in there?"

"My gran told me about those old horrors," another whispered. "If they're coming back..."

Rowan swallowed, lowering himself on the bench. He hadn't wanted to call the ferret in front of everyone, but that voice... scared him. And now there would be questions before he and the others had answers, especially with all the tall tales Elara found about shadow beasts that used to terrorize the town.

The sight of shiny black shoes against the gravel ground pulled his attention to Mr. Steelwright, standing in front of him, his eyes wide as he looked back at the forest.

"I. Yes, I'm fine," Rowan replied, clutching Jimson's arm for support. "Just a bit drained."

"Pretty sure giving someone a substance that would sprout an entire forest would take it out of anyone." Marley piped up. She shot Rowan a sidelong glance.

"Of course. Of course," Mr. Steelwright said. "I don't think the people in our lab had nearly the success you did. Granted, that was all metallurgical work, but still." He paused, eyeing Rowan for a moment. "But I heard you shouting out for help. Then that creature appeared. What happened?"

A lump formed in Rowan's throat. He looked at his friends, but they didn't even know what he'd heard. And if he waited, and they spent weeks looking all on their own, they'd probably never find the answer.

"I heard a voice," Rowan finally said.

"You heard a voice?" Marley asked.

Elara looked at Mr. Steelwright, then at Rowan. "Rowan, should we... uh."

Mr. Steelwright kneeled, meeting Rowan's level. There was an eagerness in his eyes as he asked, "What did it say?"

Rowan looked at Marley, then Elara, and shrugged. "It asked me what I sought," he said slowly, "and why I wanted the trees to grow."

"Fascinating," Mr. Steelwright murmured. He leaned in closer. "What did it sound like? And what did you tell it?"

Marley sat down next to Rowan. "Woah there, Mr. Steelwright. Rowan's pretty exhausted. Maybe we keep the questions to when he's rested and—"

"It was like it spoke through me," Rowan said. "I could feel it in every bone in my body."

Mr. Steelwright smiled. "Excellent, and that creature?"

"It's mine," Rowan admitted. "And it's safe." He looked at his friends, then added. "It's something from the forest. Something that's been there for decades. Maybe even longer."

"I think that's enough for now," Jimson said, squeezing Rowan's shoulder.

Clanking grabbed Rowan's attention as a set of large automatons approached the forest, their arms shifting into long rotating saws.

"Perfect timing," Mr. Steelwright said, standing. "We'll clear out these woods you've created and smooth out the land. Plenty of lumber to get our facilities up and running." He looked out at the crowd and snapped his fingers. "Calder! Why don't you accompany Mr. Mosswood back to the greenhouse and ensure he gets settled?"

"That's alright," Jimson said, helping Rowan to his feet. "I've got it. We don't need your son's help."

Calder paused and looked down at the ground, clearing his throat.

"Very well," Mr. Steelwright said. "We'll reconvene after you've regained your strength. I'd love to hear more about these... discoveries."

As they walked around the newly formed forest and back onto the path that led to the greenhouse, Rowan couldn't help but notice the glinting automatons already at work on each farm. Even the Evergreen farm had a large automaton, running its mechanical arm through the dirt and pulling weeds.

"Bet your dad is pretty happy to have one of those automatons helping," Rowan said.

Jimson let out a low chuckle. "More like over the moon. All the growth those plates caused made it tough for them to keep up. He'd never let me, but he'd need at least one extra pair of hands if they hadn't come."

As they approached the greenhouse, Rowan spotted a small patch of browned grass where he buried a sigil plate.

"Oh great," he breathed, kneeling and digging up the plate. It was more corroded than he'd expected to see, the edges of the metal breaking off as he pulled it from the ground.

"What's wrong?" Jimson asked, crouching beside him.

"How long ago did we install these plates again?" he asked.

"Been about... a month or so?" Jimson said, raking his hand through his hair. "Why?"

Rowan gestured at the ruined metal. "They're degrading too fast. We didn't account for the automatons. They're basically walking alchemical constructs. All that alchemy in one place, and with the woods..."

He shook his head and climbed to his feet. "I'll need to rework the whole matrix."

"But you should rest," Jimson said, following behind him as they ducked inside the greenhouse. "You literally summoned an entire forest."

"I know," Rowan said, opening drawers in the apothecary cabinet and grabbing scraps of metal. "But if I don't do this now, then those plates could give any second. Your dad's is the closest to the forest. I don't want anything to—"

Jimson spun him around, meeting him face-to-face while he put his hands on Rowan's waist. "It'll be okay. We can get Marley or tell the automaton to get off the property. You don't have to do everything by yourself."

"But I do," Rowan murmured, his gaze dropping to the curve of Jimson's lower lip. "There's no one who can do the botanical part. If I don't, then—"

Jimson closed the distance between them, pressing his lips against Rowan's. Rowan melted in Jimson's grasp. The stress. The anxiety. It all faded away. Strong arms tightened around Rowan, hands splaying across the small of his back as he pushed into the kiss.

The world beyond the greenhouse walls fell away. Nothing else mattered. His hands gripped Jimson, pulling him in as the man's coarse beard tickled his face.

He could have stayed like that forever, wrapped in Jimson's arms. But the sudden fizzle and popping from outside broke their kiss apart.

Rowan spun toward the source of the noise and spotted the farming automaton outside the window, on the field, sparking and smoking.

"What the..." Jimson muttered.

"No, no, no," Rowan breathed, already moving before his brain could catch up. He burst outside as the automaton jerked and crashed face-first into the soil, limbs still twitching.

Braided Alchemical Practices

R owan wiped a bead of sweat from his forehead, leaving behind a smudge of dirt as he leaned back from the workbench with a huff. A pile of corroded sigil plates lay in front of him, each another failed attempt at what felt like days of trialing new etchings and blending components.

Elara perched on a stool next to him, eyes glazed over as she thumbed through another dusty botanical alchemy tome of Rowan's. "You know," she said, snapping the book shut and stifling a yawn, "when you said I could come over to 'procrastinate' on packing, I didn't think you'd put me to work. I don't understand how this alchemy makes sense to you. Quantum is all math. Whatever this is... I have no idea."

Rowan chuckled, pushing away from the table and stretching. "You're telling me. Doesn't help that none of these are working. Good thing we got those automatons off the fields, but the farmers are already up in arms. Once we get into harvest season, they'll be knocking down my door and dragging me out."

He picked up one of the damaged plates, the once shiny metal with intricate etchings now nothing more than a pitted, warped piece of junk. "We're missing something here. Something that would hold the energy better."

The greenhouse door swung open, and Marley walked in, her overalls grease-stained, her purple hair pulled back in a messy bun. "Mr. Steelwright is going to be the death of me. That's the fifth automaton to fail this week." She plopped into a chair next to Elara, resting her shoulder against her. "Any luck?"

Rowan sighed, raking a hand through his hair. "No. I've done all I can think of with the botanical matrix. Elara couldn't find anything wrong with the metallurgical side. We just need to contain the excess energy. Or maybe..." He eyed the etchings on the plates once more, frowning. "If we could move..."

He scooped up one of the unused metal plates, angling it to catch the light coming through the greenhouse windows. "What if the problem isn't the forest side of the equation at all? We created the sigil to prevent the forest from extracting energy and nutrients from the fields, but the issue now is that there is an excess of energy with nowhere to go."

Elara sat up straighter, eyes widening. "Wait. Sort of like you are creating a spatial resonance field without a dispersal agent?"

Rowan frowned. "A what? I mean, yeah, I think so. If the automatons are constantly channeling alchemy to work, then the sigils are just bouncing the energy back into the automatons and overloading them."

Marley crossed her arms and slouched in her chair. "So we need some kind of safety release, like a pressure-relief valve."

"Exactly!" Rowan said, placing the plate on the workbench and picking up one of the etching tools. "But botanical doesn't have anything like that."

"Nor metallurgical," Marley grumbled. "I mean, not for alchemical energy. Maybe I could rework the pressure ones, but I don't know where to start."

Elara laughed, staring up at the ceiling. "You won't believe this."

"What?" Rowan asked.

"This is going to sound wild, but quantum displaces

and untangles energy all the time. That's literally all it does."
She got up, crossed the room, and picked up the plate.
"Would it be out of the question to fit in a little quantum
into this sigil?"

"A triple-discipline matrix," Marley laughed. "Wow,
we're getting real fancy now. Why don't we just bring in the
bio and psych disciplines while we're at it?"

Rowan frowned and looked down at the plate in front
of him. "Or... two double-disciplines on both sides of the
plate. Your quantum could entangle the two, right?"

Elara's eyes lit up, and she nodded. "Entanglement
is easy. If we did that, I'd still have room for the energy
displacement."

"Perfect," Rowan said. "Marley and I will keep our
matrices the same; then, we need a matrix that will circle
around mine and be on the inside of Marley's."

Elara nodded and turned back toward Marley,
nudging her out of the way as she rummaged through her
satchel, producing a battered quantum alchemy manual. "I
think I can do that. I just need to reference a few things and
check on the components."

She flipped rapidly through the pages, muttering
under her breath. As she did, the door to the greenhouse
swung open once more, and Jimson ducked inside, Calder
trailing behind him.

Jimson was just as dirtied as Marley, with grease
and sweat clinging to his shirt. Rowan let his eyes linger

for a moment before eyeing the ever-pristine and severely out-of-place Calder.

"Got any good news?" Jimson asked, resting his hands on his hips as he smiled at Rowan. "All this soldering got my shop piping hot, and it doesn't help that I've got townsfolk coming to me asking when they can use their automatons again."

Calder cleared his throat and stepped beside Jimson, hands behind his back. "Indeed, I would like an update to report back to my father." His eyes narrowed as they swept over the piles of corroded metal. "I hope you've seen some progress, yes?"

Marley rolled her eyes and pushed herself up from her seat. "Actually, we were just about to test something. Come on, this might be something worth your attention."

She walked past him, patting him on the shoulder and leaving behind a noticeable grease stain, before heading back out the door.

Calder wiped at the stain, then quickly gave up and straightened his back, eyeing Rowan for a moment before marching outside.

Rowan gathered his etching tools, components, plates, and the small metal chunk they'd kept from the forest and stepped beside Jimson, leaning in for a kiss. "Everything alright?"

"It will be," Jimson said, holding the door open for Rowan.

They assembled in the open field just beyond the greenhouse. Rowan knelt in the dirt, smoothing out a large circle before carefully transcribing the complex matrix he'd started inside. Marley and Elara joined him, both kneeling and clearing space for the plates.

"Wait," Calder said. "Three of you?"

"Keep up," Marley said. "Your dad will want a full report of this." She then turned and started etching in her designs, her hands moving with a practiced ease. In contrast, Elara was more hesitant, often pausing as she picked up her book and double-checked a line or two.

Despite that, the three of them worked in harmony, switching between plates and the center etching, weaving in their disciplines between the larger geometric shapes of the elements. Once Rowan finished his final touches to the botanical sigil, he stood back and took in their work.

"Alright," he announced, sharing a glance with Marley and Elara. "Let's give it a go."

Rowan placed the components on the sigil. Compost and water were used for growth, and metals formed the barrier. He settled in the middle of the sigil, with Marley and Elara on the edges, their hands on the etched plates. Then he grabbed the last component, the chunk of metal from the forest, and held it in his hands. It didn't give him the same rush as the refined powder had. Still, it was enough to stabilize and ground himself as tendrils of green energy traced into the sigil.

He felt the edges of blue and violet energies, both somewhat erratic and struggling to hold. The moment his energy touched theirs, it calmed, and power surged through the sigils. His energy braided with Marley's and Elara's, each joining into one solid indigo tendril, drawing a path that moved along the center sigil and then the two untouched plates. Marley or Elara didn't need to move this time. Instead, it was as if the three of them could move the energy anywhere they wanted, focusing on one plate, then seamlessly appearing on another plate, filling it with energy.

It was different this time as if adding Elara made their energy stronger. Soon, Rowan lost all sense of self. He was Marley, and Elara, and himself all at once. They were the sigils, and the metal, and the earth.

"You test my patience, small one," a voice tore through his mind.

Their energies unraveled, and Rowan snapped back into his mind, opening his eyes to find the sigil glowing with a bright indigo light.

The shadow ferret appeared at his side in an instant, looking left to right, just as Rowan did, looking for the source of that voice.

"Why did you stop?" Marley asked, breathing heavily.

"Did... did you hear that?" Rowan asked.

"Hear what?" Elara asked, frowning as she looked down at the glowing sigils.

The hair on the ferret's back smoothed, and it looked

up at Rowan, head cocked to the side. Then it made a few quick chirping sounds before diving headfirst into the center of the sigil.

"What the—?" Rowan asked, backing up as the ferret vanished in a flash of indigo light.

"Where'd it go?" Marley asked.

A flash of light formed behind Marley, and the ferret shot out of the ground several yards away, flinging into the air before landing on its feet. It ran back toward them, making the same chirping sounds as it did it again, vanishing and appearing even farther away and shooting higher into the sky.

"What is it doing?" Calder asked.

"I think it's helping," Elara laughed. "And that means the plates are doing their job. Looks like the little guy might be charging them up. See how he's getting closer to the woods each time?"

As if to prove her theory, the ferret dove into the plates once more and rematerialized several yards deeper into the tree line.

Jimson helped Rowan to his feet, smiling wide. "So the three of you did it then! That means we can get the automatons back on the fields, right?"

Marley grinned. "And we saved that one"—she nodded to Calder—"from the pitchforks."

"We have to test it first," Calder said, stepping forward and eyeing the plates. "With the automatons. Before we tell everyone this is working. I mean."

"Of course," Rowan said. "Marley and Jimson can bring one by later and we'll confirm it holds."

"You just don't want to admit we saved you," Marley said, eyeing Calder.

He opened his mouth, no doubt readying for a scathing retort. However, the reply was drowned out by a thunderous rumbling that reverberated through the ground.

Birds shook loose from trees, covering the sky as they cawed and shrilled with their alarms. Rowan readied himself for some massive bear beast to come barreling out from the woods, but none came.

"What the hell was that?" Marley asked.

"I don't know," Rowan said, frowning at the direction the sound came from. "But that didn't feel natural."

Elara nodded. "We'll need to tell my mother about this. Something strange is going on."

Familiar Variations

Rowan shifted from foot to foot, adjusting the suspenders of his green overalls as plumes of coal smoke drew in closer to the train station. He hated goodbyes, and this one stung.

To his side, Marley fidgeted with loose strands of her purple locs, her usual happiness dampened. Even Jimson was quieter than normal, standing stoically as the three of them clustered around Elara.

"Well, this is it," she said, her blue eyes red from tears. She shook her head and straightened her shoulders.

"It'll be over before you know it, cuz," Jimson said, nudging her shoulder. "You'll be back up here, showing us all your new quantum finds in no time."

Elara chuckled. "I know, but the Steelwrights..."

"Will be fine," Rowan said. "We'll make sure they don't do anything they aren't supposed to."

Marley smirked and cracked her knuckles. "And if they do..."

Elara laughed and pulled Marley in for another kiss. "Don't hit them too hard. I don't want to hear you getting locked up."

"Not a chance," Marley scoffed, waving her hand. "They won't see it coming."

"You just focus on graduation," Rowan said. "Refine that wormhole retrieval, and Dean Vayu will have to graduate you."

The whistle from the approaching train cut through their banter, followed by the squeal of brakes as it came into Frostfern Station.

Elara bit her lip and pulled away from Marley. "I will," she said to Rowan before turning to Marley. "And you better write me. At least twice a month. I don't want to hear from the newspapers that this town is becoming automaton central. You hear me?"

Marley grinned and stepped close to Elara. "Oh, I like this assertive side." She wrapped an arm around Elara's waist and pulled her in for another kiss. "Tell me, what will you do if I don't?"

The train whistled once more, noting its imminent departure.

Elara dove in and hugged Rowan, squeezing him tight and nearly headbutting him as the scent of lavender and old books assaulted his senses. "I'll miss you, Ro," she whispered. "You and Marley made everything here even better than I imagined."

Rowan squeezed her back. "See you soon."

She pulled away, turning and hugging Jimson next. She threw her arms around his broad shoulders and squeezed. "Hug me back," she demanded.

Jimson laughed, wrapping his massive arms around her. "We'll be down in a few months. Bet you won't even miss us."

With a roll of her eyes and one last kiss from Marley, Elara boarded the train, reappearing at a window just as it pulled from the station. The three of them stayed, waving until the train disappeared around the bend, swallowed up by the mountains.

"Well," Marley said, wiping her damp cheeks. She looped her arms through Rowan's and Jimson's, anchoring herself between them. "Looks like I'm the third wheel now. You two better not think of getting rid of me."

"Get rid of you?" Rowan feigned a gasp as he clutched his chest. They headed out of the train station and down the path toward the town. "We'd never do such a thing. But now that you say it, aren't there some automatons in need of your attention?"

"Ha, ha, hilarious." She pulled free and faced the two of them as she walked backward. "I suppose so. See you later?"

"Of course," Jimson said. "Swing by the farm. We're having a big roast, and you know my mom would want you there."

"Perfect," Marley said. "I wouldn't miss her cooking for the world." She waved at the two of them, putting her hands on her hips as she said, "Well, gents, those hunks of metal aren't going to fix themselves. I'll let you off the hook today, Jimson, but I'm gonna need some heavy lifting tomorrow. Later." With a final salute, she pivoted on her heel and raced off toward town, leaving Rowan and Jimson as they headed to the greenhouse.

They walked in silence, Rowan enjoying the smell of wildflowers and the warmth of Jimson's hand as they strolled along the path. Unfortunately, that silence didn't last long, as the sound of snapping branches and rustling leaves raced toward them from the woods.

"What the?" Jimson said, stiffening as he stood in front of Rowan.

A figure exploded from the forest, staggering onto the path before them. Rowan frowned, taking in the disheveled person with scratches and grime covering their face.

"Tamsin?" Rowan cautiously asked, eyeing their torn

animal skins. "Everything alright?"

Their eyes were wide as they looked over their shoulder at the looming trees. "The beasts," Tamsin rasped, swaying on their feet. "I-I can't stop them."

"Beasts?" Rowan echoed, his chest tightening. Memories of the massive bear resurfaced, and the thought of another one chasing him down made his blood run cold.

Jimson reacted first, rushing forward to steady Tamsin before they toppled over. "It's okay. Just tell us what's happening."

Tamsin gulped down ragged breaths, their eyes shifting between Jimson and Rowan. "Beasts, like the one you fended off months ago. There are more. They keep appearing. I've been trying to hold them back, but I can't anymore. There's too many."

"Hold them back? By yourself? How?" Rowan asked, imagining several bear-like creatures descending on Tamsin.

Tamsin stood up straight. "I haven't been entirely truthful," they admitted. "I might not have alchemy, but you're not the only one the woods gave a shadow to."

"What?" Rowan asked.

To illustrate their point, Tamsin raised a hand, fingers splayed toward the sky. A tendril of shadow unfurled from their palm, coalescing into a large, winged raven that settled on a high branch.

Blue eyes regarded Rowan as the bird ruffled its

feathers.

"The forest chose me, as it chose you, to watch over it and protect it," Tamsin said. "But now, the creatures are restless. And I can't stop them."

Rowan's breath caught in his throat as realization dawned. That voice he'd heard was connected to this, to Tamsin.

Before he could ask, a roar tore through the woods, and trees cracked and shifted.

"Dammit," Tamsin said, facing the trees. "It caught my scent."

Whatever it was came barreling toward them, and Rowan could only dive out of the way as a massive shape burst free from the forest.

It skidded to a halt, turning around. It was a boar, larger than anything he had ever seen, with wicked curved tusks jutting from its frothing jaws. Its beady eyes burned a bright red, like hot coals. It reared up on its hind legs, slamming them down with enough force to send tremors through the ground.

Tamsin pushed past Jimson and thrust their arm toward it. Their shadow raven hopped off the tree and grew in size as it dove, but just as it was about to snap its jaws at the boar, the beast knocked it to the side with a massive tusk. The raven careened and tumbled onto the ground, vanishing in a heap of mist.

Instinct took over, and Rowan reached within, calling

for the ferret. Shadowy tendrils appeared in front of him, weaving together to shape his little friend. He willed it to grow, and it did, becoming larger with every passing second. Rowan didn't need the metals or the powders like before. The ferret seemed to desire to protect him, and that helped. In no time, it was nearly as tall as the boar itself.

The ferret darted forward, a blur as it leaped over the beast and sank its teeth into the boar's bristly haunches. It screamed, bucking and writhing, but the ferret gripped on, wrapping its body around the boar.

Then, with a sickening crunch, the boar twisted, its jaws clamping down on the ferret's paw. A lance of pain stabbed Rowan's mind, and he doubled over, gasping as the ferret kept its bite but growled in agony.

He had to help. Had to do something. Dropping to his knees, he dug a finger into the dirt, frantically sketching earth, water, and fire symbols. It was crude, and he didn't have any components, but he had to try. Dirt flaked up, corrupting his lines, but it didn't matter. The sigil would hold true in his mind. He spat on the ground, an offering of water, before slamming his hand onto the sigil.

"Please work," he mumbled.

The voice didn't speak this time, but he felt it, waiting for him to ask. A torrent of energy rushed through him, setting the sigil ablaze with green energy. A pulse rippled out from the sigil, and he could feel the seeds, lying dormant in the ground, waiting to be called on.

He focused near the boar's feet and poured energy into the seeds. Vines burst from the earth, wrapping around the boar. His shadow ferret seized the opportunity, wrenching its paw free from the beast and leaping clear of the vines moments before it constricted the boar, pulling the beast to the ground.

The boar shifted, squealing as it thrashed against the vines before it fell still and breathed heavily.

"Now what?" Jimson asked.

"I'm sorry," Tamsin said, extending a hand toward the boar.

It squealed again, a high-pitched whine that dug into Rowan's mind. It pulled a few vines free from the ground before streaks of red light tumbled out from its eyes. Lines of fire swirled and tunneled into Tamsin's hand, a burning vortex fueled by the boar's screams.

When the last of the fire was absorbed, the beast's body crumbled into a pile of ash, and Tamsin fell to the ground, their arm blackened and burned.

Rowan rushed over, and he and Jimson helped Tamsin sit up.

"There will be more," Tamsin rasped. "They keep coming, and I can't stop them all. I... I need your help."

Rowan swallowed hard, his mind reeling at what had just happened. He glanced at Jimson, reading the fear on his face. If more things like this came out of those woods and descended on Frostfern...

Rowan squared his shoulders and nodded at Tamsin. "Tell me what I need to do."

SIGILS FOR SPIRITUAL
ATTUNEMENT

R owan groaned as he woke, his muscles aching from the day before. He blinked, wincing from the morning light as memories of the previous day came flooding back. Tamsin hadn't been easy on him, spending hours of training on summoning his ferret and willing it to change in size. It was exhausting, and now, he contemplated lying in bed for the foreseeable future.

It only helped his desire to remain bedridden that a large arm was wrapped around him, comforting him as

Jimson lay beside him.

"Morning," Jimson murmured, squeezing Rowan and nuzzling into his shoulder. "You wouldn't stop tossing and turning."

Rowan rolled to his side and wrapped an arm around Jimson, pulling him closer, feeling the warmth of his bare chest. He breathed in, savoring the scent of pine and sawdust that clung to Jimson's skin, with a hint of something sharp and metallic—remnants of all the work on automatons threatening to take over.

"Just sore. And confused," Rowan said, swallowing hard. His fingers absently traced the contours of Jimson's back as he spoke. "I mean... a guardian of the woods? What does that even mean? Do you think Tamsin even knows?"

Jimson's hand found Rowan's, intertwining their fingers. "It's all new to me," he said. "But you'll figure it out."

Rowan sat up and looked out the window toward the forest. Roots breached the soil, and he wondered just how deep they buried into the ground. He mentally mapped the pathways of each of the roots as if he were tracing a sigil with his energy, feeling his way down to waters and mineral-rich earth.

"Do you think you could talk to that voice you heard?" Jimson asked, his voice pulling Rowan back to the present. "I mean, that's what I'd do."

Rowan considered it for a moment, his mind racing. If he could connect with that voice, which was somehow part of the forest, then that might just be the answer. He'd need a sigil, something that would amplify the connection...

He turned to Jimson, a smile on his face, and planted a kiss on his lips. "You're a genius!" As he pulled back, he jumped out of bed, putting on his clothes as, he said, "Help me with breakfast, then I'll go try to talk to this voice before Tamsin brings on a whole stampede or something."

The two of them moved in tandem in the kitchen, dancing around each other with ease as they chopped vegetables and fresh bread or watched the stove as the eggs cooked. Rowan prepared a kettle of water and crushed some dried nettles and chamomile before dumping them in.

"What are those for?" Jimson asked.

"Nettles for soreness and chamomile to help relax," Rowan said.

As they ate, Rowan drew out plans for his sigil. "I don't think it'll need a botanical matrix. Just simple elements to focus on," he mused, absently stirring his tea. "Maybe just earth and spirit."

Shortly after, Rowan stood alone in the woods. The air was a heavy fog that carried damp earth and pine as the birds sang their morning trills. He'd found a small clearing and used a stick to etch into the soft, mossy loam.

It was a simple outer ring. Earth for stability and spirals of spirit to connect. He felt odd not adding more, but there was nothing more he needed, and the more complex, the more his mind would focus on that.

He pulled out a small pouch of dried yarrow, the only thing he could think of that might help, and sprinkled the delicate white flowers over the sigil.

He sat in the middle, pulling out a small shard of metal from the forest and holding it in his hands. It pulsed with energy, ready for him to use the sigil he sat inside.

Rowan took a deep breath and closed his eyes, focusing on the metal in his palm and the earthy scent rising from the ground. His energy sank into the earth, filling the sigil with a brilliant green glow.

At first, there was nothing. The sigil held firm in his mind, but nothing came or responded. Then, gradually, a sense of something vast stirred at the edges of his consciousness. He reached out to it, but it was like smoke, fleeting every time he tried to hold it in his mind.

"Please," Rowan whispered, his voice barely audible. "I don't understand."

A rumble passed through the earth, vibrating up through Rowan. The voice emanated through him, causing an ache in his bones.

"Seeker. Guardian. Watcher. What roots do you wish to reveal?"

Rowan frowned. What? He considered for a moment,

then said, "The beasts. Why are they waking? What did we do?"

A sigh rustled through the leaves overhead. "A sapling only sees branches, not the forest entire."

Rowan's mind raced. What did it mean by that? He was undoubtedly the sapling in this scenario, but the forest entire? He looked around, eyeing the trees, their trunks, the ground. Everything was connected through roots to underground streams, mycelium networks that spoke to each other, death and decay feeding new life. He knew this.

"Does it have to do with the metal? It's a part of the balance, right?"

"What is exposed may be taken, but what runs deep maintains balance. The veins of the earth run deep," the voice intoned, "lest the shadows grow long."

Before Rowan could respond, an ethereal screech tore through the air, like the call of an elk but magnified tenfold. Rowan lost grip of the sigil, and the surrounding light, along with the voice, vanished.

Stumbling to his feet, disoriented from the concentration of his magic, Rowan called his shadow ferret to his side. Shadowy wisps formed into his familiar friend, which he willed to the size of a large dog before the two of them raced toward the source, branches whipping past and undergrowth crunching beneath their feet.

Rowan skidded to a halt as they broke through another clearing. A massive elk, its hide covered in moss with stones jutting out of its flesh, stood trapped against a tree. He'd expected to see Tamsin facing off with it, but it was a hulking farming automaton looming over the creature, its metal arms raised to strike.

Without thinking, Rowan sent his ferret racing forward. It grew as it ran, matching the automaton in size as it slammed into its side. The machine staggered, its swing knocked off course as it turned its attention to this new threat.

Rowan focused on the connection with the ferret, their minds working as one as the ferret bit into the cold metal and felt the crackle of energy in its jaw before dodging an attack from the elk.

Movement to his left caught his eye as Tamsin burst into the clearing, bow at the ready. Their eyes met, and Tamsin called his raven to join in the assault as they knocked back an arrow.

Rowan could barely keep up fighting off the automaton as Tamsin and their raven tried to fend off the elk. Metal clanged, and beasts screeched. With every hit the ferret took, Rowan felt as well, and soon, his muscles ached even worse than this morning as he gritted his teeth.

Finally, with a great heave, the ferret toppled the automaton. It crashed to the ground, twitching and sparking. The elk threw off the raven with its horns and took the opportunity to bolt into the underbrush, leaving only the sound of breaking branches in its wake.

As the dust settled, Rowan slumped to the ground, exhausted. Tamsin approached the automaton cautiously, poking it with their bow as their raven shrank and landed on their shoulder.

"This isn't the first one I've seen acting strangely," they said grimly. "Your Steelwright friends have some explaining to do."

Rowan nodded, his mind racing. "They're doing something we don't know about and distracting us from it." He pushed himself to his feet. "We need to find out what's really going on."

Rowan breathed in the scent of oil as he perched on a stool in Jimson's workshop. The shadow ferret dozed in his lap, its little feet twitching as it dreamed. Marley pulled off her work gloves and sat beside him, while Jimson leaned against his workbench, frowning.

"So, what do we do?" Jimson asked, breaking the silence.

Rowan absently stroked the ferret's fur, his mind churning. "We need proof. Evidence we can take to the mayor."

Marley's eyes lit up. "I could rig up some kind of monitoring system. If we can catch these rogue automatons in the act, maybe we use that to show her. Or at least stop them before they do something worse."

Jimson nodded, straightening up. "And I'll start a log of all the weird damage I see. They've been claiming all these automatons are coming in from construction, but the damage was always a bit off from what Calder and Mr. Steelwright were saying."

"Good thinking," Rowan said. "I think I need to get in that facility and see what they're doing on the inside. If I can convince Mr. Steelwright and Calder to give me a tour, then they'd be distracted long enough for Marley to set up her rig."

"It's a plan then," Marley said. "Operation Rust Bucket is underway."

"Rust Bucket?" Rowan asked.

"It was that or Operation Steelwrong."

Rowan let out a loud sigh. "Operation Rust Bucket it is."

Steelwright Industries Refinement Facility

The Steelwright facility could not have been any more different from the rest of Frostfern, with its sleek metallic siding and sharp angles. Rowan glared at it as the shadow ferret stirred inside him, mimicking the knots that formed in his stomach. He closed his eyes and inhaled, breathing in the last vestiges of summer and centering himself before playing the part he and his friends agreed to.

Mr. Steelwright waited at the entrance, his smile not quite reaching his eyes. "Mr. Mosswood. I'm pleased you've finally asked to see our little operation."

Rowan forced a smile, holding back the desire to call forth the shadow ferret. "Thanks for dropping everything on short notice. I'm excited to see what you've done with the place."

Calder appeared, holding the doors open. His usual crisp suit seemed slightly rumpled, and he held his shoulders higher than normal. "Rowan. Good to see you."

There was a smile on his face that made Rowan pause. It wasn't the usual fake smile like his father, but more... genuine?

"Follow me," Mr. Steelwright said, wrapping an arm around Rowan and steering him inside. "And be careful not to stray into the production areas."

Past the doors, there was a cacophony of clanging metal, hissing steam, and the low thrum of massive machinery. Not only were automatons working about, but workers brought in from Neosilica, handling heaps of familiar blue-green ore. Even at a distance, Rowan could feel the energy emanating from it.

"The refining process is quite involved," Mr. Steelwright started, launching into a well-rehearsed spiel. "Automatons carry out most of the dangerous works, but human intervention is still needed until we know more about the substance and its effects on our machinery."

Rowan peered off into the production, watching workers carry the ore to an automaton, who would then grind the ore or dump it into a furnace. Even as he watched, one automaton sparked and collapsed, no doubt the energies from the ore conflicting too much with the alchemy inside it.

"Fascinating," Rowan said, pulling his attention back to Mr. Steelwright. "But how are you extracting the refined essence? Crushing it or heating alone isn't making that powdered extract you gave me."

Mr. Steelwright blinked. "Ah, well... it's still in research. And proprietary, for now. I will say, though, it is a mix of heat, pressure, and carefully calibrated sigils that..."

He trailed off as if he'd realized he'd better stop before he said too much. Rowan suppressed a smile, relishing in the fact he'd caught this man off guard.

"Why don't we keep the tour going," Calder chimed in, leading them down a hall.

Rowan caught sight of a heavily secured area marked with a red RESTRICTED sign. A low, unsettling hum emanated from behind the reinforced doors, setting his teeth on edge. The ferret wriggled inside him, ready to come out and knock those doors down, and Rowan had to take a second to hold it back.

"And what's in there?" he asked after he got a grip on the ferret.

Mr. Steelwright smoothly positioned himself in front of Rowan, wrapping an arm around him. "Ah, that's just some sensitive research. I'm afraid it's a little too early in the process for a full reveal, but rest assured, you and the others will receive a full report before we put it into production."

Rowan nodded, biting his lip. If he had pressed Mr. Steelwright too much now, their tour would have ended up cut short, and his attempt to keep these two distracted would have failed. Still, he knew whatever was behind that door would tell him what those automatons were up to.

Calder cleared his throat and gestured. "Perhaps you'd be interested in our latest developments in our automation assembly? We've been working on a refined farming automaton and have been able to reduce the alchemy expenditure by twenty-five percent."

Rowan approached the assembly line, noting several automatons with soldered scratch marks or puncture wounds. "I bet Neosilica would love this research. Have you sent it to them? Even with the malfunctions here, a better output on sigils would make major improvements down south."

Mr. Steelwright's jaw tightened just enough for Rowan to notice. "Not malfunctions, just minor glitches. And we're working on it."

Calder shifted uncomfortably, avoiding Rowan's gaze.

Next, they stopped in the alchemy lab, which was a small glassed-off room with black benches filled with chalk drawings of various metallurgical sigils. Stacks of books piled in one corner, and when Rowan approached, his stomach turned over. Tucked away in that corner, someone was working on botanical sigils, albeit crude and very formulaic.

He pointed to a particularly sloppy sigil. "Is this an experimental array?"

Mr. Steelwright's composure slipped for a moment, red flushing his face before he calmed and strained to speak. "We're considering some options with our automatons."

Rowan traced the array with his finger, noting the sharp angular edges and recognizing the extraction sigil. "This looks familiar. Did you base this off my extraction final?"

Mr. Steelwright's jaw tightened, a vein pulsing in his temple. "We are looking at extraction methods, yes. And your research notes have been... instructive."

"Wait," Rowan said, leaning in close. "If you do this, then you're going to end up hurting someone." He picked up the chalk. "Mind if I...?" Without waiting for a reply, he sketched a new sigil. "This is all wrong. I mean, this is metallurgic, so I'll leave that alone, but if you keep this, you'll make someone lose their hand. You have to separate these first, then bind them."

He finished a rough sketch, stepping back and going over the sigil. "I don't know what you're doing, but now the botanical won't backlash on you."

Mr. Steelwright's eyes widened. Then he clapped his hands together and smiled at Rowan. "Well, thank you, Mr.

Mosswood. I'm sure our researchers will appreciate that."

Rowan eyed the stack of books, which were a mix of botany, physical chemistry, and some of the old books on myths similar to the ones Elara had in her room. He had no idea what they were up to. Granted, he wasn't entirely sure what the compounds were in the ore, but the middle section of the sigil looked more like the statue of a person than an actual symbol for anything.

Calder cleared his throat. "Well, that's sort of it. I mean, unless you want to see our offices, which, I promise, aren't all that exciting."

Something else caught Rowan's eye, pinned to the wall among the other papers. It was a hand-drawn map of Frostfern and the surrounding valley, with red sketches etched out from the plant and out into the forest.

Next to it was another map, older and yellowed at the edges, showing the Azure Islands out east, far from the mainland. Someone had traced trade routes in faded blue ink between the mainland and the archipelago. But these lines were crossed out, replaced with harsh red marks highlighting mineral deposits across the islands. Notes in the margins detailed the discovery of alchemically-reactive metals.

Calder caught his eye and hung back as Mr. Steelwright stepped out of the lab. As he did, Calder whispered. "I have... concerns. About this project. I wanted to tell you, but—"

Mr. Steelwright's sharp voice cut through the air. "Well, gentlemen. I best be off. Calder, please escort Mr. Mosswood out."

"Wait, I," Rowan started, but then he saw them, Jimson and Marley, delivering a cart of scrap automatons near the entrance, their sign that Marley had finished placing the monitoring equipment. He looked back at Mr. Steelwright and smiled. "I wanted to thank you for the tour. Appreciate it."

Mr. Steelwright nodded. "You are welcome, Mr. Mosswood. And I thank you for that insight." With that, he turned and headed toward his office.

Calder led him out of the building, stepping outside and out of earshot of any workers. Marley and Jimson were just down the path, close enough for Rowan to catch up.

"Listen," Calder said, grabbing Rowan's arm. "We, uh, we need to talk."

Rowan hesitated, but Calder wasn't his father, and that look in his eye caught Rowan off guard. Behind that usual polished exterior was genuine worry. "Fine. What is it?"

Calder paced, his hands behind his back. "He's been digging underground. That's why the ground's been shaking. There are these tunnels."

"The map in the lab?" Rowan asked.

Calder nodded. "He's been stockpiling ore in the restricted room."

"What's he planning?" Rowan pressed.

"I don't know," Calder's voice cracked. "He doesn't let me go in there. But I know he wants to synthesize it."

Rowan's stomach dropped. "And sell mass-produced alchemy enhancers?"

Calder nodded. "He wants to be in front of a new alchemical revolution. One that might shift that war in the Azure Islands."

Rowan's mind raced. If the Steelwrights succeeded in creating synthetic metal, something that wasn't connected to whatever that forest being was, then what would happen? Would it be safe?

"I need to get in there," Rowan said, voice low. "I need to know exactly what he's doing."

Calder nodded, his shoulders relaxing. "I'll tell you everything I know. But we have to be careful. If he suspects we're working against him..."

"I know," Rowan said. "But there is something with that metal. Something I don't quite understand yet. Your mining has made it worse... and now this? We need your help."

Calder gave him a half smile. "Just like old times, right? Sneaking behind my dad." When Rowan frowned, he quickly said, "No. Not like that, but, well, you know what I mean."

"I do," Rowan said. "Thank you, seriously."

REGULATIONS FOR THE SALE OF ALCHEMICAL GOODS

R owan trudged forward with his bike beside him through the cobbled streets of Frostfern, legs tired and shaky. He eyed his basket, which was overfilled with delicate pastries that kept wafting their sweet, fresh, bready aroma toward him. It was another long afternoon filled with handing out his salves and tonics, only to end up with a basket fuller than the one he'd started with.

Not that he was complaining, of course, but just one of the little croissants from the bakery across from the tavern would have been enough of a payment in his mind.

He stopped outside Jimson's workshop, detaching the basket and staring down the street. From here, he could barely see the forest just beyond the river. It had been quiet for the past few days. No beasts, not even a howl, as the three of them waited for the sensors to go off. Something wasn't right, and the anticipation for the other shoe to drop was palpable.

He shook off the feeling and shouldered through the workshop door, greeted by the overwhelming tang of soldered metal. Jimson and Marley hunched over Old Man Thistle's automaton, reapplying the chest plate and tightening the bolts that would hold it in place.

"Knock knock," Rowan called out. "I come bearing way too many gifts. Hopefully, you two are hungry."

Marley's head snapped up, and her purple locs swung to one side in a smooth motion. "Please tell me there's at least one of Miss Agatha's apple tarts in there. I've been dreaming about them all day."

"I think she gave me three," Rowan said. "And those chocolate croissants, too."

Jimson set down his wrench and wiped his hands on a dirtied rag before crossing the room in three long strides. He snagged a croissant from the basket and gave Rowan a kiss. His stomach let out a loud, sonorous growl, and he patted it as he said, "Couldn't have come at a better time. I'm starving."

"Me too," Marley said, grabbing two tarts from the basket and taking a massive mouthful of one of them. "But don't expect a kiss from me," she grinned, her mouth full of apple tart.

The three of them settled into a circle of crates as they munched on various tarts, buttery scones, and flaky pastries. As they did, Rowan quickly noticed how both Jimson and Marley winced and stretched awkwardly.

"Everything alright?" Rowan asked.

"Yeah," Jimson said. "Just sore. I was hunched over Marley for the past three hours trying to make sure she didn't crush her fingers on Old Man Thistle's automaton."

"Pretty sure my hands are too tired to even cramp," Marley said, opening and closing them.

Rowan sat upright and smiled. "Well, both of you are in luck. It turns out I kept a tin of salve just for the both of you."

He dug at the bottom of the basket and pulled out a small metal tin, uncapping it to reveal a waxy substance that smelled of flowers and mint. Taking out a scoop with his fingers, he plopped it into Marley's hands. "Rub that in." He then looked at Jimson. "And you. Shirt off."

Jimson's face reddened, but he complied, pulling off his apron and then peeling off a rather damp undershirt.

Marley giggled and said, "Oh, didn't know I was going to get dinner and a show."

"Shut up, you," Rowan said, standing behind Jimson.

He took more of the salve in his hands and then slowly worked it into Jimson's shoulders.

Jimson let out a moan as Rowan worked his thumb across a particularly tight muscle, then let out a few more as Rowan worked down his shoulders and to the small of his back.

"Should I leave?" Marley teased, grinning as she worked her thumbs on her palms.

"Shut up," Jimson grunted. "Don't... stop."

Rowan caught Marley's stare, and the two of them chuckled as Rowan finished working the salve into Jimson's back.

Jimson remained hunched over, stretching from side to side as his back popped and cracked. He wheeled one arm, then the other, and smiled as he relaxed. "Might need to keep some of that on hand later."

"Yes, yes," Marley said, opening and closing her hands. "Where would we be without you?"

"Probably with perpetual back pain and carpal tunnel that you'd complain about endlessly," Rowan quipped, eyeing Marley's hands.

Marley shrugged. "It's not like they teach you any of this in Metallurgical. We're just supposed to go to doctors and complain."

"Well, you've got the complaining down," Rowan said, which he quickly regretted as he had to dodge a flying scone aimed right at his head.

The scone landed behind him, atop several instruments that blinked and flashed. "Still nothing?" he asked.

"Nope," Marley said, leaning back on her crate. "All quiet on the Rust Bucket front. But..." She reached into her pocket, pulling out a slightly crumpled envelope. "I was waiting until you showed up to mention that I got a letter from Elara!"

Rowan raced around Jimson and sat on the crate beside Marley. "Really? What does it say? Is she doing alright?"

Marley opened the letter, removing the first page, her face reddening. "Um, that's for me." She then cleared her throat and read, "And to Jimson and Rowan, I hope you two are doing well. My studies are progressing faster than expected—who knew all the multidiscipline work would pay off? I've got professors hovering over my shoulder, asking if I can review some of their more theoretical works. Early tests of my final are promising, too. If I keep at it, I might graduate by the end of the year, but I don't want to bore you with the details."

"Aw, but I miss it when Lars goes on her tangents," Jimson chuckled.

Marley continued, "Marley has caught me up a little, but please be careful. Our mutual friends are definitely up to something, and I hope it gets resolved posthaste. I miss you all terribly. Best of luck, and I hope to see you soon,

Elara."

An ebbing silence filled the workshop as Rowan leaned back and replayed Elara's words, imagining her sitting at her desk or in the library, writing it out when she could have been outside enjoying the weather or out with friends.

"We should write her back," Jimson said. "We won't be down there for a few more weeks."

Rowan nodded, then let out a loud yawn. "Maybe tomorrow?"

As the yawn circulated the room, Marley stretched and picked up a small screwdriver. "You two lovebirds head home. I've got a few tweaks I want to make, then I'm calling it."

"You sure? We can stay," Jimson said, grabbing a button-up shirt from the floor near the stairs.

Marley shooed them with her hands. "Positive. Go now before it gets too dark." She winked at Jimson. "Pretty sure he'll love it."

"Love what?" Rowan asked as Jimson wrapped an arm around him and led him out of the workshop.

The two of them walked down the dirt path to the greenhouse, Jimson wheeling the bike as Rowan rested his arm around Jimson's waist.

As they approached, and the sun crested the mountains behind them, Rowan noticed something new hanging above the weathered boards of the porch.

A beautifully crafted two-person porch swing with honey-colored wood that gleamed in the fading light.

"Wait. What?" Rowan breathed, pulling free from Jimson and stepping onto the porch, noting the intricate leaf patterns carved into the armrests. "When did you make this?"

Jimson ducked his head and set the bike beside the house. "Been working on it. Nevs wants me to do more practical work, so I've been making benches and trunks when Marley doesn't need help. I figured we could use a spot to relax after a long day."

Rowan ran his fingers over the smooth wood, a smile stretching across his face. "It's perfect." He sat, tugging Jimson onto the seat beside him, then slowly letting the bench sway under them.

Jimson put an arm around him, and Rowan nuzzled into Jimson's shoulder, peering out toward Frostfern as the sun dipped below the mountains, painting streaks of orange and pink in the sky.

"I could be here forever," Rowan said. "Reminds me of the swing where I grew up, south of Neosilica. Mom and I would stare out at the fields that stretched on for forever."

Jimson played with Rowan's hair, curling it with his fingers. "What was she like?"

"She was amazing. Always helping with her salves and potions. She never went to Flamel, but that could have fooled anyone with how much she knew." Rowan sighed, playing with the buttons on Jimson's shirt. "She'd take me foraging with her, taught me everything I ever wanted to know."

"Sounds like a dream for you."

"It was," Rowan said. "But she never got a chance to open an actual shop. Not without a 'real' alchemist. Funny, since she'd have ways of explaining alchemy that no teacher could."

"Is that why you do it? Make all the salves and tonics?"

"Yep. She might not have had the chance, but I do. And I can't think of a better place to live than here, once everything settles with the Steelwrights, I mean."

Jimson pressed his lips against the top of Rowan's head. "I think I'd like that. And I'll have a shop of my own here soon."

Rowan tilted his head up, meeting Jimson's brown eyes. "Really? I mean, Nevs isn't going to chase you out of town once she teaches you everything?"

"Nevs is a traveler. She settled in Frostfern a few years ago because they needed her, but she's already looking for her new place to call home," Jimson said. "And I can't imagine being anywhere else, with anyone else."

Rowan shifted to meet Jimson's gaze, then pulled him in for a kiss. "I'm so happy I found you."

"Me too."

They swayed back and forth on the swing as the stars above glinted and fireflies danced at the edge of the forest.

Rowan wished nothing more than to stay in the moment for all of eternity.

ALCHEMICAL ENTRAPMENT

"Steady now," Rowan said, leaning behind Jimson's broad shoulders, his chest pressed against Jimson's back. The soft lantern light above cast shadows across the table, which was filled with little cylindrical tins, and Jimson held a large pot above them.

"You'll want to pour slowly," Rowan said, taking in the salve's sweet lemon and herby scent. "If you go too fast, you'll trap air bubbles."

Jimson carefully poured, his usually deft carpenter's hands trembling slightly as he tipped the pot. "Like this?"

A dollop of salve plopped unceremoniously into the tin, splattering over the rim before knocking it onto the floor. Jimson winced. "Ah, damn."

Rowan laughed, collapsing into Jimson's back. With a warm chuckle, he said, "Almost. Here, let me take over." He took the pot from Jimson and shifted in front of him, feeling Jimson press up behind him and watch over Rowan's head. Rowan poured a thin stream of the herbal mixture, watching as it settled smoothly into the tin.

Jimson leaned down and gave Rowan a kiss on the cheek. "I don't know how you make it look so easy. I can carve and chisel all day, but pouring salve is apparently not on my list of skills."

Rowan laughed, leaning back and planting a kiss on Jimson's lips. "It's all practice. You should have seen me when I first started. I once spilled my mom's entire batch of fever reducer all over the floor. Smelled like yarrow and ginger for weeks."

"Well," Jimson said, wrapping his arms around Rowan's waist and giving him a squeeze. "I want to help, so I'll just have to keep practicing then. Next time you make a batch, pull me out of the workshop, okay?"

Rowan spun around in Jimson's arms, facing the burly man and looking into his warm brown eyes. "I think I can pencil you in for a few more lessons." Rowan grinned, poking at Jimson's arms. "As long as I can salvage some of the salve before you dump it all onto the floor."

"Oh, you're in trouble now," Jimson said, a glint in his eyes as his fingers found Rowan's sides.

Rowan squirmed and tried to free himself from the barrage of tickles, but only made it worse.

Then the greenhouse door burst open, startling them both. Rowan pulled free from Jimson, nearly knocking over a rack of drying herbs as Jimson turned toward the door, stepping between the noise and Rowan.

Marley stumbled in, her eyes wide and sweat on her brow. She pulled back her locs and held up a small device, its screen flashing an angry red as it emitted a series of beeps. Her ferret automaton ran around her heels, flashing the same red light pattern with its eyes.

"It's happening," she panted. "They finally set off the sensors. Something's happening in the woods."

Rowan's stomach dropped. He knew the peace wouldn't last, but a part of him had hoped. "Let's go. We need to catch them in the act."

Jimson nodded. "Should we find Tamsin first? We might need them and their raven."

"No time," Marley said, showing the screen. "Whatever's happening, it's big."

Rowan took a deep breath, centering himself. He closed his eyes for a moment, reaching out with his mind to that familiar presence that sat in the dark. In response, shadows coalesced beside him, taking the form of the ferret. It grew quickly, expanding from a small, wispy shape to the size of a large dog, its blue eyes glowing.

It hopped over to the little automaton ferret, sniffing at it, tail twitching as the automaton's eyes continued to flash.

"Alright," Rowan said. "Let's go."

Without another word, they slipped out into the night, following the path that led toward the forest's edge. They plunged into the forest, Rowan and Jimson following behind Marley as she held her flashing device in front of her, leading them. Mist clouded their way, consuming the path behind them and swallowing up the greenhouse.

"Just through here," Marley called out, her breath heavy. She veered sharply to the left, ducking under a low-hanging branch.

Rowan followed close behind, the shadow ferret keeping pace beside him as they broke through into a clearing.

The once peaceful glade now lay in ruin. Massive tunnels gaped in the earth like open wounds. Tree stumps stretched on into the dark. Piles of stone and uprooted trees littered the ground, with chunks of shimmering ore that glowed a soft blue.

Automatons filled the area, several carrying armfuls of the ore into the tunnels.

"What have they done?" Jimson asked.

Marley kicked over a sensor she'd stuck into the ground. "They dug under and completely avoided the sensors."

"But the beasts," Rowan whispered, kneeling to press his hand to the earth. "They would have attacked."

A sharp cry cut through the air, and Rowan looked up to see one of the beasts, a fox with a pair of glowing tails, captured in some kind of metal cage, being carted off by several automatons into the tunnels.

Before they could say another word, there was a loud screech. Across the clearing, a massive raven landed on two of the automatons, beak pecking at them.

"Tamsin," Rowan said, standing.

Even from this distance, Rowan could see both the bird and Tamsin were struggling. And more and more automatons crawled out from the tunnels to flank them.

Without a second thought, Rowan surged forward. "We have to help. Come on."

Jimson picked up a fallen branch, hefting it like a club. "Right behind you."

Marley raced to Rowan's side, pulling out small disks from her pockets as her little ferret ran beside Rowan's. "Kept some of these on hand, just in case."

Rowan commanded his shadow ferret ahead, willing it to grow even larger as it slammed into the nearest automaton. The machine staggered back, its gears grinding in protest as the little automaton ferret joined in and jumped on it, pulling wires and gears from its neck.

Jimson swung the branch with all his might into the

midsection of an automaton, nearly tearing the thing in two as it sparked and collapsed.

Marley's blue alchemical energy flashed as she tossed little metal plates like discs, each one springing to life and ensnaring an automaton long enough for Jimson to come in and knock them out.

Tamsin broke free from the automatons holding them down, and for a moment, it seemed they might turn the tide.

But then, a concussive bang rattled Rowan's mind, followed by a bright white light. As Rowan tried to orient himself, he heard Tamsin let out a blood-curdling scream.

Their shadow bird crumpled to the ground, trapped inside a net that crackled with white energy.

"No!" Rowan yelled as Tamsin collapsed to the ground.

Automatons closed in on the raven, pulling at the net and dragging it toward one tunnel. Others closed in on Tamsin.

Rowan turned to Jimson and Marley. "Get Tamsin out of here! I'll go after the raven!"

Before they could protest, Rowan was already moving. He and his ferret tore after the retreating automatons.

As they got closer, the shadow ferret lunged forward. Rowan dropped to his knees, his fingers digging into the soft earth as he hastily sketched out a sigil. Green energy poured out of him, filling every line as he willed the forest to respond to his plea.

Vines and roots erupted from the ground, writhing like serpents as they tripped and tangled the fleeing machines. His ferret clawed at the net in an attempt to free the raven, but it recoiled, shrieking in pain.

Rowan leaped forward, reaching for the net and wrapping a hand around it. The metal was searing hot, blistering his palms, but he gritted his teeth against the pain and pulled.

With a sound that bore into his ears, the cage came apart in his hands. The raven let out a slow breath before dissipating in a wisp of smoke.

"We did it," he whispered.

The ground beneath his feet rumbled and gave way. Before Rowan could save himself, he fell into a massive tunnel, his ferret racing to keep debris from falling onto him. The fall left him breathless, lying in the dark, gasping for air.

"Pity," a man's voice said, cutting through Rowan's gasps.

Rowan looked up to see Mr. Steelwright standing at the edge of the collapsed tunnel. Mr. Steelwright's usually impeccable appearance was slightly disheveled, with dirt covering his suit and his hair out of its perfect placement.

"I was hoping it wouldn't have to be you," he said, the look in his eyes something that truly chilled Rowan to the bone. "But you've left me no choice."

He raised what looked like a modified rifle with an unusually wide barrel, the kind Rowan had seen automatons use to launch containment nets. Rowan's heart leaped into his throat as he realized Steelwright wasn't aiming at him, but at his ferret.

"No!" Rowan shouted, struggling to free himself from the debris. "Don't—"

Bright white light filled the space, and pain exploded through Rowan's body, a searing pain that tore at his flesh. A scream caught in his throat as he reached for his ferret, now trapped in the same white net as the raven had been.

The last thing he saw before the darkness crept in was his ferret's blue eyes, wide and frantic.

Shadow Work

Senses ebbed back into Rowan's mind, pulling him from unconsciousness. He was in the forest with his friends. And then—the acrid tang of burnt metal and antiseptic hit his nostrils.

He blinked his eyes open, squinting at the harsh light above him. He was on top of a cold metal slab with wires snaking across the floor to a panel of blinking machines.

As he tried to piece everything together, he reached out to his shadow ferret. But there was nothing in the dark corners of his mind where the creature should have been.

"Little one?" Rowan whispered, his voice hoarse. "Where are you?"

He'd hoped for an answer, a little hop from the darkness, and his friend slinking up to greet him. But there was only silence. He closed his eyes, concentrating with all his might to summon even a wisp of his companion. But no matter how hard he strained, there was nothing there to call.

"No. No. No," Rowan muttered, swinging his legs off the slab and planting bare feet on a cold metal floor. He shivered, noting he was in some strange thin gown and his clothes were stacked on a chair next to a wall covered in books.

As he dressed, he eyed the books, noting titles like Quantum Resonance and the Search for Eternity, Spiritual Alchemy of Old, and Deific Lore.

"What were you up to?" Rowan wondered aloud.

He turned, looking at the slab he'd been lying on, and eyed the intricate pattern etched into the metal floor. Rowan's breath caught as he knelt, running a hand along the unmistakable lines of an alchemical sigil.

He'd never seen one so intricate. The outer ring incorporated the classical elements, but they were woven into spirals of spirit in a fractal pattern that made his head spin. The inner matrix was a labyrinth of symbols and lines that were beyond any discipline he knew. It almost looked like some kind of artwork rather than alchemy, with faces and trees blending together.

"This was never about the ore," Rowan said, slowly piecing everything together. "They knew about the voice in the forest before I did. He used us—used me."

Before Rowan could fully process, a mechanical grinding noise sounded on the other side of the metal slab. He stood up, eyeing an automaton in the corner of the room, jerking to life.

He spotted a metal rod, sharpened on one end, used to etch the sigil onto the floor. Rowan grabbed it and frantically etched a simple growth sigil, certain he'd be able to dredge up vines to capture the automaton.

He pressed his hand down on his sigil, but where his magic had once flowed, it now sputtered and strained to fill the markings.

"Come on," he growled, forcing every ounce of his will into the attempt. The sigil glowed for a moment, then dissipated entirely, leaving Rowan gasping for air.

The automaton lurched forward, its arms extended. Rowan gripped the metal rod, swinging upward and connecting with the automaton's chest with a resounding clang.

It left a barely noticeable dent in the machine's sturdy frame, but it was enough to momentarily throw it off balance. Rowan ducked under its flailing arms and sprinted for the door.

He burst into the hallway of the Steelwright facilities,

heart pounding in his chest. Without pausing to catch his breath, Rowan wedged the metal rod between the door handles, noting the RESTRICTED sign scrawled on the door, hoping it would at least slow it down.

Stepping back, he realized how silent it was. During the tour, machines were whirring, and metal was clanging. Now, papers were strewn across the floor, and equipment lay overturned.

"Hello?" Rowan called out. His voice echoed throughout the empty space, but there was no response. "Is anyone there?"

Rowan started toward the exit. Every shadow forced him to pause, half-expecting another automaton to lurch out at him.

A muffled sound caught his attention as he passed the alchemy lab. Rowan strained his ears to listen. There it was again—a voice, familiar and comforting.

"Rowan? Can you hear me?"

His heart leaped at the sound of Jimson's deep baritone. "Jimson!" Rowan called back, spinning around to locate the source of the voice. "Where are you?"

He raced down a small hallway, skidding to a stop in front of a door barricaded by a hodgepodge of office furniture. Cabinets, chairs, and even a small desk had been piled haphazardly against it.

"Looks like they used whatever they could find to lock you in," Rowan said, bracing himself against a heavy filing cabinet. He pushed with all his might, muscles straining, as he slowly cleared a path to the door.

The moment there was enough space, Rowan yanked the door open. Massive arms wrapped around him in a bear hug, threatening to squeeze the air from his lungs.

"Sorry," Jimson mumbled. "We didn't get to you in time, and then the automatons... they—"

"No," Rowan said, pushing back. "It's not your fault." He looked past Jimson and spotted both Marley and Tamsin slouched in a pair of office chairs.

"What happened?" Marley asked. "My alchemy doesn't work. I tried getting us out of here, but it kept failing."

Rowan's heart sank. So it wasn't just him.

"Mr. Steelwright took my ferret," Rowan said. "When we freed Tamsin's raven, he used some kind of device on mine. It hurt... and I don't remember what happened after that."

Tamsin spoke. Their voice was barely above a whisper. "The forest. It's so quiet."

"Do you still have your raven?" Rowan asked.

Tamsin closed their eyes. After a long moment, they nodded. "It's there. Hidden. I don't think I could call it if I wanted to. It's like... like trying to grasp smoke."

Rowan squared his shoulders. "I'm going to get it back," he said. "I have to."

"Where do we even start?" Jimson asked, his hand

finding Rowan's and giving it a squeeze.

Rowan closed his eyes, reaching out with his mind as he had before. He searched for that ancient, resonant voice that had spoken to him. At first, there was nothing but silence. Then, faintly, barely above a whisper, he heard it:

"Help."

"We start by getting out of here," he said firmly. "And then... then we go to Neosilica."

"Neosilica?" Marley asked. "You think they'd go there? Why? Wouldn't they want to lie low?"

Rowan shook his head. "It's the only place with the resources to handle the ore. And they would need to keep appearances. They'll expect us to follow. No doubt they'll try to arrest us."

"We'll need Elara," Marley said. "Without your ferret or the ore, we don't stand a chance without her."

They made their way through the abandoned facility's corridors, their footsteps echoing off metal walls as they traced the path back to the entrance. The four of them stepped out into the dawn light, and Rowan was drawn to the forest. No birds sang, and the leaves were already turning yellow well before they should be.

It was as if he were staring at a tomb on the verge of collapse.

"What have they done?" Tamsin whispered.

Rowan's fists clenched at his sides. "Do what you can to keep the forest alive while we're gone. We'll fix this," he said. "We have to."

Manufactured Heating
Sigils

The clatter of wheels against rails continued to speed up as Rowan slid open the compartment door, a satchel of herbs slung over his shoulder.

Their room was better than the one he'd had at the front of the train all those months ago, but it was still small, lit by a single lantern that barely helped against the darkening sky outside.

Jimson lay sprawled on the bed, a damp cloth draped over his forehead, his skin a sickly tinge of green.

"Hey," Rowan said softly, setting his satchel down. "Still feeling like you've been through a butter churn?"

Jimson cracked open one eye, the corner of his mouth twitching in a failed attempt at a smile. "More like I've been strapped to a water mill. But I'll live... probably. How many more days of this?"

"Four. At least," Rowan chuckled.

As Jimson groaned over that news, Rowan reached into his bag. "There was enough time at this stop for me to run and grab a few herbs that might help. Fresh ginger and mint, to be exact."

He pulled out various jars and his mortar and pestle, measuring and mixing with practiced ease. In no time, he had crushed a wet paste of ginger, peppermint, and chamomile flowers. He then grabbed a kettle, noting the simple sigil the train company had etched for any alchemist to use without going to the kitchens. After filling it with water, he focused on the sigil, his magic still weak, but easily tracing the lines and soon enough bringing steam out from the top.

He'd wondered how many uses that sigil would have before it gave out, corroding the metal and pouring hot water over some unsuspecting victim.

"Alright, sit up," Rowan said, pouring the concoction and the water into a mug and holding it out. It sent a sharp, sweet smell into the air, clearing Rowan's nose and mind. "And careful, it's hot."

Jimson pushed himself up on his elbows, grimacing slightly as he took the mug. "Thanks."

Rowan smiled and patted Jimson's leg. "There's some chamomile in there too. It should help, but you should get some rest."

"What about you?" Jimson asked, looking out the window. He'd barely had a chance to enjoy the mountains as they passed, and now they couldn't see anything. "It's well past sundown."

"I just need some air," Rowan said, packing away his things and stuffing them under the bed. "I'll be back in no time."

Jimson set down the mug and leaned back on the bed, staring up at the ceiling. "Okay. Love you," he said sleepily.

"Love you too."

Rowan slipped out of the compartment and into the narrow corridor, using the walls to steady himself as the train jostled him left and right. He passed through several sleeper cars, then a few empty passenger ones, before reaching the observation deck.

Glass curved up and around the top of the car, revealing a clear, starry night overhead. He found a booth and slid in, sprawling out and staring high into the sky.

In the silence, with no one else around, he felt the pain grow in his chest. It was a void that hadn't gone away since he'd lost his ferret. No matter where he was or what he was doing, the pain was still there.

He did his best to focus on the stars, tracing constellations and recalling the names of plants that bloomed when that constellation was high. He wasn't sure how much time had passed as the landscape outside changed from mountains to plains under bright moonlight, but a voice finally pulled him from his thoughts.

"Couldn't sleep either?" Marley asked as she plopped into the seat across from him.

Rowan sat up, blinking as he shook his head.

Marley looked around the empty observation cart, then leaned in. "We're finally south enough that our alchemy shouldn't go haywire."

Rowan nodded. "I got through a simple heating with no issue earlier."

"Perfect timing for some maintenance on Sir Gearington," Marley said, pulling off her ring. Blue energy glowed as the automaton ferret appeared on top of the table, eyeing both Rowan and Marley.

The sight sent a sharp pain through Rowan's chest, though he did his best to conceal it. He held out a hand to the metal ferret, letting the creature sniff it. "Still as spirited as ever, I see."

Marley laughed, placing her bag on top of the table and pulling out various components.

Rowan stroked under the ferret's chin. "Of course, you get a name like that."

Marley pulled out a foldable mat and chalk and got to work sketching out a sigil.

Rowan watched as she deftly traced the elements of earth, water, spirit, and fire around the elemental ring, then leaned in close as she worked through the complex symbols of mechanics.

She placed some mounds of scrap metal and a small container of oil around the sigil before picking up Sir Gearington and putting him in the center of the ring.

Placing her fingers on the sigil, Marley breathed in, and Rowan watched the blue glow of her magic seamlessly trace the lines. There were no sparks or fizzles like there had been when they were in Frostfern.

Instead, the ferret lifted, hovering in the air as the oil and metal floated around him. Tiny paws played with the metal as the oil seeped into the metallic flesh, then bits of metal stripped free from the ferret, only to be replaced by the floating bits.

When all was said and done, the ferret sat on the table just as sparkly as he had been the first day Rowan had seen him, and the leftover scraps and oil looked old and discolored.

Marley blinked her eyes open and leaned back. "Well, that was long overdue."

Before Rowan could respond, the door to the observation deck slid open, and a group of passengers spilled out, their excited chatter filling the space.

Rowan and Marley quickly cleared the table, shoving any hint of alchemy into Marley's bag while Sir Gearington transformed back into a ring.

"Did you hear about the big announcement?" one of them said, sliding into a booth near the front of the car, holding a large glass of amber liquid that sloshed all over.

"I heard it's going to change everything!" one other said.

"My cousin works for those Steelwrights," another chimed in. "Says it was a major breakthrough. Saying alchemists won't even need sigils anymore. Can you imagine?"

Rowan and Marley exchanged a look, a lump forming in Rowan's throat.

"Wasn't he up north a few weeks ago?" one of them asked.

"He was. I heard a rumor that showed back up in Neosilica with something big. Tried to hide it, but my friend James said he saw a bunch of automatons blocking off the street."

The doors behind Rowan slid open, and Jimson stepped out, looking a little less green. He slid in beside Rowan, a half-full mug in his hands.

"There you are," Jimson said. "I never got to finish this. Could you heat it up?"

"Uh, yeah," Rowan said, pulling chalk from his pocket and drawing a quick heating sigil.

"Feeling better?" Marley asked.

"Yeah," Jimson said, picking up his steaming mug and taking a sip. "This tonic works wonders."

Voices from the other table picked up again, and they overheard one saying. "Well, I, for one, would love for it to be a full-on automaton workforce. Let me spend all day enjoying the parks."

"Or bars," another one chimed in.

"What's that all about?" Jimson asked.

Marley leaned in. "Apparently, the Steelwrights have some big announcement planned."

"That can't be good," Jimson said.

"No," Rowan agreed. "It can't."

Marley pulled a crumpled letter from her pocket. "Elara warned me about this. Said she couldn't write much, but things have been changing in the city. More automatons, more restrictions." She glanced at the other passengers. "We should be careful when we arrive."

Rowan leaned against Jimson, taking comfort in his arm as the three of them fell into silence, staring out the window.

As the first hints of dawn painted the sky, Rowan blinked and sat up, yawning. "Well, I guess now is as good a time to sleep as any."

"I'm gonna stay up and catch breakfast," Marley said. "You two go get some beauty sleep."

Rowan followed Jimson back through the carts and

into their room in a sleepy haze. Before he knew it, he was pulling off his shoes as Jimson pulled something out of the overhead bin.

"So," Jimson said, holding something in his hands. "I, uh... I made something for you."

He held out a small wooden figurine. It was a ferret intricately carved from a block of dark wood.

"I know it's not the same," Jimson said. "But I thought maybe it could keep you company until we get him back."

Rowan swallowed around the lump in his throat. "It's... how... when?"

"I had to keep my mind off throwing up," Jimson laughed. "It helped."

"It's perfect," Rowan said, running a finger along the edges. He leaned in and kissed Jimson, smiling as Jimson's bushy beard tickled him.

They settled into bed, Jimson's bearish arm wrapped around Rowan, his body warm and comforting as he pulled Rowan in close.

"You know," Rowan said after a while, still holding on to the ferret. "I never named him. After all this time, I didn't even think about it."

Jimson breathed heavily against the back of Rowan's neck, already fast asleep.

"That'll be the first thing I do," Rowan said, turning the ferret figurine over in his hands. "When I get you back."

FLAMEL UNIVERSITY

Rowan stretched his stiff back as the train came to a halt at the station in Neosilica. Through the window, he looked out at the metropolis of metal and glass that spanned high into the sky. Odd, he thought, this place felt more foreign and cold after only a few months away than he'd remembered.

"By the gods," Jimson breathed, his face pressed against the window. "This place is amazing!"

Rowan laughed, picking up his luggage and heading to the door. "Maybe we'll get you up to the top of one of those towers. That's a sight you don't want to miss."

As they stepped off the train, Rowan breathed in, inhaling the acrid smog that carried throughout the city from the industrial park. It was a far cry from the crisp, pine-scented air of Frostfern.

Jimson did the same, only resulting in a fit of coughs.

"It takes some getting used to," Marley said, patting him on the back as she joined them on the platform.

Advertisements lined the station walls, hawking everything from beauty treatments to pocket-sized automatons that could hunt down any vermin, no matter the size.

Jimson nearly left his luggage behind, eyeing each flyer, the newsstand, and the cafe.

"Whoa, this place is incredible," Jimson exclaimed, nearly tripping as he craned his neck to look above him. "Is that a big balloon?"

Marley snorted, grabbing Jimson's arm to steady him. "Airship. They're supposed to be able to take you from one end of the city to the other faster than anything else." She looked toward the automatons patrolling the station. "How about you keep your eyes on the ground? Steelwright's machines are everywhere."

As they started toward the exit, Rowan's amusement quickly faded. Steelwright automatons stood near the exits, their polished metal bodies drastically different from the automatons that had initially populated the station. Their eyes glowed, too, as they stopped everyone exiting and looked them over before ushering them along.

"When did they take over the station?" Rowan muttered, instinctively reaching for his shadow ferret. The pain hit him, and he stopped, bumping into several people who were making their way to the exit.

"Last month," a woman whispered as she hurried past. "And it gets worse every day."

Marley pulled Rowan and Jimson to the side wall. "Looks like they've been busy. We need to find a way out of here before—"

"Attention, citizens," several of the automatons said with a unified voice. "Please present identification for routine scanning. Failure to comply will result in detainment."

"What do we do?" Jimson asked.

Marley looked overhead, then left and right. "This way," she said, pulling them away from the crowd.

She led them down a service corridor, slipping under a railing. Rowan's heart pounded as they slid through a side door, emerging into a narrow alley that reeked of rotting garbage.

"That was close," Rowan said, looking up and down the alley. "How'd you know to go this way?"

Marley shrugged. "There had to be a service exit. City planning is just another kind of engineering."

"Great," Jimson said, his eyes wide. "Well, what now?"

"Those automatons were clearly looking for us," Rowan said. "We need to get to Flamel, but we should try to keep off the main roads. Too many eyes."

They started down the alley, slipping through crowds and into other side streets. After pausing for a moment to orient themselves, Rowan nodded to a small cafe down the street.

"If we get a chance, I'd love to take you there sometime," Rowan said. "They have the best coffee. And they make these amazing chocolate croissants."

"And we have to take them to Old Hags," Marley laughed, "That's where Rowan got so drunk he tried to serenade a streetlamp."

"Okay, look, how was I supposed to know the whisky was that strong?" Rowan laughed.

Jimson chuckled. "Well, I'll have to see it if we get the chance."

They pressed on, passing by another set of alleys until they spotted Steelwright Industries headquarters down the street, looming high into the sky with red brick siding and tall panes of glass. Rowan's stomach churned at the sight, even more so at the large number of automatons only a few blocks away patrolling the perimeter.

"Is it even bigger than when I left?" Rowan asked.

Marley nodded. "Last time I was down here, they were expanding. I'm guessing they're putting all that grant money to use pushing out all the competition. Titanium

Innovations was already struggling a few months ago when I checked in."

They hurried past, keeping their heads down as they skirted down the streets and deeper into the city.

Once they reached the inner city, past the industries, and into the greener part of Neosilica, the air carried a crackle of alchemical energy that made Rowan's hair stand on end. This close to the university, after being so far from hundreds of alchemists, the residual magic they left in the air sent a buzz in his bones.

"Is that normal?" Jimson said, pointing toward the main gates.

Ahead, the usually desolate garden square, save for graduation day, was filled with people carrying signs. The gates to Flamel, which were brass and covered in ornate elemental sigils, were closed, and the crowd shouted, their signs aimed toward the campus.

"No more automatons," someone shouted, followed by. "Stop Steelwright and do something."

"Well, this is bad," Rowan said, leaning toward Marley.

Marley nodded. "We're not going to get in there unless..." She looked around, then pointed. "There, hurry up and join them."

A group of students started into the crowd, weaving closer to the gate.

The three of them rushed ahead, following in their wake as they approached the gates.

For a moment, he was sure there would be automatons waiting to check them; instead, it was normal campus security. And after Marley flashed her alumni insignia at them, they got in without question and the gates closed behind them.

Jimson let out a shaky breath. "Well, that was easy."

Rowan headed down the cobblestone path. "We're not out of it yet. With that many people around, I can bet the Steelwrights know we're here. We need to find Elara, fast."

"Do you know her dorm room?" Rowan asked.

"I do," Marley said. "But it's the middle of the day. If she isn't in the lab, then she's in the library."

They made their way down the path, breaking into a massive open campus with dozens of concrete slabs for alchemical practice intermixed with walking paths and grass.

Around the quad were the dorms, several stories high, with windows filled with anything from sigils to silly drawings and even flags from various countries.

Students hurried past, their arms filled with books or alchemical components as they raced off to the towering buildings just beyond the quad. Rowan caught snatches of their hushed conversation,

"Did you hear about Professor Valeria?"

"They say one of her students figured out some kind of energy transference."

"Could you imagine it? Sending energy miles away without wires?"

Rowan caught Marley's eyes and grinned. "Sounds like someone's final is coming along well."

"Did you expect otherwise?" Marley laughed.

They walked past the dorms and toward the academic buildings, which were three towers that twisted high into the sky with a massive clock on all four sides of the middle tallest building. Behind them was a gigantic, bulbous, metallic library that peeked out on either side. On the grounds leading up to the buildings were gardens filled with flowers that seemed to grow two sizes bigger than normal.

"Are those bluebells?" Jimson asked, stopping to run a hand along the fist-sized flower.

Rowan nodded. "Professor Ramsey was always good at getting things to grow out of season."

"Gents, I know we love to stop and smell the roses, but let's find Elara first."

They made their way inside, walking up the swirling staircase until they finally reached the Advanced Quantum Studies department. To their right was a lab filled with chalkboards covered in sigils and various machines, and Elara stood in the center of it all.

"Elara," Marley called out softly, stepping into the lab.

Elara's head snapped up, her eyes wide. She nearly knocked over everything in her path as she crossed the room and wrapped her arms around Marley.

"What are you doing here?" she asked.

Before anyone could respond, a sharp voice cut through the air. Rowan's blood ran cold as an automaton voice spoke through the speakers:

"Attention all students and faculty. The campus is now under lockdown. Please do not assist or aid any suspicious individuals and remain in place until further instruction."

Elara pulled back, her face pale. "They know you're here."

"No time," Rowan cut in, his mind racing. "We need to see the dean. Now."

SNARES AND ILLUSIONS

Rowan jumped as the lockdown announcement sounded once again through the lab in the Quantum department.

Elara waved her hand to the rest of them and whispered, "This way," as she led them out into the hall and toward a small stairwell. "It's one of the side exits that locks on the outside."

They could hear a rising commotion outside as they descended, a clang of metal feet marching. Jimson found Rowan's hand and gave it a squeeze as the four of them paused in the stairwell.

"We're not safe here," Rowan murmured. "We're trapped..."

"Steelwrights are making the place a cage," Marley said, pulling back her purple locs into a ponytail. "One that I'm keen on breaking out of."

They emerged outside, nearly colliding with a group of wide-eyed students racing to get indoors. Panicked whispers reached their ears, and the group pushed past them and into the building:

"Did you hear? Some fugitive alchemists are on campus!" one of them said.

"I heard they were behind the train derailment a week ago."

"No way, I bet it's that weird fox thing again. You saw it, didn't you? The thing had two tails!"

"No, it didn't, Soren. Stop making stuff up."

Rowan's stomach churned as he held the door open for them. If only they all really knew.

Once they all passed, Jimson leaned in close to Rowan. "Think they noticed we were out of place?"

Elara laughed. "You kidding me? They're a bunch of sophomores who barely even looked at us."

As they rounded the corner to the main entrances of the towers, they noted a collection of automatons blocking off the entrances.

Rowan stopped in his tracks. There was no way they

could get through there.

"Reports say they went into the quantum tower," a familiar voice said.

Through the automatons, Rowan spotted Calder's familiar blond hair marching toward the tower from which they'd just come. A surge of emotions ran through Rowan—anger, betrayal, and a twinge of something he couldn't quite name. "Sweep the area again. They can't have gone far," Calder commanded.

"The library," Elara hissed, pulling them back. "We can at least hide better there. But they'll be on our heels if we don't distract them."

Marley smirked, pulling out a piece of chalk from her pocket. "Ro, you got some seeds on you?"

"Yeah, but I'd need water," Rowan said.

"Leave that to me," Marley said, kneeling and etching out a sigil. "They have some pipes below us that carry water. One or two bolts loose, and you'll have a leak."

Rowan reached into his pocket and pulled out a handful of seeds and a bit of his own chalk, drawing a sigil of his own.

"Don't let them know where we are," Elara said.

Marley placed her hands on her sigil. It glowed blue, and after a minute, she said, "Okay, I found a spot right near the front entrance of the admin tower. If I just," she paused, tilting her head to the side. "There. Water is leaking under them. Rowan, go."

Closing his eyes, Rowan pressed his hands onto the sigil, his energy filling the lines. His mind traveled into the soil, pulling the seeds with him, and he mentally bore toward the leaking pipe.

Once there, he strained, forcing the seeds to pull in the water and grow until vines burst from the ground and wrapped themselves around automatons.

Chaos ensued as automatons fell to their knees, and Calder fended off several vines that seemed keen on holding him down.

Any automatons who weren't constricted by the plants were now racing to help the others, pulling and tearing at the vines while Calder shouted for help.

"That should be enough for now," Elara said.

Rowan blinked his eyes open and backed away from his fading sigil.

They turned and raced off to the library, bursting through the doors and catching their breath.

From behind the circulation desk, a tall woman with flowing orange robes and a tight bun stepped out, placing herself between the four of them and the others in the library.

Rowan knew her. After years of dodging her as he stayed up late studying, or the time she kept him there for hours, scraping away the last remnants of the sentient fungus that had learned to read in the library. Head Librarian, Sage Lumina.

"What are you four doing? Don't you know there is a lock—" Lumina paused, eyeing Rowan, Marley, and then Jimson. She squared her shoulders and held out a hand, an orange energy forming at her fingertips. "Oh, I see."

"Wait, no, Sage," Elara said, holding up her hand. "Please, we're not dangerous. We just need to see the dean."

Sage Lumina drew a sigil in the air in one swift move, trailing glowing orange energy. Lines of fire and spirit combined, followed by intersecting triangles.

Pillars of light appeared around the four of them, burning hot and encapsulating them within.

"Dean?" Lumina called out. "What do you want me to do with these fugitives?"

A man walked forward, bald and wearing a deep purple suit that complimented his dark skin. Dean Vayu caught Rowan's eye and then said, "Thank you, Iris, I'll take it from here."

Sage Lumina turned and snapped her fingers as the pillars vanished.

"Rowan?" Dean Vayu said. "Seems you have some explaining to do."

"We need to talk," Rowan said, looking out toward the crowd of people in the library. "In private."

The dean looked out the doors behind Rowan, noting the approaching automatons, and nodded. "Yes. That would be best." He turned toward Sage Lumina. "I'll need your office. Just for a little bit."

Sage Lumina cleared her throat and pulled a key from her pockets, handing it over to Dean Vayu as she glared at Rowan.

They followed the dean as he stepped through a heavy oak door, closing it behind them. Rowan's words tumbled out before the door even latched, holding nothing back as he caught Dean Vayu up to the Steelwrights' taking his ferret.

"...and that's why we think he is trying to do something with the forest or my ferret. I mean, you've heard his announcement, right? That's not because of that powder he refined," Rowan said, his voice cracking. He paused, the weight heavy in his chest. "It's not just about the magic or the forest. That ferret... it was a part of me. Losing it feels like losing a piece of myself. They are messing with something they don't understand, and I don't know what will happen if they succeed at whatever they are trying to do."

Marley stepped forward. "It's all true, I promise. I saw it all firsthand."

Jimson, who had been standing quietly beside Elara, chimed in, "Sir, he's right. The people of Frostfern are at risk of losing their crops again. And for what? Power? It ain't right."

Dean Vayu listened, his face steeled. When he finally spoke, he walked around Sage Lumina's desk and plopped into her chair. "I had my suspicions. But this is worse than

I feared. Still..." He paused, pondering his words. "Shadow familiars? I barely believe you, let alone would a council of alchemists. Do you have any proof of their existence?"

"Well," Rowan started, his heart sinking. "No. Mr. Steelwright took mine."

"Then exposing them won't be simple," Dean Vayu said.

"So help us," Marley interjected. "You have the authority to make the council listen."

The dean sighed, rubbing his temples. "I wish that were so, but we'd be playing right into Steelwright's hands if we did that. With nothing tangible, he'd move to remove me from my seat."

After a moment of silence, Elara spoke, "So we get proof then. The council would listen then, right?"

The dean nodded. "They would."

"Then we'll do it," Jimson said firmly, resting his arm around Rowan. "No matter what."

Dean Vayu pushed himself up from his seat. "Very well. But you cannot leave here looking like this. Miss Frost, stand next to me and learn this sigil. It might need some maintenance depending on how long you take."

Rowan watched the dean raise his finger, purple light streaking across the air as he drew a sigil without the need for chalk or components.

Spirals of spirit filled the air, and then a central pattern that was hard to focus on as the dean deftly drew. Even Elara squinted to see it before the dean had finished.

With a wave of his hand, the sigil duplicated, then duplicated again until there were four identical sigils, which moved in the air to hover over the four of them.

A sensation washed over Rowan as the sigil disintegrated above him, dropping fine particles of purple energy on him. It felt like a mist settling on his skin.

"This isn't foolproof, but it should deceive the automatons and anyone who isn't face-to-face with you. If Miss Frost needs to reapply the sigil, then it needs to be on a small piece of parchment with ink that contains a little blood from everyone. This should last a week; after that, you'll need to carry the parchment around with you at all times."

Elara nodded, then frowned. "But how come I still see everyone clearly?"

"Because the four of you have the same sigil. You'll need to entangle the sigils you make, Miss Frost. I'm certain you'll figure that out between the three of you."

He scrawled on a piece of paper and pressed it into Rowan's hand. "Go here for the night, tell them Teddy sent you, and they'll board you."

Rowan swallowed hard. "Thank you. When I have my ferret back, we'll find you."

The dean smiled and rested a hand on Rowan's shoulder. "Please, be careful. I wish I could help more, but my hands are tied with the council. Anything I do until the four of you are caught will be recorded."

They left the office moments after the dean, stepping into mayhem as dozens of automatons filled the library.

"I know they're in here," Rowan heard Calder call out.

Rowan led the others down a row, hoping to reach a side exit, when an automaton rounded the corner, staring directly at him.

His heart beat loudly in his chest as the thing scanned him up and down, and then it said, "Civilians, for your safety, please proceed to the main entrance."

"Guess it worked," Marley mumbled in his ear as they cautiously walked to the front of the library.

Sage Lumina gave them a strange look as they passed her, but she kept silent as they joined the others.

Calder barely glanced at the four of them, walking past them to peer out into the rest of the library. Rowan noticed Calder's shoulders relax slightly as the automatons returned to him empty-handed.

"We have complied with your search," Dean Vayu said. "But as you can see, the fugitives are not on the premises. Not anymore, at least. Thank you for your diligence, but may my students return to their studies?"

Calder closed his eyes and let out a slow breath. When he spoke again, his voice was calm. "Yes. Of course. Thank you, dean. If you happen to come across them, please come to me first, okay?"

"Of course," Dean Vayu said slowly, escorting Calder

and the swath of automatons out the library doors.

Rowan looked down at the piece of paper in his hand. "Let's get out of here before Calder changes his mind."

ALCHEMICAL FEATS IN ROSEN PARK

Rowan inhaled the scent of freshly brewed coffee and warm chocolate croissants, which soothed his racing thoughts. He picked at the edge of the flaky pastry as he sat across from Jimson in a cozy booth at the small cafe beneath their hotel. Just beyond the window, the bustle of Neosilica's morning rush started picking up.

He'd rather be back at Frostfern, tending to his plants and enjoying the sunrise as it peered in over the mountains. But this would have to do.

Jimson let out a sigh as he took a bite of his pastry. "By the gods, Ro. I've never had anything as good as this."

Rowan chuckled, staring into Jimson's eyes. "Now you know why I wanted to bring you here."

He relaxed into his seat, sipping on his latte and savoring the fact that he wasn't in a rush off to some job, panicking he'd be late. Yet, they had their own worries. Ones that nagged at his mind the moment he spotted an automaton in the crowd of people passing by.

"I was thinking," Rowan started, leaning forward, "we should split up today when we scout. We'd cover more ground if the four of us weren't together."

Jimson reached across the table, his calloused hand resting on Rowan's. "We can talk plans later when we're back upstairs, yeah? I thought you wanted to come down here to relax?"

Rowan sighed, the warmth from Jimson's hand easing his tension. "You're right. I just... I can't shake the feeling like we're out of time. We don't know what they're doing. What if—"

"We have to be strategic. You said that, remember? If we watch them every waking minute, then all logic will go out the window, and we'll move too early." Jimson traced his hand in circles on the back of Rowan's hand. "We have time."

They finished their breakfast in a comfortable silence, catching each other's eye and smiling as some new person came into the shop, often in a rush.

Back in their hotel room, they found Marley hunched over at the small desk, fiddling with a small device. Elara sat cross-legged on the bed, surrounded by a sea of papers and books.

"There you two are," Marley said, not looking up from her tinkering. "How was breakfast? Those croissants are everything, right?"

Jimson patted his belly. "They're lucky I have some self-restraint. Downed three of them before I stopped myself."

"Well, no time like the present to scout," Rowan said, reaching for his bag. "I was thinking we might split up. We can cover more—"

"Nope," Marley cut him off, setting down the device. "You two are taking the day off."

Rowan blinked and took a step back. "Wait. What?"

Elara looked up from her papers, a smile tugging at her lips. "Marley and I were talking, and we think we can handle the scouting for today. And Jimson hasn't even seen Neosilica. You should show him."

"But—" Rowan protested, only for Marley to cut him off again.

"Nope. No buts. We've been doing this for a few days, and you and Jimson keep getting in the way. You're wound up, and he's a lost puppy wanting to take in the sights. Take a break, and enjoy the city for a day. Besides," she added,

"Elara and I need to test something out."

She reached into her pocket and pulled out the familiar ring, twisting it and setting it on the bed. In seconds, the silvery ferret automaton stared back at Rowan, its mechanical eyes glowing softly.

"Sir Gearington?" Jimson asked. "What are you doing with him?"

"Marley and I modified him with a quantum screen," Elara said. "He'll sneak into the Steelwright facility while we watch and map out his moves. By the end of the day, we should have the entire building mapped out."

Rowan eyed the ferret, which fell over as it scratched the back of its ear with its foot, making a soft metallic clang. "Fine. But be careful. And if you're not back here by nightfall—"

"Yes, yes. You'll burn the whole place down looking for us." Marley rolled her eyes as she smiled. "Now you lovebirds go, enjoy the city."

Floating lanterns bobbed overhead as the two of them walked through the park gates. Jimson stared, wide-eyed, at the towering trees with leaves that shimmered like polished copper, their branches intricately tamed into sculpted spirals and swoops. Before them, a fountain stood with a massive shimmering pool filled with ducks, who occasionally dodged the various streams of water that defied gravity as they twisted and looped in impossible patterns.

"How...?" Jimson breathed.

Rowan grinned, approaching the edge of the pool and pointing at a small alchemical inlay on the cement. "Water alchemy. The park officials need to recharge them every few hours, but see the patterns the water makes?" He pointed at the water as it danced in the air. "The water recreates these sigils, making a sort of anti-gravity effect."

Jimson shook his head, a smile tugging at his lips. "Alchemy is so cool."

Rowan nodded. "If only it worked this well up in Frostfern. This doesn't even scratch what it could do. Water purifying, proper transportation, and simple luxuries like kettle heaters. I mean, the list goes on."

"And I would love to hear about every single one," Jimson said, grabbing Rowan's hand.

They strolled through the park, Rowan pointing out the various alchemical marvels and statues that dotted the landscape.

"And who's this?" Jimson asked, stopping in front of a copper statue of a woman, holding open a book and pointing up to the sky, the start of a sigil glowing above her finger.

"That's Naomi Flamel, founder of Flamel University," Rowan said. "She was a refugee from the wars. Came here when she was just a teen and proved herself when she outperformed even the king's alchemist. She caught the princess's eye not too long after that, and the queens of Rosen turned this city into a haven for alchemists to learn and grow."

Jimson nudged Rowan's shoulder with his own, then wrapped his arm around Rowan's waist, looking up at the statue. "Isn't that perfect?"

For a moment, Rowan let himself get lost in the beauty of it all. The statue in front of him, the topiaries swaying in the wind, it all melted away his worries about the Steelwrights. Here, with Jimson by his side, he could almost pretend they were just another couple enjoying a lazy afternoon in the park.

Almost.

A scream pierced through the air, followed by a stampede of feet as a group of teenagers burst from a nearby copse of trees, their faces pale.

"Monster!" one of them shouted, his voice cracking. "It's coming!"

Rowan frowned at Jimson, and then, without another word, they both took off toward the trees.

They stepped onto a small path, racing through the park forest.

Ahead, they spotted what the teens were running from, and Rowan's heart caught in his throat. A two-tailed fox spirit, its fur a shimmering silver, crouched low to the ground, its ears flattened against its skull.

"Is that...?" Jimson whispered.

Rowan nodded, his heart hammering in his chest. "One of the spirits from Frostfern. The Steelwrights must have caught it after all." His stomach churned at the thought. "Looks like they didn't keep it captured for long."

The fox's sapphire blue eyes locked onto Rowan's. For a moment, he felt a connection, a tug at the back of his mind that was achingly familiar. Not quite the same as his ferret, but similar enough that he could feel its fear.

Then, without warning, the creature turned and darted deeper into the woods, its tails streaming behind it like silver ribbons.

"Wait!" Rowan called, racing after it. He ran off the trail, Jimson close on his heels.

They wove through the underbrush, ducking beneath low-hanging branches as the fox stayed just ahead of them, leading them farther on.

Finally, they stumbled into a clearing. The fox stood at the center, its tails flicking erratically behind it. And there, nestled in the grass at its feet, was a litter of silvery kits.

Rowan stopped dead in his tracks, eyeing the kits, which were no bigger than his palm, their fur a downy white that trailed mist. They mewled softly, their tiny paws kneading the air.

"What... What do we do?" Jimson asked.

The mother fox stared at Rowan, her stance solid over

her kits but not aggressive. Slowly, Rowan lowered himself to the ground, his hands held out.

"It's okay," he said, his voice soft. "We're not going to hurt you."

The fox tilted her head, considering. Then she stepped forward, her nose twitching as she sniffed his outstretched fingers.

A jolt of energy raced up Rowan's arm, setting his nerves alight. For a moment, he could see through the fox's eyes—the clearing a kaleidoscope of colors, magic pulsing in veins of blue beneath the earth. It was like the connection he'd had with his ferret, but different and alien.

He gasped, and the connection snapped like a rubber band as the fox pulled away. She shook her head, then regarded him, her blue eyes boring into his own.

"Ro?" Jimson asked, his hand gripping Rowan's shoulder. "What is it?"

Rowan shook his head as thoughts and emotions that weren't his bubbled to the surface. "She's... afraid. She wants us to help."

An image surfaced in Rowan's mind. He was trapped in a cage in a room full of other animals. Then he was free and running on top of roofs. Running from... something metal.

"The automatons," Rowan said, the realization punching him in the gut. "They're looking for her."

Jimson stepped away, grabbing loose branches and

dragging them into the clearing. "Then we need to help them. Hide them. If we make a barrier, they'll be safe."

Rowan nodded, grabbing onto one stick and laying it on the ground. "I've got an idea." He positioned other sticks around the clearing, breaking branches and forming long arcs and intersecting lines. After a few moments, he stood on the edge of the clearing. "It isn't perfect, but it'll have to do."

He waved Jimson to his side of the sigil, then pressed his hands to the sticks. Green energy flowed out of him and into the sigil, shakily leaping from broken branch to branch.

"It's," Rowan struggled to say. "It's not stable."

Suddenly, he felt warm fur press against his face. The fox nuzzled against him, and as she did, power flowed through him, surging into the branches.

Shoots of green broke free from the ground, twining together in a dense thicket. Vines with long thorns wove through the branches, and soon enough, there was only a tiny opening where Rowan and the fox's head touched.

Rowan felt the energy wane and the thicket take root. Then he slumped back, chest heaving, as he looked at the fox one last time before she turned and ducked through the opening, returning to her kits within their newly fortified shelter.

Jimson was at his side in an instant, helping him to his feet. "You did it," he murmured. "They're safe."

"For now," Rowan said, the images of automatons still in his mind. "But we can't let them find her." His mind raced, piecing together the images. The fox in the cage. The bright light. His shadow ferret next to him, gnawing at the metal bars, eyes wide with fear. "We need to stop them. Now."

Jimson nodded. "We'll have the layout tonight. Then we can—"

"We need Calder," Rowan said, steeling himself. "The layout will only help so much. But we can get to Calder, and we can get answers."

Jimson tilted his head. "You don't mean..."

Rowan nodded. "I do. We grab Calder. Tonight. Tie him up if we need to, and get my ferret back."

Defense Against
Automatons

Rowan rested his back against the brick wall of a narrow alley, breathing in the acrid exhaust from the nearby manufacturing plants. He and his friends waited in the shadows, hidden from the neon lights that shone in this part of town that promised fair hotels and cheap gambling. It wasn't the sort of place he'd visited when he was in school, nor a place he'd ever planned to come to.

"You sure he's here?" Jimson asked, peering out into the street as two burly men hauled a drunk patron out of the bar and tossed him onto the rain-slicked cobblestones. The man lay there groaning as passersby stepped around him without a second glance. "Seems a bit... rough."

"Bet you Calder didn't want dear old Dad's money to pay for his first apartment," Marley said.

"You alright there, Ro?" Elara asked, looking him up and down. "You look sick."

Rowan managed a weak chuckle. "Oh yeah, nothing like waiting to ambush your ex in a grimy alley to really calm the nerves." He touched the worn sigil paper in his pocket—their disguise from Dean Vayu was already starting to fade after two weeks, but it would have to last just a bit longer.

Marley laughed. "This was your idea. Too bad we don't know which room he's in; otherwise, I could just pummel him until he talks. But then I'd need to fix the locks to this main entrance when we're done."

"I mean," Jimson grinned. "I don't mind that idea."

Rowan feigned a gasp and clutched his chest. "Why, Jimson, I never pictured you as the violent type. Are you jeal—?"

"Shh!" Elara hissed, peering around the corner. "He's coming."

The four of them leaned against the walls as Calder passed by. Rowan's breath caught in his throat as he spotted the blond man flanked by automatons.

"Okay," Calder said, spinning on his heels. "I'm home.

Safe and sound. Maybe go on patrol or something."

The automatons stayed still. "Request denied. We are to stay with you until you enter the premises."

"Fine, whatever, watch me walk inside then. Hopefully, the doors don't attack me," Calder said, stepping up to the entrance.

"Alright, Rowan, that's your cue," Marley muttered. "Let's hope this plan of yours works."

"Be careful," Jimson murmured, quickly squeezing Rowan's hand.

Rowan breathed deeply and stepped out of the alley, adjusting the borrowed maintenance uniform that hung loosely on his frame. He approached Calder just as he reached the entrance, his heart pounding in his chest.

"Halt," one automaton said, swiveling around to face Rowan. "Identify yourself."

"Uh. Evening, sir," Rowan called out to Calder, pitching his voice lower and rougher than usual. "I'm afraid there's been a bit of a situation with the main entrance."

Calder paused, his brow furrowing as he turned. Even from this distance, Rowan could see the dark circles under Calder's eyes. "What sort of situation?" Calder asked.

"Some hooligans messed with the locking mechanism. Looks like amateur alchemy, but the specialist won't be here till morning."

Calder sighed and looked up at the building. "Great. I could look at it if you—"

"You could, but do you want to be liable if you damage the locks any more than they are?" Rowan asked.

"Fine. Look, I just want to get to bed. You got keys to another entrance?"

"I do, sir," Rowan replied, pulling out a ring of keys from his pocket. "There's a service entrance 'round back."

Calder looked past Rowan's shoulder toward the alley. For a moment, Rowan thought Calder might refuse. Then, with a nod, Calder walked toward Rowan and said, "Fine. Lead the way. Automatons, come on."

As Calder approached, he frowned, looking at Rowan's face as he blinked. "Wait. Don't I know you from somewhere?"

Rowan shook his head and looked down at the ground, trying his best to avert his eyes. His heart stopped as he spotted their last protection— the sigil paper—had fallen when he grabbed his keys, its purple glow now fading into a puddle at his feet.

Rowan caught Calder's eyes, and his mouth fell open. "Wait. Rowan?"

The automatons all turned toward Rowan, shouting. "Fugitive Rowan Mosswood, you are under arrest. Do not resist."

The automatons surged forward, their metal limbs whirring as fingers reached for him. Rowan leaped back, swinging his ring of keys at the closest automaton, knocking it off course.

"Help!" Rowan shouted, his voice cracking.

Jimson burst from the alley, wielding a metal pipe. He brought it down on an automaton's head with a resounding clang, sending it staggering back.

A flash of purple erupted from the alley, followed by another flash beneath the feet of one automaton. It didn't even have time to react as half its body slipped through the portal before it closed, leaving the torso behind on the sidewalk.

Marley raced out from the alley, throwing a sigil plate at the other, blue energy sparking as tendrils of metal wove around the automaton, trapping it.

"Wait!" Calder shouted as Jimson approached him. "Stop!"

Rowan opened his mouth, ready to tell Calder to just give up and go peacefully. However, the words died in his throat as he caught sight of one automaton raising its arm, revealing a cannon-like apparatus where its hand should have been.

"Look out!" Rowan cried, lunging forward and tackling both Jimson and Calder. A bolt of crackling energy sizzled overhead as they tumbled to the ground in a heap.

The impact knocked the breath from Rowan's lungs as he landed on top of them.

Calder was the first to scramble out from under him, Jimson grabbing at his heels as Calder pulled a piece of chalk from his pocket.

"Stop him!" Rowan shouted, but it was too late. Calder slammed his hand down on the sigil, and blue light formed.

Rowan expected some kind of trap to wrap around him and the others. Unlike Rowan, Calder had all the metal components he'd need right there in the street.

Instead, he heard a distant metal crunching.

He looked up to see the cannon-armed automaton collapsing to the ground, its body crushed by some unseen force.

Silence fell, broken only by the ragged sound of their breathing. Rowan stared at Calder, his mind reeling. "You... you helped us?"

Calder's shoulders slumped. The fight drained out of him. "I've been trying to find you," he said. "Warn you about my father. He's..." He trailed off, shaking his head.

"He's what?" Marley demanded.

Calder looked down the street. "Not here. There'll be more soon. My apartment's just up there. We can hide until they finish sweeping the area."

"Fine," Marley said. "But if this is some kind of trap, pretty boy, I'll turn you inside out, you understand?"

Calder paled and nodded. "They'll come to my door, but once they see I'm fine, they'll go."

They made their way inside after Marley deftly fixed the main entrance locks. Rowan kept his eyes on the back of Calder's head as they ascended the stairs in a tense silence, pausing only briefly as Calder unlocked his apartment door.

Unlike the dingy building, Calder's apartment was rather pristine. Granted, Rowan could tell there were plenty of alchemical adjustments that made his space sleek, with metal tables, walls, and cabinets.

Calder had them wait in the kitchen as the automatons came and went. As the automatons left, he ensured the door was locked before gesturing to a cluttered desk filled with notes and strange sigils.

"What is all this?" Elara asked, leaning in to study the complex arrays.

Calder tapped an intricate sigil filled with fractals and repeating patterns. "This is what my father's been working on. He wants to harness the spirits. From what I can tell, this would absorb them."

"Absorb them?" Rowan asked, imagining his ferret being pulled into this sigil. "How?"

"The fractals pull them in," Calder explained, tracing over the sigil. "Like how we use our energy to trace the lines, this works by making the spirit's energy fill the sigil, until they reach the middle, where he would stand."

Knots formed in Rowan's stomach. "He thinks this will make him like them. Like some kind of god," he breathed.

Jimson frowned. "But why?"

Calder leaned back and shook his head. "Power?

Control? I'm sure he's convinced himself it'll cure world hunger or something, but he just wants it for himself."

Marley crossed her arms. "And we're supposed to believe you don't want that? After everything you did to Rowan?"

Emotions surfaced in Rowan's mind. Feelings he'd thought he'd forgotten. Nights his stomach churned, convincing Marley to stay up late to do Calder's homework. And the dread he'd had when Calder nearly paid off his debt to the school and the overwhelming sense he'd be trapped in that toxic relationship forever.

Calder's shoulders slumped. "I know," he looked at Rowan. "I was just as manipulative as he is, and I'm sorry. I'm trying to do better and want to make this right."

Rowan's heart clenched, old wounds opening again.

"Fine," Rowan said at last. "I'm willing to trust you. For now. But if you betray us..."

Calder let out a sigh. "I won't. I swear it."

Elara looked down at the papers. "How long do we have? Before he activates the sigil?"

"He won't tell me when, but I suspect he's almost got the last of the sigil figured out. A day, if we're lucky?"

Marley peered out the window, down at the street below. "Then we need to move fast."

Jimson nodded. "We need to get in there and release those spirits before he can do anything to them."

"Think that will be enough evidence for the council?"

Elara asked.

"A city full of forest spirits?" Rowan said. "It better be."

PREPARED SIGILS

Rowan looked up at the sky, holding back his nerves from his friends while he eyed the hues of lavender that hinted at dawn. He breathed in the salty air from Neosilica's port and steadied himself on the docks as his eyes fell on Steelwright Industries.

The burnished metal and glass facade loomed over him, its darkened windows reminding him of the lifeless eyes of the Steelwright's automatons. They were nothing like the eyes of Marley's ferret, which had just as much life in them as his own shadowy ferret friend.

He adjusted the strap of his satchel, pushing down the pain in his chest and feeling the weight of components and pre-prepared sigils he'd made for their little heist.

"You alright?" Jimson whispered, leaning in close to Rowan. "This place looks about as inviting as a thornbush."

Rowan managed a weak smile and leaned into Jimson. "Ready as I'll ever be, I guess."

Marley adjusted her bag, pulling out a small jar of metal bits. "If we wait any longer, then the snakes inside this thornbush will notice."

As they started toward the side entrance, Calder grabbed Rowan's arm. "Remember that night we snuck into my father's garage?" he whispered, voice barely audible over the waves lapping against the dock. "When we were supposed to be 'studying'?"

The memory hit Rowan like icy water. Late nights hunched over sigils he barely understood, fingers brushing as they reached for the same book, and how quickly they forgot about studying. He nodded, not trusting himself to speak.

Calder continued, "He has some of the same tricks here. We'll need to keep an eye out for them. Trust me, and we'll get your creature back."

Rowan hesitated, old wounds threatening to rip open again. He glanced over at Jimson, then at Marley and Elara, his friends willing to break into a building to help him. These were the people who stood by him, who'd shown him what friends really were.

"Okay," Rowan said to Calder. "I'll trust you. For now."

They reached a gated entrance with sharp wiring across the top. As Calder had predicted, there wasn't a single person watching this entrance. These docks, which used to carry merchant ships to the Azure Islands, have been abandoned since the conflict. Now, with Neosilica's airships dominating commerce, this particular port had fallen into disuse.

Marley stepped forward, unscrewing her jar and pulling a slip of paper out. "Watch and learn, Calder. Maybe I'll make you an expert alchemist after all."

She licked the back of the paper and slapped it onto the lock while dumping out a handful of metal filings into her hands. Her brow furrowed as she placed her hands on the paper and closed her eyes. Blue light flared, and the metal in her hand melted, trailing down her fingers and into the sigil. The lock clicked open.

"Your turn, Elara," Marley said, nudging Elara's shoulder.

Elara pulled out five small bits of paper and a lump of charcoal. The bits of paper turned purple, and she handed one to each of them.

As Rowan grabbed his, he noted how everyone else seemed to blur around the edges, and his eyes wanted to trail off them.

"It won't last long, but keep them on you until the paper disappears," she said.

They reached the metal door to the building, and Marley picked the lock again before they stepped inside.

They navigated corridors lined with humming machinery, the fluorescent lights shining a sickly white above them. Every turn on the polished tile floor was empty, and with it, Rowan felt his insides twist.

"Patrol," Jimson hissed from the back of the line they'd formed. He pointed toward an intersecting hallway, and Rowan could hear the rhythmic clanking of automaton feet grow louder.

Rowan scanned the corridor, spotting a supply closet. He yanked it open, ushering the others inside before squeezing in himself and easing the door shut, holding his breath.

Elara stuck another sigil on the door, light glowing purple as the frame seemed to vanish altogether.

Pressed close in the dark, Rowan felt the warmth of Jimson at his back. He focused on the rise and fall of Jimson's chest, breathing the man's scent as he tried to slow his own racing heart.

"Well," Marley whispered, her voice cutting the tension, "this is cozy. Reminds me of that time in the library stacks during finals."

Elara stifled a giggle, and for a moment, the frame appeared again before vanishing. "Shut up. I'm trying to concentrate."

The automaton patrol passed, their footsteps receding into the distance. Rowan counted to ten before tapping on Elara to drop her alchemy. He cracked the door open, peering out into the empty hallway. "Clear," he whispered.

They raced down the hall in the opposite direction of the automatons, rounding a corner and nearly colliding with a bleary-eyed technician, his arms full of papers. The man blinked at them, frowning as he stared at the mess of papers on the floor.

Rowan's mind raced, panic clawing up his throat, before he blurted out, "Maintenance crew! We, uh, need to check the pipes."

The technician eyed them, then his gaze slid to Calder, and his eyes widened. "Ah, Steelwright's son!" He rushed to pick up the papers and moved out of their way. "Of course, of course. Sorry I was in your way. Please, carry on." He rushed past them without another word.

Rowan sagged against the wall. That had been too close.

"Quick thinking," Jimson said, squeezing Rowan's shoulder. "Though I'm not sure 'checking the pipes' is the most convincing excuse in a place like this."

"Well, fine then. Next time, I'll leave the lying to you. Granted, you didn't convince anyone when you took Marley's secret chocolate stash."

"Hey," Jimson grinned. "She basically left them out for

anyone to take."

"I definitely did not," Marley said. "I still expect a replacement. With interest."

Calder cleared his throat. "We should keep moving."

They pressed on, Calder leading them through to the center of the building, where the labs were.

Rowan's stomach twisted as he peered into the labs. There were several piles of metallic leaves, no doubt experiments mimicking his final exam. However, those leaves looked brittle and covered in rust.

"What are you doing here?" he asked.

"My father was impressed with your final. He wanted to recreate it but have something that could properly siphon metals without dying outright."

"And instead of hiring the grad who made the final," Marley paused, glaring at Calder, "he decided it made more sense to do it himself, knowing nothing about plants?"

"Well. It started with plants," Calder said, his voice trailing off.

He cautiously walked forward, clearing his throat as they passed by another room. Inside was a cage containing three boars, each with tusks of metal.

"He tested animals?" Elara said, peering through the glass. "But-But that's..."

"Unethical? I know." Calder said. "The only reason he slowed down was because of the metal you found in Frostfern."

Bile rose in Rowan's throat. "This is wrong. This isn't progress. It's testing sigils without a care for who or what it hurts."

There was a clang of metal behind them. Rowan turned, but nothing was there.

"We need to keep moving," Calder said. "Main lab is up ahead."

They stepped through a set of double doors into a cavernous space filled with the whirring and clanking of machinery. Rows of cages lined the walls, and Rowan's heart leaped into his throat as he saw various spirit animals from the Frostfern forest trapped within. An elk with moss-covered horns, a bird made of fire, creatures that he'd never even believed existed months ago reduced to specimens in some lab.

But no sign of his ferret.

Marley examined the locks on the cages. "I could get these open, but it might trigger an alarm. There's wiring I don't think I can bypass."

"We need a diversion," Elara said, her eyes scanning the room. "Something to distract security while we free them."

"We could start a fire in the supply closet," Jimson said.

"Oh, I like where your head's at," Marley grinned.

"Or," Calder spoke up. "We could set off the alarms without actually starting a fire."

"No fun," Marley said.

As they debated options, a curved etch on the floor

caught Rowan's eye. He crouched down, tracing his fingers over the lines dug into the concrete. A complex sigil full of fractals and spirals. His blood ran cold as he recognized elements from Calder's notes.

"He's already drawn out the sigil," Rowan whispered.

Calder's face paled. "I didn't... It was still just a drawing last time I saw it."

A familiar chittering sounded from the doors. Rowan's head snapped up, his heart leaping into his throat as a small black shape bounded into view. His ferret raced toward him with bright sapphire eyes.

"Little one," Rowan breathed. "You're safe." He reached out, fingers trembling. The pain in his chest subsided, replaced with a growing warmth.

But the shadow ferret skidded to a halt, just out of reach, its eyes glazing over in a vacant stare. Shadows trailed around it, swirling and blurring the edges as the ferret grew in size.

"I'm afraid your little friend answers to me now," a voice boomed from the doorway, echoing off the metal walls.

Mr. Steelwright stood there in a pristine black suit, his hand outstretched toward the ferret.

The shadow ferret swelled to a monstrous size, darkness oozing from its pelt like oil as it jerked its head. It snarled, baring dagger-sharp teeth.

Drawing in the Air

The shadow ferret charged Rowan, its form shifting and blurring as tendrils of black smoke trailed behind it. He dodged out of the way, time slowing as the ferret flew past him and skidded on the floor.

Rowan's heart beat heavy in his chest, seeing his once companion with kind sapphire eyes now burning blue with a rage he'd never seen before. It bared sharp teeth at Rowan, letting out deep, guttural growls.

Rowan peered past the ferret toward his friends. They all knew what had to be done. He didn't need to say it—they needed to distract the ferret while Elara worked to bind it. Jimson was the first to take a step toward the ferret, readying himself to draw its attention. Elara dropped to the ground, quickly drawing out a sigil.

Five automatons burst through the door before they could execute their plan, their metal bodies gleaming as their eyes glowed red.

"Intruders! Halt!"

The smell of ozone hit Rowan's nose as Marley's mechanical ferret sprang into action, its metallic form trailing blue alchemical energy as it tore the arm off the closest automaton.

The ferret growled once again, and Rowan's hand slipped into his satchel, fingers wrapping around a jar.

"You can't stop progress," Mr. Steelwright's voice boomed from behind Rowan.

"You've lost it!" Marley shouted.

"Lost it? Don't you see? With these spirits, we'd finally be able to end scarcity! The metals from the forest were just the beginning. We could heal the sick. End hunger. Alchemists would truly be gods!"

Rowan's stomach churned, taking his eyes off the ferret for a moment to see the spirits trapped in cages. This wasn't progress. These creatures would be torn apart, their energy used up. Then what?

"This is wrong," Rowan said. "You'd destroy something before we even learned what it was."

"For progress, I would do anything," Mr. Steelwright said, raising his hand. The shadow ferret whined, then growled again at Rowan.

"Father, stop!" Calder's voice cracked as he threw one of the entrapment plates at Mr. Steelwright.

The ferret turned, moving like puppet strings, reeling into the air and catching the flying plate with its teeth.

"Do you want to be on the wrong side of history, son?"

"Do you forget what happened when we went to the Azure Islands?" Calder asked. "How many more have to suffer before you see?"

Mr. Steelwright glared. "History will see me right. Those metals have changed everything. Once the council sees the truth. Once I show them—"

Rowan pulled the jar from his satchel. He had to do this. Had to harm what he came to save if he had any chance. Tears stung his eyes as he licked the back of a rapid-growth sigil and slapped it on the jar, flinging the glass at the ferret's feet.

"I'm sorry," he whispered.

The jar shattered, shards of glass skittering across the concrete. In an instant, vines burst from the muddy mixture, coiling and twisting around the ferret and pulling it to the ground as it writhed, black smoke steaming off the plants.

"Rowan, look out!" Jimson shouted.

Rowan turned to see an automaton's metal fist

swinging right toward him. He ducked just in time to feel the rush of air as it passed inches from his face. Jimson barreled into the machine, knocking it over before he jabbed his makeshift bat into the thing.

"Thanks," Rowan gasped.

Jimson smirked back at him. "What are boyfriends for?"

Mr. Steelwright sauntered forward, laughing. "Already willing to turn on your little friend?"

A flash of blue light from Rowan's left grabbed his attention. Marley knelt shoulder to shoulder with Calder, their hands pressed to the floor, a sigil glowing beneath her palms. Metal flooring writhed and twisted, forming a barrier that sealed the door shut from another wave of advancing automatons.

"That won't hold them long," she warned, sweat beading on her brow.

Elara shouted, slamming her hand to the ground as the last standing automaton approached her. Purple light flared beneath Elara's hands, and the automaton paused.

Gears whirred and groaned, and the automaton collapsed in on itself, chest caving in and forming a small heap of metal that slammed to the floor.

"Nice one," Marley grinned.

Mr. Steelwright clapped his hands, stopping in the center of the room, a broad smile on his face.

"No matter how much you try," he said. "I will show

the world what you and your friends would rather hide."

He let in a sharp breath, and the ground glowed. In seconds, the floor sigil was filled with a brilliant blue light.

The air grew heavy, and Rowan strained to breathe as if some kind of physical weight were on his chest.

Then came the pull.

It was as if hooks tore into him, pulling at something inside him. He tried to resist, digging in his heels, but his knees buckled, and he slammed into the ground.

"Rowan!" Jimson yelled, lying on the floor near him, reaching out.

Whatever this sigil was, it was pulling on Jimson, too, trying to rip something out of them. But the others stood at the edge of the sigil, just out of reach.

The caged spirits wailed, bashing against their enclosures. One particular spirit, a turtle nearly three times the size of any Rowan had ever seen, glowed brightly before tendrils of light poured from it, draining into the sigil.

It vanished before his eyes, the bright light winding through the sigil before reaching Mr. Steelwright, who breathed in the energy, his skin glowing faintly.

"Can you feel it, Rowan?" he asked. "This is the future!"

Rowan's mind raced, searching desperately for a solution.

More tendrils of light pooled off another spirit, a massive elk with drapes of moss hanging off its antlers.

If Rowan didn't stop Mr. Steelwright, then he'd claim them all. If only he could free—

"Marley!" he shouted. "The cages!"

Marley looked at the cages and nodded, a grin on her face. She pulled out the last of her components and sigils from her bag, blue alchemical energy crackling around her hands as she cut into the locks. Doors flew open, and each spirit backed out, pulling free from the sigil.

Freed from their prisons, Rowan could feel each of them, a swirl of images and emotions. They surged past Rowan, ramming into Mr. Steelwright and breaking his connection to the sigil.

The hooks in Rowan vanished, and he could breathe again, the world growing brighter and warmer.

Mr. Steelwright traced a sigil in the air, his blue magic tinged with coils of black. A stream of fire flung toward the vines holding the shadow ferret, freeing it.

The spirits swirled Rowan, forming a shimmering barrier against the shadow ferret's attacks and Mr. Steelwright's haphazard sigils.

"No!" he roared, stepping back toward the sigil. "You can't deny the future!"

"This isn't progress," Rowan shouted through the spirits. "We need to study them, not exploit them."

Mr. Steelwright cut more sigils in the air, metallic spikes flinging toward Rowan and his friends.

The elk jumped in the way, deflecting the brunt of the

spikes while taking one to the side. It let out a strange howl and staggered.

"The barricade!" Calder shouted.

Rowan glimpsed behind him, spotting Calder's flickering alchemy against the automatons as they broke through, tearing through the makeshift wall he and Marley had made.

Rowan couldn't stand behind the spirits as Mr. Steelwright continued his attack. And now his friends were protecting him from the automatons. They were surrounded.

"Use the sigil."

The voice came from the spirits, resounding in his mind.

He looked down at the etchings in the ground, the sigil that Mr. Steelwright had made to siphon the spirits' energy.

No. He couldn't—

The shadow ferret leaped into the air, biting down on a bird made of fire.

The spirits wouldn't last. If he didn't act now, they would all be lost, and what would happen to his friends?

Steeling himself, Rowan closed his eyes. He filled the sigil with energy, a green hue glowing beneath him.

"No!" Mr. Steelwright shouted. "What are you—"

The sigil filled his mind, and the room glowed in a brilliant light. Unlike before, none of the spirits resisted, each slipping into the sigil and flowing into him.

He felt the voice in the woods stir, a faint heartbeat from hundreds of miles away. He was here, in Neosilica, and there, in Frostfern among the leaves, running through the woods, flying over the mountain.

His hand moved of its own accord. The tip of his finger warmed as it traced a sigil in the air, unlike any he had learned at Flamel. It was an image of a turtle, traced in a language he'd never seen, but he felt as if he'd always known it. The sigil hung there for a moment, then Rowan grabbed it, and as he did, Mr. Steelwright lifted in the air.

Rowan spoke, the call of beasts on his tongue. "Return our sibling to us."

He pulled, and light pooled out of Mr. Steelwright, forming the turtle, who swiftly joined the light inside Rowan.

The man crumpled to the ground.

The light within Rowan grew bright, then burst in a wave of energy, washing over the room in shimmering gold. Automatons fell to the ground, sparking as their alchemical energy overloaded.

Rowan's knees buckled. He would have fallen if Jimson hadn't raced over to him and caught him, holding him close.

"I've got you," Jimson murmured, his beard tickling Rowan's cheek. "You did it, Ro."

Near-hysterical laughter burst from Marley's throat.

"What in the hell was that?"

Elara joined in, and soon, they were all laughing.

Calder crouched next to his father. "He's out cold. We'll need to get him into custody while we can. Marley, you don't have any more of those traps, do you?"

Marley pulled a plate from her pocket. "One left, but I hope—"

Her words died on her lips as her gaze focused on something behind Rowan. "Oh, no."

Rowan turned, spotting a small, still form lying amid the debris. His shadow ferret, wisps of darkness trailing off its fur like smoke.

"No," he breathed, stumbling out of Jimson's arms. Tears blurred his vision as he knelt by its side, his fingers curling around the shrinking ferret's fur.

"Please," he whispered, his voice cracking. "Please, no."

BRAIDS OF SPIRIT

Rowan knelt beside the unresponsive shadow ferret, heart pounding heavily against his ribs. The lab around him was destroyed—overturned tables and equipment smashed on the floor, sparking heaps of automatons, and the etched sigil in the cement glowed a faint green as sparks of energy arced, making his skin tingle.

He cradled the shrinking, limp form in his hands. The ferret's once-sleek shadowy fur was now a dull gray, and wisps of shadow trailed off its body like smoke. Its chest barely moved with shallow, labored breaths.

"Come on, please," Rowan whispered, his voice cracking. "Stay with me."

Jimson crouched beside him, placing a warm hand on Rowan's shoulder. The touch grounded him, pulling him out of his spiral.

"Is it...?" Jimson's voice trailed off, unable to finish the question.

Rowan shook his head, unwilling to voice his fear. He stroked the ferret's head, recalling the first time the ferret appeared and all the memories since then. The lump in his throat grew, threatening to choke him.

"You sneaky thief," he murmured, a chuckle escaping him. "You stole breakfast that first time we properly met. I was so confused."

Elara knelt on his other side. "Remember when we tried to catch him? He was so persistent about getting back in the shadows."

Marley stood a few paces in front of Rowan, twisting her ring. "There has to be something we can do," she looked at Elara. "Some sigil or—"

Marley's voice was muffled in Rowan's ear as the air shimmered, and speckles of white light pulsed around him. Ethereal forms materialized around them—the forest spirits appearing from inside Rowan, answering his call.

The mossy elk towered over them, its antlers draped with lichen and tiny pink flowers that glowed. A fiery bird perched atop a sparking automaton, its wings trailing spiraling embers that fizzled on the ground. The turtle with a shell of starlight stood beside the elk, its neck stretching and peering at the fallen ferret.

As the spirits gathered, the lab faded. The scent of fresh dirt and fallen leaves filled Rowan's nostrils. He could hear the rustling of wind through branches and feel a storm in the air.

"What's happening?" Jimson breathed, his head swiveling, staring into a strange ghostly forest overlaying the lab.

Before Rowan could respond, tendrils of light unfurled from the spirits. The threads of light came together in a dance, braiding into a single, pulsing strand of energy. As the energy streamed off the spirits, they seemed to fade, their edges blurring and dimming.

"No, wait," Rowan said, eyes wide as he stared at the elk. "You're vanishing."

The elk knelt in a bow to Rowan, the air crackling with magic as colors swirled and danced around them like a bright aurora.

"They do this for you," a low, resonating voice spoke in Rowan's mind. "Accept their gift."

The braided light plucked free from the spirits, leaving behind shadows of their former selves. The cord gently snaked toward Rowan, one end pressing to his chest and the other to the ferret's.

Rowan gasped as he felt the ferret once again.

Memories flooded through him—racing through the dark forest, chasing fireflies, the thrill of the hunt thrumming through their veins, the joy of curling up in Rowan's arms when he was asleep and didn't know.

The emptiness in Rowan's chest filled with warmth and life, like barren ground bursting into bloom after the first spring rain.

"Rowan?" Marley asked, her voice distant. "Are you okay?"

He blinked, coming back to the destroyed lab. The ferret in his hands stirred, eyes fluttering open. That familiar sapphire gaze met him, and Rowan couldn't help but grin. Anguish melted away, and tears spilled freely down his cheeks. "You're back."

The ferret let out a soft grunt, nuzzling Rowan's palm and yawning widely. Then it dissolved, sinking into Rowan's shadow and nestling in Rowan's mind.

A name echoed in his thoughts, carried on by little tendrils of shadows.

"Wisp," Rowan said aloud, the name feeling right on his tongue.

"What?" Jimson asked.

"His name is Wisp," Rowan said, wrapping his arms around Jimson, his tears soaking into Jimson's chest. "He's back."

"Is he okay?" Elara asked.

Rowan nodded, taking a moment to look up at Elara.

"He will be. In time."

Jimson squeezed Rowan and brought him in for a kiss. "You did it! You saved him!"

"We did it," Rowan said, looking around at his friends. "I couldn't have done it without all of you."

Marley pumped her fist in the air. "Take that, Steelwright jerk! I mean... No offense, Calder."

"None taken," Calder said quietly, biting his lip as he eyed his unconscious father.

Rowan stood at the edge of a raised platform inside the Public Health and Safety building, flanked by his friends. The past few days had been a whirlwind of hearings and meetings, culminating in this public address that he wished would end. Wisp stirred in his mind, still weak from the fight but mentally comforting Rowan.

Eager faces stared up at them, hands raised. Journalists clutched notepads and pencils, while others held brass contraptions with horn-like amplifiers to catch their responses.

A woman stood, adjusting her wire-rimmed glasses. "Lydia Thornbrook, Neosilica Times. Mr. Mosswood, how do you respond to rumors that Steelwright Industries was experimenting with forbidden alchemical practices?"

Rowan bit his lip. He'd prepared for this question.

Dean Vayu and the others warned him they'd ask, but he still hesitated before speaking. "I can only say what I know, which is that Steelwright Industries was grossly misusing natural resources and harming animals. I can't say what the investigation will find, but I will fully support any findings."

Another reporter shouted, "What about the strange creatures reportedly seen in the city? Are they connected to Steelwright's experiments?"

Elara fielded this one. "Flamel University already put out a statement acknowledging the existence of these forest spirits, native to the Frostfern region. We are handling their capture and return to their natural habitat."

"And the automatons?" someone else called. "Will they be decommissioned?"

Marley shook her head. "Nope. I've left Titanium Innovations to work with Calder Steelwright on a project to reprogram them. We're in the middle of stripping the forest metals from the automatons, and we have approval from the city to cycle them into improvement projects around the city."

The questions continued, and there was a blur of inquiries about Steelwright's arrest, the future of the company, and the implications for alchemical research. Finally, the head of public safety, a large woman with short-cropped hair and a gold nose ring, stepped up in front of the crowd and spoke. "That's all the time we have. Thank you. We will have another meeting when we know more."

As they stepped off the stage, Jimson leaned in close to Rowan. "You did great up there," he said, his breath warm against Rowan's ear.

Rowan smiled, his shoulders slumping. "Thanks. I'm just glad it's over."

They made their way out of the building, breathing in the cool autumn air.

"Well," Marley said, stretching her arms above her head, "that was certainly an experience. When can we stop with the whole 'Heroes of Neosilica' thing?"

Elara laughed, linking her arm through Marley's. "Soon enough, my hero."

As they rounded a corner, Rowan took in the coppery towers of Neosilica and the clean street ahead of them. He couldn't help but marvel at how much had changed in just a few short days. A handful of friendly Steelwright automatons assisted citizens carrying produce to markets, cleaning streets, and replacing bricks on pathways.

Rowan shook his head in wonder. "You really outdid yourself, Marley."

"I mean," Marley started, chest puffing out, "these are just the first few. There is still a lot to do to fix everything Mr. Steelwright did. But it's a start."

"I'm just glad Calder brought you on to help," Elara said, bumping Marley's shoulder. "Which means you get to spend more time with me here."

Jimson wrapped an arm around Elara and squeezed. "Once winter break hits, the two of you better come back up to Frostfern."

"Oh, definitely. Elara told me you go all out on the winter celebrations," Marley said, rubbing her stomach. "I'm dying to try these famous ginger cakes."

They rounded a corner and spotted Calder overseeing a group of automatons digging into the stone paths and planting shrubs. He looked taller, somehow, as if a massive weight pulling him down was finally freed.

He smiled when he caught sight of them, a spring in his step as he approached.

"Rowan," Calder said, his voice slow and careful. "I was hoping I'd run into you before you headed back to Frostfern."

Jimson took a small step forward, clearing his throat. "Calder," he replied, keeping his voice calm. "How are things going?"

Calder smiled up at him. "Good, actually. Challenging, sure," he admitted. "But good. We got approval from the city to plant more green spaces. They recognize that with all the added automatons, they can really focus on the city's quality of life."

Rowan nodded, genuinely impressed. "That's... actually really cool, Calder. I'm glad you're able to spin Steelwright around."

Calder's shoulders relaxed slightly. "I wanted to thank

you," he said. "For giving me a chance to make things right. I know I don't deserve your forgiveness, but—"

Rowan held up a hand. He met Calder's gaze and gave him a smile. "You're trying. That counts for something."

"So, uh," Marley started. "When's your dad's hearing?"

"Marley!" Elara said, elbowing her.

"What? We should know," Marley said.

Calder nodded and cleared his throat. "They're still collecting all the evidence. His defense lawyer thinks the prosecutor already has enough to lock him up, but I heard they are still investigating some things he did in the Azure Islands."

Jimson frowned and folded his arms. "How do they keep someone like that locked up? I mean, he's an alchemist, right?"

"It's not easy," Rowan said.

"Well," Marley started. "He'll have round-the-clock monitoring. They'll need to keep him away from anything sharp and keep his nails short, too. No metal. Strict diet. Once he gets sentenced, they'll send him to one of the far-off prisons."

Calder nodded, a sadness flashing across his face. "He deserves it."

Rowan bit his lip, then met Calder's gaze. "If there is anything you need. Know you have us."

He looked at his friends, and they nodded without hesitation.

Elara grinned. "You're one of us now."

Calder beamed. "Thanks. That... that means a lot," he paused for a moment, then added, "When are you headed back?"

Rowan rubbed the back of his neck. "Dean Vayu is getting the council together to talk. After that, Jimson and I will be on our way back to Frostfern."

"Good. Good," Calder said. "I have a few tweaks to make, but I want to send up some automatons. Figure Steelwright Industries can set things right up there."

"Yeah," Rowan smiled. "I think they'd like that."

COUNCIL OF GRAND
ALCHEMISTS

Rowan breathed deeply as he approached the grand council chamber at the top of the towers of Flamel University. Massive intricately carved oak doors loomed before him, geometric alchemical symbols glowing a soft purple. He traced his fingers over a spiraling etching of aether, feeling a faint tingle of energy.

He pushed the doors open, and the hinges creaked, echoing through the cavernous room beyond. Soaring marble columns stretched toward a vaulted ceiling painted with constellations and mythical beasts. Stained glass windows cast colorful patterns across the polished white stone floor.

A crescent-shaped table of dark wood sat at the far end of the chamber. Seated in high-backed chairs with intricate carvings and sigils were the most distinguished alchemists in all of Neosilica—the Grand Council. Rowan's palms grew clammy as he approached, very aware of their gaze on him.

Dean Vayu rose, his deep purple robes swishing as he smiled. "Rowan Mosswood," he intoned, his rich baritone filling the chamber. "Welcome. Thank you for meeting with us. Please allow me to introduce you to the council. You already know Sage Lumina."

He gestured to the librarian with steel-gray hair pulled into a tight bun.

Lumina's piercing gaze reminded Rowan of a hawk eyeing its prey. She inclined her head slightly, the light glinting off her wire-rimmed glasses. "Mr. Mosswood," she said crisply.

"Sage." Rowan gave a slight bow, swallowing hard.

Dean Vayu then gestured to a wiry tan man with wild red-and-gray hair and a neatly trimmed beard. "This is Sage Aldric Ember, the head of Neosilica's energy management."

Ember's amber eyes flickered like flames as he regarded Rowan. "So," he said, his voice cracking, "you're the one who's been stirring up trouble in the north."

Next was a woman with flowing white hair and rich dark skin with robes of sea green. "Sage Cordelia Brooks, the CEO of Brooks Purifications, is working with the city to improve our city's water supply."

"Welcome," she said, her voice melodic. "I'm intrigued to hear your reports, Mr. Mosswood."

Finally, Dean Vayu gestured to an elderly man whose sparse, wispy white hair floated around his head like a cloud. "And Sage Edwin Zephyr, our consult and elder of the council."

Zephyr nodded to Rowan sleepily but didn't say a word.

Rowan bowed deeply. "It's an honor to meet you all," he managed, keeping his eyes off the empty chair next to Sage Ember, where Mr. Steelwright had likely sat.

Dean Vayu smiled. "Thank you for coming, Rowan. We'd like to discuss your findings in Frostfern."

As Rowan straightened, he recalled his time away from Neosilica. The dilapidated greenhouse, the pull from the forest, and Jimson. He'd gone to pay off his schooling but found so much more. And now, he stood before the most powerful alchemists in Neosilica, with the spirits of an ancient forest dwelling within him.

"The discovery of forest spirits right here in Neosilica was quite the surprise, Mr. Mosswood," Sage Lumina said, leaning forward slightly. "I'm curious. What sort of things have you discovered in your time at Frostfern?"

Rowan cleared his throat. "Dean Vayu sent me there to study the magic. That far north, alchemy is sporadic and often fleeting. I'd assumed it was bad soil composition, but the woods in Frostfern contain something else."

"The metal," Sage Ember interjected, "which Mr. Steelwright abused."

Rowan bit his lip. They knew about the spirits, but he wasn't sure they were ready for the truth. "The metal isn't what caused the spirits. It's just an artifact. There is something there. A deity in those woods, and it talked to me."

Sage Brooks frowned and looked at Sage Zephyr. "So, your hypothesis was true?"

Sage Zephyr smiled and leaned forward. "That deity bonded you, yes? A familiar?"

"This is ridiculous," Sage Lumina said. "Forest spirits are one thing. Echoes of magic from the metals. But a deity?"

"I'd like to see this familiar of yours," Sage Zephyr said to Rowan.

Rowan closed his eyes and reached inward, grasping the thread that connected him to Wisp. It felt different now, stronger. He tugged gently, willing Wisp to appear.

For a moment, nothing happened. Rowan could feel the council's eyes on him, waiting.

"He's still weak," Rowan said, focusing harder, offering his own strength. Sweat beaded on his brow, feeling as if he were trying to pull a mountain.

Then, in a swirl of shadows, Wisp materialized beside him, racing forward and hopping up on the table. He regarded them with his blue sapphire eyes as tendrils of smoke curled off him and covered the table.

The council members leaned forward, their eyes wide.

"Remarkable," Sage Zephyr breathed. "Familiars like this were thought lost when the last god died. Gifts they bestowed on the witches of old."

"It would seem not all the gods are gone," Sage Ember said.

"This doesn't prove that," Sage Lumina said. "We need further research."

Before anyone could say more, Wisp vanished, melting into the table and slipping back into Rowan's shadow.

"The new bonding is strange," Rowan said. "It will take some time to get used to and for Wisp to recoup his strength from whatever Mr. Steelwright had him doing. Before, he could grow two times the size of a bear."

"And the other spirits?" Dean Vayu asked. "We know there were others Mr. Steelwright captured."

Rowan placed a hand over his heart. "They're here, with me. After reshaping the bond, they became shadows of their former selves. I believe they need to return to the forest to become whole again."

"Perhaps it would be best if you remained here, under

our care and study," Sage Lumina suggested.

Rowan's jaw clenched. "With respect, Sage Lumina," he said, struggling to keep his voice level, "these spirits long for the forest. They're not specimens. I'd like to see them return home."

Dean Vayu nodded. "Rowan is right," he said. "The spirits are not ours to keep. However, I would like to discuss the fox spirits who have made residence in Rosen Park."

"Yes?" Rowan asked hesitantly.

"We would like them to remain here. We'll keep the woods preserved and only observe them, but the kits have failed our capturing efforts, and I suspect moving them may be more harmful than good."

"And you want what, my blessing?" Rowan asked.

"You have a connection to the spirits that none of us have," Sage Zephyr said. "If anyone can speak for them, it's you."

Rowan frowned, seeking the right answer. A low, resonating voice spoke deep in his mind. Distinct but clear.

"Yes," Rowan said. "But you must protect them."

Dean Vayu clapped his hands. "Perfect, then that brings me to my next point of business. Your actions in Frostfern and against Mr. Steelwright have proven you worthy of consideration as a junior council member."

Rowan's breath caught in his throat. A junior council member of the Grand Alchemists?

"It's a great responsibility," Sage Ember started. "But

continued education of magic would be best supported by the resources of this council."

Rowan swallowed hard, his mouth suddenly dry. "I... I'm honored," he managed. "But I'm not sure I'm qualified."

"I couldn't agree more," Sage Lumina said.

"But his friend," Sage Brooks said. "Marley Argentum claimed he could draw sigils in the air."

Sage Lumina pursed her lips. "Then prove it. Mr. Mosswood, if you will." She gestured to him.

Rowan hesitated, then raised his hand. He focused, trying to channel his energy into a basic sigil to alter the wooden table. Green sparks sputtered from his fingertip, fizzling out before they could form any lines. He tried again, but failed. He shook his hand and sighed.

Then he felt it. A whisper in the back of his mind, like a breeze rustling through leaves. The spirits came forth, guiding him. He let his hand move of its own accord, tracing a sigil he'd never seen before without elemental rings or discipline. It traced an intricate shape of a turtle, fractal patterns on its shell woven through with spiraling lines that shifted as they hovered in the air.

As he completed the last line, the sigil pulsed and came to life, swimming up high toward the ceiling. It disappeared, a small cloud taking its place above them, gray and heavy. It hovered for a moment, then rain fell between Rowan and the council, splashing on the floor and table.

The council members exchanged glances, but none of them held back their shock.

"I suppose that answers that," Dean Vayu said, laughing.

"Dean, I would like to know if others can learn this," Sage Lumina said.

"As would I," Sage Brooks said.

"I assume you already planned on returning to Frostfern, yes?" Dean Vayu asked.

Rowan nodded. "I've made something for myself there. I'd like to stay if I can."

"Perfect. We will extend your stipend and provide funding for research," Dean Vayu said. "And, of course, with your acceptance to the council, consider your original debt to the university settled." He smiled. "We would like you to learn as much as you can, and we will send students at the start of spring for you to instruct."

"Wait, what?" Rowan asked, momentarily stunned. "Students?" He imagined himself standing at the front of a classroom, trying to corral a bunch of eager young alchemists.

"You are one of the few botanical alchemists left," Sage Lumina said. "Introducing the next generation of alchemists to the magic you've found will only help in further conservation and preservation. We will not keep this knowledge to ourselves, like former council member Steelwright."

"A Junior Grand Alchemist like yourself deserves the opportunity to foster minds," Sage Ember said. "And who knows, perhaps we'll discover more deities out there. You can't be having all the adventures by yourself."

Rowan's heart hammered in his chest as he gave the council a slight bow. "I won't disappoint, Grand Alchemists."

Dean Vayu stepped away from his chair and walked over to Rowan, handing him a small gold ring with simple etchings of the elements on it. It was smaller, without the inlaid gems of the Grand Alchemist, but still a clear indicator that he was part of the council. "This is a lot to take in. Take your time and settle into Frostfern. You have the winter to acclimate. As for the students, I was a nervous wreck my first semester, but they are there for the same passions you have. Remember that."

Rowan smiled, joining Dean Vayu as he led him to the doors. "Thank you, Dean. I won't let you down."

UNCERTAIN AND CERTAIN SIGILS

Rowan rushed into their hotel room, frantically grabbing at his suitcase. The clock on the wall was most certainly mocking him as it ticked away.

Jimson raced in after him, eyeing the little stubs of paper on their nightstand. "I thought the train was leaving tonight."

"So did I," Rowan said, his stomach churning. He wasn't sure if the upset was the nerves or the dozens of flavors of ice creams they were just indulging in at a shoppe with a device that could mix and match any flavor imaginable.

Granted, ice cream for breakfast wasn't the wisest choice, but it was their last day, and Rowan thought it'd be cute. He reached for the tickets, pointing at the timestamp. "Yep, that's morning. And this is the only train headed that far north for the next week."

Jimson pocketed the tickets and grabbed his own suitcase, stuffing it full of clothes and souvenirs.

"Have you seen my green button-up?" Rowan called, pulling open the closet and tossing clothes in the air.

"You mean this one?" Jimson held up a shirt, which Rowan grabbed while Jimson wasn't looking. Rowan and Jimson pulled at the same time, causing them to tumble, tripping over each other and landing on the floor.

For a moment, they just stared at each other, breathless. Then Jimson laughed, rolling off Rowan.

Rowan grinned, pushing himself onto his elbows. "I don't think now is the time to... you know..."

"Ha ha," Jimson said flatly, planting a quick kiss on Rowan's lips before standing. "Get packed before we miss the train and get stuck here."

They packed in record time, clothes and souvenirs flying into their suitcases haphazardly. As they raced down the stairs of their hotel, luggage banging against their legs, Rowan's mind whirled with everything that had happened the past few weeks.

The streets of Neosilica were bustling, the air thick with the sweet smell of breakfast vendors and the sharp metallic tang of alchemy. They rushed by several markets they'd had the luxury of visiting the past week, filled with little automatons and cafes with alchemical drinks guaranteed to give you any mood you wanted to have.

As they hurried along, Rowan felt a pang of nostalgia. "There are some things I'm going to miss. The energy. The innovation."

Jimson nodded, his eyes lingering on a shoppe window displaying intricate wooden carvings enhanced by delicate alchemical sigils. "Gave me a lot of ideas for projects back home. I just wish I got to see one of them at work."

"We'll be back," Rowan said, placing an arm around Jimson's and pulling him along. "At the very least, you need to be here when Elara graduates."

Jimson pulled his gaze from a small stand with spinning automatons that hovered in the air. "I'd like that," he managed to say. "And who knows, maybe they'll take some of my carvings."

As they reached the tops of the steps to the train station, sweating from carrying their luggage, Rowan caught sight of a familiar streak of purple hair.

"Marley!" he called out, waving frantically.

Marley turned, her face lighting up as she spotted them. She elbowed Elara beside her, who looked up from the book she'd buried her nose in.

"There you are!" Marley shouted back. "Train leaves in ten minutes!"

As they approached, Rowan saw Calder hanging back, his hands shoved deep in his pockets.

"Cutting it a bit close," Elara said, stuffing note cards in a textbook titled The Uncertain Sigil: Principles of Probability in Quantum Alchemy.

"Lost track of time," Jimson admitted, rubbing the back of his neck sheepishly. "That ice cream shoppe of yours is dangerous."

"Ah, you found Frosty Fredd's," Marley grinned. "Did you try the bacon and fish flavor?"

Rowan made a face. "Unfortunately."

The train whistle blew, cutting through their banter. Rowan's stomach lurched as he realized this was it. They were really leaving.

Marley was the first to move, wrapping Rowan in a bone-crushing hug. "Just like last time," she said.

"Yeah, except without the bag of dirt," Rowan said, holding back a lump forming in his throat. "I'll miss you."

"You better take care of him, big guy," Marley said, her arms reaching around Jimson.

As they hugged, Elara approached Rowan. "Write us," she insisted. "I want to hear all about your research. And... everything else."

"Of course," Rowan nodded. "And I want the same from you. Keep us posted on your studies."

Calder cleared his throat and held out a hand. "I, uh...
I hope you have a safe journey. The automatons are already
loaded and programmed to depart at Frostfern. It's not
nearly as many as last time, but it's a start."

Rowan knocked his hand away and pulled him in for
a hug. "Thank you. Seriously."

Calder's stiff arms softened, and he squeezed Rowan
back. As he peeled away, Jimson swept him up with one arm
and gave him an enormous bear hug. "You better come up
for the Winter Festival, too. You're family now."

"I... Uh..." Calder said, gasping for air. "I will."

The last boarding call echoed through the station.
Jimson rested a hand on Rowan's back and said, "Well,
we've got to go."

With one last wave to their friends, they boarded the
train. As it pulled away from the platform, Rowan pressed
his face to the window, watching as Neosilica's towering
spires faded into the distance.

"You okay?" Jimson asked, lying back on the bed in
their sleeper car, unwrapping a ginger candy and popping
it into his mouth.

Rowan took a deep breath, considering the question.
"Yeah," he said finally. "Part of me wishes we could have
stayed longer, but it'll be nice to get back to the calm."

Jimson nodded. "It's been quite the adventure, hasn't
it?"

Rowan laughed softly. "You could say that."

They both lay in bed, watching the countryside roll by outside their window. Rowan marveled at how easy it was to lie there in silence with Jimson, enjoying the moment.

Soon enough, the ginger candies weren't cutting it. Rowan hopped up, guiding Jimson to the observation deck and ordering them a ginger fennel tea.

"My hero," Jimson said, carefully bringing the tea to his lips.

While Rowan didn't need it for the motion sickness, the sharp ginger, licorice, and honey were the perfect afternoon tea to help shed the remnants of nerves that clung to him.

Five days passed in a blur, with them spending their mornings in the dining car, learning card games from an older couple traveling to the Svalla Coast, and ending each night wrapped in each other's arms beneath the stars. Now, they were sitting side by side in their usual booth on the observation deck, gazing out at the rugged mountainside.

Jimson pointed out toward the distant peaks and smiled. "Almost there. Can't wait to be back in our bed."

Wisp materialized in front of them, staring out the window with his little paws on the windowsill.

Rowan rubbed the back of Wisp's ears. "Maybe we can convince your mom to make that bilberry pie."

Jimson shook his head. "Out of season, but her cloudberry upside-down cake is amazing."

Rowan rested his head on Jimson's shoulder. "I've never had cloudberries."

Rowan's breath caught in his throat as the train pulled into Frostfern Station, and they stepped off. The platform was packed with familiar faces, all waiting for the automatons and deliveries to unload from the train. He spotted Old Man Thistle eyeing up one of the new automatons, his craggy face leaning in with a grin. Miss Juniper oversaw a group of young boys unloading crates of fresh produce and packing them on the cart handcrafted by Jimson.

"Welcome home, dears," she said, approaching and patting Rowan's cheek. "We've missed you. I'd love a fresh batch of your salve once you settle in. My knee's been acting up."

Rowan smiled. "Of course, Miss Juniper. I'll start gathering the herbs tonight and have a batch ready in a few days."

They made their way through the crowd, fielding questions about their time in Neosilica. By the time they reached the edge of town, Rowan's cheeks ached from smiling. The familiar sights and sounds of Frostfern washed over him, and he realized how much he'd missed this place.

They walked down the path to the greenhouse, trailing the luggage behind them as Wisp bounded beside them. In no time, Rowan was reclining in the kitchen, sipping on a warm chamomile tea. He peered out the window into the forest.

"Ro?" Jimson asked. "Everything okay?"

Rowan rubbed his chest, a swirl of energy fluttering his heart. "They're not ready."

"What?"

"The spirits," Rowan said. "They're not ready to go back."

Jimson sidled up to Rowan, pouring himself a mug of tea. "Then don't rush it." He pressed a kiss to Rowan's temple. "They'll let you know when they're ready, and we're not going anywhere."

Voice of the Forest

Rowan walked through the forest, mist curling around his ankles as he passed by massive mushroom caps and ferns. This far in, ancient trees as wide as his home loomed before him, gnarled branches reaching high with yellow and orange leaves painting the canopy.

Wisp loped through a pile of leaves, rustling through them before finding his way back to Rowan and rubbing against his leg. It was comforting to see him so much these past few days, exploring the greenhouse and watching Rowan prepare his most recent batch of herby salve to relax tense muscles.

In the distance, a lone bird trilled its morning song, the melody echoing through the trees. The spirits stirred inside him, anxious and ready.

Leaves crunched behind him, and Rowan turned to spot Tamsin approaching. Their weathered face softened, and a small shadowy raven landed on their shoulder.

"Is it time?" Tamsin asked, falling in step beside Rowan.

Rowan nodded. He swept the forest, noting that even in autumn, the colors of the woods were duller and muted more than he would have expected. "It is. The spirits are finally ready."

Tamsin gestured ahead. "There's a clearing this way. It's where I first found the voice of the woods."

They took the lead, taking Rowan deeper into the forest to a clearing surrounded by the tallest of the forest's trees. Their trunks were so wide it would take a dozen people to encircle them, their bark etched with strange patterns that shifted and danced in the streams of light that shone through the canopy.

Rowan's heart thundered in his chest as the spirits swirled inside him, eager for their release. He closed his eyes, drawing in a deep breath and centering himself.

"Ready?" Tamsin asked.

Rowan smirked. "Ready as I'll ever be. Though birthing a bunch of forest spirits isn't something I ever thought I'd be doing."

Tamsin laughed. "I suppose nature has its ways of surprising us."

Rowan focused, calling forth the spirits one by one. The mossy elk emerged first, its antlers dripping with lichen as it bounded into the clearing, feet thudding on the soft ground. Next came the fiery bird, wings trailing spirals of embers that danced in the air before it perched up high. Others followed, flooding out of him, until finally, the starlight turtle formed, its shell glittering.

Rowan stood there for a long while, watching as the animals took in their surroundings before vanishing into the forest. As each one left, color seeped back into the land. Leaves grew more vibrant, the air became denser, and tiny purple and pink flowers bloomed in the clearing.

An emptiness filled Rowan. It wasn't like the hollowness he'd felt when he lost his ferret, but more like the sensation after letting out an overdue breath.

A voice rumbled beneath him, the deity of the woods rousing to life as it touched his mind.

"You have done well, young alchemist," the deity said.

Tamsin jumped, looking left and right, then meeting Rowan's gaze. "I can... hear them."

The deity continued. "I feel life back in my veins in a way I have not felt in centuries. I felt we were on the verge of being forgotten, but you saved them... saved me."

Images formed in Rowan's mind, visions of the

woods, of Frostfern, and the mountains.

"You have done something I thought couldn't be done," the deity continued. "Something that, with practice, could bring back the others."

"So you agree, then, with what the Sages want?" Rowan started. "To help me teach others?"

"They need you." The vision in Rowan's mind expanded, showing towns connected by a network of magic in the earth. Each place felt dormant, like something slumbered beneath, slowly feeding off the magic.

"This is... incredible," Rowan breathed. "But I'm just one person. I can't do this all."

"You are the catalyst," the deity replied. "I will teach you, and you will teach others. The journey may start with you, but once the others wake, other guardians will follow where you leave off."

"But that would mean leaving here again, right?" Rowan asked a pang in his chest. "Don't you still need me?"

"The forest will always need guardians," the deity replied. "But your path is just beginning. You've laid strong roots here. I must guide you on how to tend them, then, in time, I ask you to only start the seeds elsewhere for others."

The deity's presence faded from his mind, and the clearing grew brighter. Wisp hopped happily around, chasing after Tamsin's shadow raven as birds sang overhead.

"I'll tend to the forest," Tamsin whispered. "Whenever you choose to go."

Rowan met Tamsin's gaze and nodded. "There's still much to do here, things I need to learn before I'm ready."

"I'll help," Tamsin said, guiding the way out of the clearing, "with whatever you need. You'll know where to find me."

With that, Tamsin waved him off, their shadow raven flying behind them as they vanished into the woods.

As Rowan made his way back to town, his mind buzzed with what he'd just experienced and the path he'd have to take. Someday.

The familiar cobblestone streets of Frostfern came into view, and his heart warmed at the place he now called home.

Miss Juniper waved from her produce stand, a smile on her face. "There's our alchemist," she called out. "Jimson's been looking for you."

Rowan grinned, selecting a ripe apple from her display. "Better see him then. You know, I might need to pick up a few more apples later to whip up a nice pie. Keep some for me?"

She chuckled. "You know where to find me, petal. And don't think I've forgotten about that new salve you promised. My knees could really use it."

"You're first on the list," Rowan assured her. "The herbs should be properly cured in a few days, then I'll bring it straight to you." He continued down the road.

Rowan waved at Old Man Thistle, who was stepping

out from the tavern with a slight wobble in his step. Before the old man opened his mouth, Rowan nodded. "I know, I know. Jimson is looking for me."

The old man scratched his head, but Rowan hopped by him, turning down an alley.

Fresh-cut cedar filled his nose as he approached the workshop. Inside, he spotted Jimson hunched over a workbench, gently carving a flat piece of wood.

"Hey there, cutie," Rowan said, leaning against the doorway.

Jimson jumped, nearly dropping his chisel as he quickly covered his project with a tarp.

"You're back!" Jimson said, hastily wiping his hands on his apron as he approached. "I was thinking we needed to send out a rescue party."

Rowan laughed, kissing Jimson on the lips. "Me? Lost? Never. But the spirits are back where they belong." He ran a hand along Jimson's arm, playing with his arm hair. "What's this you're working on?"

"It's, well... it's a surprise. For you." Jimson glanced at the covered project, then back at Rowan. "Actually, it's ready now. Want to see?"

"Absolutely."

Jimson grinned, grabbing the tarp-covered object. "Perfect. Come on, follow me."

"Where? What—"

Jimson was already out on the street, practically

bouncing as he led the way.

Rowan strained to keep up, his curiosity growing with each step. As they entered the town square, he spotted many familiar faces waiting for him. Miss Juniper and Old Man Thistle stood in the front of the crowd beside the mayor and nearly a dozen others.

"What is this?" Rowan asked, his heart racing.

Jimson whipped the tarp away with a flourish, revealing a beautifully crafted wooden sign. Mosswood Apothecary was carved in elegant script, bordered by intricate vines and leaves that Rowan recognized from his own botanical sketches. A small ferret curled around the base of the letters.

Rowan frowned, his breath caught in his throat, tears springing to his eyes. "What... What is this?"

Jimson set the sign beside him and took Rowan's hand. "You've done so much since you got here," he breathed. "You helped nearly everyone in town, so we wanted to give something back. I hope you like it."

"I love it," Rowan said.

Mayor Frost stepped forward and smiled. She gestured behind her, where the crowd parted to reveal an empty storefront. "The town of Frostfern would like to offer you this place to house and sell your goods, Mr. Mosswood," she announced. "It's the least we can do for our resident alchemist. And," she added with a smile, "it'll be nice to have all your concoctions in town instead of stored up in that greenhouse of yours."

Rowan looked out at the sea of smiling faces, overwhelmed by the outpouring of support. These were more than just neighbors or customers—they were his friends, his family.

He cleared his throat, tears slipping down his cheeks as he addressed the crowd.

"I don't know what to say," he began. "I didn't know what life would be like after graduating from Flamel, but I never imagined I'd find a home, a community that accepted me so fully. I... Thank you."

The crowd erupted in cheers, surging forward to embrace Rowan and offer their congratulations. Jimson beamed, his arm around Rowan's waist.

"Guess I have a new project now," Jimson said. "While you get your concoctions ready, I'll install shelves and displays. How does that sound?"

Rowan smiled. "It sounds perfect."

WINTER BANDS

R owan pulled down a few sprigs of dried elderflower and peppermint from the rafters, savoring the rich scent that clung this high in his apothecary. The familiar aroma brought back memories of his mother's small workshop, where herbs had hung just like this, though her rafters had been lower and more cramped than the ones in this bright space. He climbed down the sturdy cedar ladder past the new shelves filled with multicolored glass bottles that caught the light from the frost-etched windows. His mother would have loved this place—proud he finally made the place she dreamed of.

He smiled, measuring the herbs, his fingers deft as he poured the contents into individual sachets. Rowan adjusted his glasses and tucked a stray lock of hair behind his ear, which had grown long in the winter months. He laid the herbs on a pre-etched sigil and offered a little of his energy, filling the sigil and giving the tea mix a soft glow before packaging them away. His special "Frost Ache" blend was quickly becoming a winter favorite here in Frostfern.

"Now, Miss Juniper," Rowan explained, sealing the box, "this tea is stronger than your normal tea. One satchel per cup, steeped for three minutes, and your aches should go. I put in a little boost to help you fend off that cold going around, too."

Miss Juniper smiled, tucking the tea away in her heavy petticoat. "What would we do without you, petal?"

Rowan chuckled, clearing off his workspace. "I owe all of you, truly," he said. "This is... everything I wanted."

As Rowan stepped away from the counter, Wisp materialized, chittering mischievously before pouncing on a pile of dried rosehips, scattering them across the polished wood table.

"Hey, you little monster!" Rowan said, playfully swatting at the creature as he scooped up the wayward herbs.

Miss Juniper laughed. "He's turning out to be a little troublemaker."

"You could say that again," Rowan said as Wisp vanished underneath the table, clinking around in the glass jars below.

The bell above the door jingled, and a gust of frigid air blew in as a snow-covered Jimson entered. Rowan's heart did a little flip at the sight, the man's broad frame filling the doorway. Snowflakes clung to his dark curls, and his cheeks were ruddy from the cold, accentuating the dimples that appeared as he smiled. His well-worn wool sweater stretched comfortably across his chest and soft belly.

Jimson pulled off his coat, shaking it free of snow and standing next to the small wood-fire stove. "Festival preparations are in full swing. You should see the ice sculptures Calder did—they're incredible!"

Rowan watched as Jimson held out shaky hands to the fire, then brushed back to his pocket as if checking for something.

"Everything alright?" Rowan asked, raising an eyebrow.

"What? Oh, yeah, all good," Jimson said quickly, pulling a small pocket watch and checking the time. "Elara and Marley should be here soon. Ready to head over?"

Miss Juniper shuffled to the door. "Thanks for the tea, petal. I'll be back for some more of that salve when you make it."

"Of course," Rowan waved, "Check back in a couple days."

The old woman wrapped her coat tight around her and braced for the cold, smiling back and giving Jimson a wink. "See you both at the festival."

Rowan grabbed his coat and scarf, bundling up and following Jimson outside. The cold nipped at him as Wisp bounded across the top of the snow, completely unbothered. They made their way down the cobblestone streets, evading the busy market square, for now, their breath puffing out in little clouds.

"Now those are excellent," Rowan marveled, pointing to an ice sculpture of a leaping stag near the festival's entrance. As they watched, the sculpture slowly shifted, head and legs moving. Rowan noticed the blue sigil at the base, a simple automation sigil that would fizzle out in a day or two. "Bet you haven't had moving sculptures before."

Jimson shook his head, a smile on his face. "Nope, and everyone loves it."

They walked up the path to the train station, passing by children making forts with the newly fallen snow.

They reached the platform as passengers began disembarking. The crowd was larger than usual, with many returning to their families for the festival. A streak of purple hair caught Rowan's eye. Attached was Marley, in a burgundy pantsuit under a tailored purple greatcoat, racing toward them with Elara in tow.

"Surprise!" Marley said, spinning in front of him. "What do you think? Purple really is my color, right?"

Rowan laughed, pulling his friends into a tight hug. "You look stunning. Glad you two both made it up here."

Elara smiled up at him, looking stylish in a fitted navy coat and sleek boots with a bright blue necklace. "The snowstorm almost kept us down in Derca for a week, but they sent some new automatons—thanks to this one here—ahead to clear it."

"What can I say? Give me the resources, and I'll fix the problem," Marley grinned.

A familiar metallic scrabbling sounded in Marley's purple satchel. Then Sir Gearington burst free, landing on the ground with a clang and sniffing around. Wisp jumped out from Rowan's shadow, chittering excitedly as he tackled the ferret. The two ferrets wove between legs and luggage, getting lost in a mound of snow.

"Just like old times," Jimson chuckled. "I don't think I'll ever get how you gave that little thing so much life."

"It was a fluke if I'm being honest," Marley admitted. "Even the automatons I make now don't act like he does."

They set off toward town, passing by the old Steelwright factory, which was now a farmer's hub. Half the building was now fashioned with sliding doors, open with heat billowing out as automatons ground dried wheat to flour.

"Glad Calder's been up here fixing this place up," Elara said.

"You're telling me," Jimson said. "My dad's never been

happier. Process, mill, and package all in one place and let the farmers work together instead of shipping it all south."

"And he got rid of all the spirit-capturing devices?" Marley asked, peering inside.

"Yep. Actually," Rowan paused. "Tamsin has been working with him to fix the place up."

"And I've seen Calder join Tamsin in the woods, too," Jimson added. "You'd think that boy would buy something other than a suit, especially if he's chasing after Tamsin."

Marley wrapped a free arm around Jimson. "You're telling me love is in the air?"

Jimson tripped, nearly falling in the snow.

Rowan eyed Marley, then Jimson. "What has gotten into you today?"

"Nothing," Jimson said, regaining his composure.

Elara laughed quietly.

"Okay, you all are weird," Rowan said when no one spoke.

They dropped off the luggage at the mayor's home, and the four of them made their way back to the town square as the sun fell past the mountains. Colorful banners fluttered between buildings, with stitched designs of snowflakes that the children had done in school. Spiced cider and fresh pine filled the air as they passed by the temporary food stalls and seating.

It was already a hive of activity. Townsfolk were gathering around long trestle tables glittering with candlelight, with pints in hands as music played. Evergreen boughs hung on buildings and temporary booths.

Children shrieked as they chased each other in a lively game of ice tag, their cheeks rosy as they puffed in the chill air.

Marley, of course, joined in the first activity, dominating the snowball fight. She crowed in triumph as her snowball took out a child half her age.

After a pint or two, Rowan found himself roped to Jimson and ready for a three-legged race. They hobbled and lurched toward the finish line, only to collapse in a fit of laughter as others passed.

Soon enough, the bonfire was lit, and everyone gathered around for warmth.

Mayor Frost stepped onto a podium, her arms outstretched, calling for silence. "Friends and family of Frostfern. We gather on the coldest night to celebrate the turning of the seasons. This year was a bounty, not only in harvest but in friendship."

She turned, her gaze finding Rowan in the crowd. "As we warm at the Great Frost Fire, I want us to recognize Rowan Mosswood. In his short time here, he has truly helped us grow for the better. Rowan, would you join me up here?"

Rowan felt his face heat as he made his way to the front of the crowd. Mayor Frost grasped his hand, her grip firm and warm. "Thank you, Rowan. For everything you've done and everything you continue to do. Frostfern is a better place because of you."

A cheer tore from the crowd, and Rowan blinked back tears. He looked out over the sea of smiling faces, feeling a rush of love.

As the cheers died down, Mayor Frost turned to the crowd once more. "And now, I believe we have one more piece of business before we start the dance. Jimson?"

Jimson waded through the crowd, looking uncharacteristically nervous. He reached into his pocket, pulling out a small wooden box.

"Rowan," Jimson began, his voice rough with emotion. "It is a tradition in Frostfern to mark a love at the Winter Festival. I knew I'd be standing here with you from the moment I met you. You bring a light into my life that I can't imagine a future without."

He opened the box, revealing a simple wooden band nestled in deep blue velvet. "I carved this ring from a branch of the oldest tree in the forest. May our love strive to endure as long as this tree and weather any storm. Rowan Mosswood, would you like to live the rest of our days together?"

Steam clouded Rowan's glasses as tears fell from his cheeks. "Yes," he managed, his voice breaking with a laugh. "Yes, a thousand times over!"

The crowd erupted in cheers and whistles as Jimson surged to his feet, gathering Rowan into his arms and spinning him around. Jimson planted a kiss on Rowan's lips, his beard tickling Rowan's face.

"To Rowan and Jimson," Marley shouted, a pint held high in her hands. She wrapped an arm around Elara.

"Hear, hear!" Elara responded, clinking her mug against Marley's.

The cheers dwindled, and Jimson slid the ring on Rowan's finger. It fit perfectly snug, vibrating from an old energy.

Mayor Frost stepped forward, speaking above the crowd. "Well, this calls for a celebration, no?" She looked at Elara. "Dear, mind getting this dance started?"

Elara nodded, and Jimson pulled Rowan off the podium, positioning the two of them around the bonfire with the other dancers.

"I have to admit," Rowan said. "I haven't gotten any better at dancing."

Jimson laughed. "Nor have I, but does that matter?"

The music played, and they danced well into the night.

Before You Go

Thank you for believing in Mosswood Apothecary! All of the support has transformed this serial into a piece of art I am so happy to have made, and I am truly grateful for each one of you.

If you've enjoyed your visit to Frostfern, would you consider leaving an honest review on your preferred platform? As an independent author, reviews and recommendations are like little seedlings that grow and help others discover these stories, which in turn grow this community of readers.

From the bottom of my heart, thank you for being part of this journey.

May you carry a little dirt with you where you go,
JP Rindfleisch IX

ACKNOWLEDGEMENTS

In a valley, far in the northern mountains, near an ancient forest where shadow ferrets dance, lays a little shop with a simple sign on it that says, Mosswood Apothecary. They say the owner of that shop makes all sorts of salves and tonics for the people there, and because of him, the town is flourishing like never before.

Thank you Ever After Cover Design for crafting a cover that captures the essence of this story. Brett Mitchell Kent, your chapter icons and interior patterns were a perfect addition through these pages, making every turn a new delight. And to Agustina Ballester, your illustrations breathed life into Rowan, Jimson, and the entire cast, making them step from imagination into reality with such vivid grace.

Kat Betts from Element Editing Services, your guidance helped this story grow from seedling to full bloom, suggesting the perfect additions to make this tale flourish. Your keen eye and dedication transformed these pages into something truly special.

Christine Daigle, your beta reading and unwavering support helped this story through its early stages. Your feedback was invaluable.

To all the Vella readers who followed Rowan's journey from the beginning, your enthusiasm and engagement helped shape this story in ways I never expected. Your love for these characters helped them blossom into who they were meant to be.

And to every Kickstarter backer who believed in this vision, you transformed this story into a work of art. Your support made this into something beyond my wildest dreams.

To everyone who touched this tale along its journey, whether through grand gestures or quiet encouragement, I offer my deepest gratitude.

Appreciate you,
JP Rindfleisch IX

KICKSTARTER CREDITS

Phoenyx Lee, my Twitch Bestie
Jessica M. Vázquez
Mari Tacken
Tyler L.
Amanda Reeves
Sofia Åsman
Pip
Meredith Anderson
Kim & Brenton Walker
Gentlevibes
Brendan Noble
Herman Steuernagel
Bli N. Kerbell
Patrick J. Murphy III
Sacha Black
Amanda Lubbers
Catherine Luzadas
Valerie Anne
Audra

Jeanna Christiansen
Christine Daigle
Liz Schreiber
Cat Stark
Cortney Babcock
Emma
Rachiel R
Malcolm Coon
Matthew Backlund
Mistress Darna Stevens
Tom Holbrook
Theo
Michael Williamson
Chase Smith
Gladys Strickland
Dana Prebis
Valerie Ozgenc
Jon and Rachelle LeFevre
Mellie

Michele Campbell
Mark Fackler
Scott Downey
Tim Schutt
Molly Fessel
Victoria P
Caris
Seattle Mike
Franchesca Caram
crispy
Elizabeth Schroder
V.E. Griffith
Lisa Bonneau
Heather Duff
Gala
Daniel To
Amber Mars
A. Benningfield
Tori Vaz
Lee Larsen
Zach Wilson
Florentina
Katie-Olive
Mackenzie Alexander
AJ Rose
Sabrina White
Christopher K. Riese
Siobhan Barry
Seth Quine

Lee Walters
Katherine Crowe
L.A. Padilla
Albert Cua
Eddie Joo
Liberty
Nicole Hoefs
Willy Traub
James Emory Joyce
Shaelei
PJ Vasquez
Kristina Leo
Holly Lewis
Stuart Butler
Isis Loux
Julia Butler
Zach T.
Katie Stonich
heather
Mark Eveleigh
Trisha Quinn
Aaron Gish
Cindy
Jeffrey Tristan Thyme
Elena Murie
Marimo
Casey White
Tayler Thompson
Caryn P.

Amanda Balter

Oh_Carol

Kytarah Ikkin

Joey Evergreen

Sophie Wyatt

Emily Pitner

Laora

Cristov Russell

Cindy Giesbrecht

Rachel Strehlow

Bert Row

Lauryn Berg

Apryl Cox

Anna

Viadu Barbosa

Sarah Battista

Sarah Harian

Bundydoc

Alexis W

Sanna Husu

Kira Bolding

Gabriela Silva

Bee Johnson

Molly Gosselin

Amanda

Stan Healy

Owen Rogers

Sunnyturbo

Jesper D

Lynnette Pritchett

Kimberly

Beata

Rachel S

Marc D. Long

Amelia

Dan

Fabienne

Polinchka

Myrthe

Devin DeMarco

Crystal Cunningham

Amy N.

Niki Kuhlman

Colin S.

Steph Dawley

Tia Luckenbaugh

Sarah

Tim Sauke

Teddy Hernandez

Sarah A. G.

Ryan C

Whitney H.

Dr. Andy Lynn

annie

Juni Bui

Angela McLean

Jade Oak

Mirage

Jason Farley

Adriana Loughridge

Michael Nachtigal

Ben Picone

Randy Goldberg MD

The Blerd Newsletter

Cassandra

Nikkii Thompson

Caity M

Brittany aka Royalty/Ruei

Heather & Kate May

Ashton

Kyo Carter

Bree Pollina

Nathan Turner

Samantha Newberry

Violet R

Sarah D.

Jes Vokoun

Ashley Kelly

Bellan

Nathan Bassett

Paige Lino

Lee Phelan

Sharon Schiffbauer

Lovis Geier

Rachel Stine

Jacklyn McDonald

Mumblefaery

Miss Sarcasm

William iam_petti Pettibone

Albert Liou

Carol Partonen

Ness

Alexandra Corrsin

Katie M. Foster

Anikó Szilas Juhász

AJ Silva

Sketchtabbi

Queen Kupo

Christina Schlickenmeyer

Natalie HW

Ashley P

Darci

Melissa Ford

Kathrine A Kirby

Xiomara Reyes

Jan B

Zach Bohannon

Moe Ridgewood

Monica Lewis

Tathra

Shannon "Beni" Nichols

Amy Wolford

Jana M

Kai'lee

Stuart

Marine L.

Natalie Duleba
Heather Close
Rebecca Woolford
souljacker85
Kelly Knight
Amsel
Jessica Hoppe
David Edmonds
Amey Gosselin
Rebecca P
Kasper Weber
K'yra Storme
Katherine Malloy
Tina M. Brooks
OGLavaKitten
Yuletidings
Axel KNG
Genevieve
TK-Sorainu
Benoît D. "Ben Libra"
Wesley "Salty" Pierson
McCreeZo
Trevor
Giulia Wood
Kevin & Ryan
CorvFel
JessiLee Morgan
John H. Bookwalter Jr.
Taylor Wilkinson

Erin Dennis
Susan Jackson
meetcue
Fenix Zoetelief
Mark Clayton
Landon King
Abigail Santos
John and Diane Rindfleisch,
 my amazing parents
Bryana Ewing
Elizabeth Noel Bennett
Pamela Franson
Erica King
Ryan Kroening
John Krugman(Hastcoat)
David A. H.
Megan
Basil
Elvi van der Zanden
Morgan G.
Emma-Jane Heaton
Sarah E.
Sabrina Wade
Christopher Mina
Alessandro Veag
Aerylaance
Bean
Kimber White
Jennifer Casas Carreño

About the Author

JP Rindfleisch is the author of queer and strange fantasy. They are the author of Mandrake Manor, The Greatest Storm Mage Needs a Break, the co-author to the Paranormal Humor series NRDS: National Recently Deceased Services, and the co-author to the Dark Urban Fantasy project called the Leah Ackerman series. To follow JP's work and find their other books, go to www.jprindfleischix.com.

9 781958 924259